burning

BOOKS BY DIANE JOHNSON

Fair Game

Loving Hands at Home

burning

by DIANE JOHNSON

Harcourt Brace Jovanovich, Inc.
New York

First edition

ISBN 0-15-114979-8
Library of Congress Catalog Card Number: 78-153687

Printed in the United States of America
A B C D E

For my friends
Alison Bishop and John Murray

burning

one

The heat in September in Los Angeles turns everything brown except where people love and water their gardens at great expense. Brown anyway if they go on vacation and get a neighbor boy to water for them. September is a good month to leave town. Those who stay are oppressed by the pervasive brownness of the scorched hills enclosing the city, and the sea is muddy, taking color from the hot, smoggy air. The pastels of the stucco houses bleach in the fierce sun to violent white and appear like vibrant purple blotches before the eye that stares at them too long.

People who live in the hills, on little green oases described by the arcs of their sprinkler systems, look anxiously at the sere horizons, at the burnt air, at the sign in front of the fire department that tells them when conditions are critical. There is always danger. The sign in front of the fire department is in the shape of a giant clock marked "low," "normal," "dry," and "danger," and because the hands of a clock always pass each point on its circumference, this fire-department sign suggests that at noon the world must burst into flames. Fearful homeowners set out ice plant, a water-loading succulent, making protective rings around themselves, and watch the sky.

Bingo Edwards watched her neighbor Max toss a lighted cigarette down the hillside into the dry brush, an antisocial act. Bingo was angry at this inconsideration because if Max would throw away one cigarette she would throw away others, and that meant Bingo would think about it, would worry, would smell things burning in the late evening. Barney would have to get up and check them, they would both worry, and this was an unneighborly thing in the Harrises, thus to jeopardize the serenity Bingo and Barney had hoped for in their new house. Also to endanger their lives and property. Bingo almost called out but then did not, because she knew she couldn't control the irritation in her voice, and though she was not someone who hesitated to criticize—critics are needed if society is to survive, she had often remarked—she held off shouting at this one nice neighbor, Max Harris, because Max had already impressed Bingo as someone who had problems coming to terms with society or, better, who had refused to come to terms with it, and this is a valuable quality in a neighbor, especially in Bel Air. Bingo loathed inconsideration but she respected desperation, which was the quality Max chiefly communicated, so Bingo did not call out.

Her irritation now shifted from this forlorn woman, who could not easily bear irritation, to the Mulholland Fire Department, whose fault it was that Bingo could see down into the Harrises' back yard at all. She and Barney had had a fine hedge until the Mulholland Fire Department had made them cut it down. It had been a high, dry, inflammable hedge, but it was one of the reasons they had bought the house—privacy and shelter from this tall hedge—and they were now shorn of it and stood, as it were, naked on their hilltop, very resentfully. The Mulholland firemen had also come and sown her hillside, against her will, with some sort of wild grass to which Barney would probably be allergic when it went to seed, and they had ordered her to plant ice plant.

And out from behind the hedge had emerged the Harrises' back yard, an affront, a surprise: just the back yard you would expect of a Beverly Hills psychiatrist, with a turquoise-blue swimming pool set in a pretentiously planted garden full of ugly, unreal California plants and a vulgar little *cabaña* for pool guests to change in, a shed for filters and pumps, a table and umbrella, Styrofoam floats in various shapes, strewn towels—all of it like an ad for back-yard living, but not Bingo's life style, certainly, and not, she would have thought from the black turtleneck and dirty Zori sandals, Max's life style either.

Bingo had wanted privacy to practice her eccentricities. She kept chickens and Eastern box turtles, a rabbit, cats. She was a henwife, she told people, laying aside a learned zoological treatise on box turtles to gather eggs and make perfect omelettes *aux fines herbes*. She also grew the herbs; she had majored in botany at Radcliffe. Except for being plain and a terrible housekeeper, she was a perfect wife. Cooked beautifully, sewed, was infinitely erudite on all subjects, was witty when she wasn't depressed.

She was feeling a little depressed now, actually, at the imminence of fire, at the planting of ice plant, at diffuse things. This week it was about hiring two high-school boys for twenty-five dollars to cut down and haul away her privacy, her hedge, and bring her eccentric back-yard clutter into full view of the neighbors. At other times she worried about overpopulation, pollution, deforestation, the war in Vietnam, crime, civil rights, impending fascism, the grape strikers, use of tear gas by the U.S. government in domestic uprisings, the quality of the education her children were receiving, the problem of waste disposal, and the powerlessness of the average voter. She belonged to organizations concerned with all of these things but did not go to meetings.

She picked a tomato off her vine and thought that she would go make some coffee, and caught herself looking over at the Harrises' again, which brought home clearly to her that she had been in some unconscious manner hoping that she would again see the naked man she had seen the day before. It is perfectly useless to conceal this sort of self-knowledge from yourself. As he apparently wasn't going to reappear, she went inside wearing a tense, attentive smile for poor Barney, whose invalided nerves had begun to fray.

None of them had been naked when they came to tell her about the hedge. Uniformed, jack-booted, with note pads, trampling in and over things right into the back yard, because they had seen her there and you don't knock coming into someone's back yard. They were led in by a magnificently handsome man with smoky eyes, piercing eyes for spying signs of combustion, and fireman's gray coveralls. Bingo was wearing her shorts made from cut-off jeans, cut off too high in the back for attractive bending over, and was embarrassed. Being plain and shy and a worrier, she felt awkward that a very handsome man had come into her yard. But he was kind and gave her the same consideration he would have given a pretty woman; he did not seem to have that secret resentfulness that Bingo sensed in many men, some curtain behind the eyes and hard edge of tone because, she had always supposed, their own wives were plain too, and this was a disappointment deeper and more vital than you liked to understand.

"This is your fire inspection, and since you're new we'll acquaint you with the rules of the district," he had told her. "No outdoor burning of any kind, no permits issued—that means *all* garden refuse must be hauled. Any garden electrical apparatus we ask you to call us to give an inspection. Naturally avoid any accumulation of newspapers or oily paint rags in the house or garage."

Bingo wiped her hands on an oily rag they had used when assembling the new hedge trimmer, apologized, assured them of cooperation. The under-firemen, in their officious way, were peering beneath her bushes and inside the covered sandbox.

"The hedge will have to come out, I'm afraid," the principal fireman had told her.

"The hedge?" Bingo stared. The lovely and flourishing green hedge that enclosed them in privacy from the prying eyes of neighbors and also spared the neighbors many things —box turtles and too-short shorts, for instance. Bingo stood outraged, but feeling, of course, that she would not wish to violate fire regulations composed for her safety and the safety of others.

"It is quite green and alive," she protested.

"It's a shame to dig out a living hedge, I know," he said, "but for fire safety we like a six-foot bare area on every property line, like a firebreak. Fences permitted, metal or redwood-if-treated; no bamboo."

"Perhaps you should talk to my husband," Bingo began, but poor Barney had just come home from the hospital and was still occasionally feverish, and it hurt him to walk. "Well, we'll take care of it, I guess," she had agreed. They had told her kindly but firmly that they would check back.

. . .

Now, in the breakfast room, Doctor Barney Edwards, recovering from blood poisoning of the leg, sat in his old college captain's chair watching Bingo out on the terrace watching something, looking down at the Harrises', but he could not see what she was looking at and had not heard about the naked man. From her stillness and from the position of her angular shoulders, which, when she was interested in something, elevated from the right to a forty-five-degree angle upward, he could see she was again staring at something downhill to the south, toward the Harrises' back yard, but he did not attempt even to speculate on what it might be. The richness and variety of her intellectual concerns confounded him and, of course, commanded his admiration. He often congratulated himself on having had the good sense to marry a clever woman instead of a pretty one. The only thing that ever could disturb the equanimous good nature for which he was beloved by his friends and patients was the presence of a woman who was both pretty and clever, and fortunately he seldom met one.

He felt a little ashamed and irreverent about the ornithological metaphor that presented itself in description of Bingo's appearance as she peered, well, buzzard-fashion down over the terrace, as if she were going to pull in her neck and spread great wings and flap away after something. Then he felt ashamed of feeling ashamed; Bingo disapproved of failures in candor. She would be the first to say that if something was true it was true, at least subjectively. It was true for Barney that she looked like a buzzard. People were always getting mad at her at ACLU meetings for saying things like "Well, it is true that Negroes have more illegitimate babies than white people," although this was objectively true and nobody could understand that no moral judgments were involved; and she did look a little like a buzzard, especially if you knew, even though her back was turned, that her nose hooked slightly.

He supposed he was getting testy and bored being laid up, especially now that he wasn't as sick as he had been. Too well to lie quietly and too ill to hobble back to work, which —though he regarded his two years in the military as dull, time-wasting, and probably immoral—he was actually looking forward to. It was healing the sick, at least, even if they were soldiers. In the meantime, fortunately, as Bingo had pointed out, he was a man of many talents and interests who could use a vacation to advantage. "Convalescence is simply wasted on the ill," Bingo had said. He thought of going to mess around in his darkroom. What was she watching, anyway?

When she came in she didn't say anything, which made him newly uneasy. She was usually good company—great company—but in a depression she hardly talked at all, and he wasn't feeling well enough yet to do all the work of getting the laundry done and fixing his own breakfast. He hoped to God she wasn't coming down with a depression.

"What were you looking at out there?"

"Oh, at our neighbors. Now that the hedge is gone we won't have any privacy at all. It makes me so mad."

"We'll put up a fence, Boo," he reassured her. "I'll build it over the weekend—I should be well by then. And our neighbors could be worse, after all. Remember when we lived in Culver City? At least this guy is a *doctor*. Even if he is a psychiatrist."

Bingo said nothing, but she did bustle around, wiped the canisters, filled a saltcellar, made Barney another cup of coffee, sat down across the pine table from him, drew the afghan she was knitting across her lap, and sighed ambiguously. Her afghan was an affectation, an anachronism to go with keeping chickens. It was just that she was tired of sweaters and everybody's feet were allergic to wool socks. She would give the afghan to her mother, who was amused by anachronistic knitted objects. In the coziness Barney decided his worries were unfounded. She was probably just getting the curse.

two

Next door, Max, who was not really Mrs. Harris, went inside because it was time for her weekly session of psychotherapy, in return for which she did the dishes and answered the phone and watered the garden and performed whatever other kindnesses, and had time to chat over the back fence with the neighbors. Though that was not really her kind of thing, it served to make the arrangement seem normal and straight. Her desperate, anguishing, powerful, passionate love for her psychiatrist bit at her chest and brought tears, and she lighted another cigarette, enjoying this customary pang of longing, always very like tears, though it was a kind of happiness over being about to go have psychotherapy with Hal Harris.

She tiptoed into the bedroom, fears gathering that he was already asleep; but no, he was stretched out on the king-sized bed, naked on top of the red bedspread, wearing a sleep mask across his forehead, though not over his eyes. He was staring contentedly at the warm gold mist of dust in front of the sunny window. The room was warm; the warmth seemed to rise from the flat red bed as off a sunny deck. Max wanted to lie against the hot surface, but her body was too bruised and made of edges. She took her sleep mask off the bureau and knelt by the edge of the bed, so that her knees touched the hem of the red spread, and laid her cheek on the edge, taking warmth from Hal's presence a foot away. The phonograph in the corner was playing Saint-Saëns, and Hal was getting an erection. He raised his head from the supine position and opened his eyes to look at the expanding tip of himself. Max's bright black eyes intercepted his affectionate glance, trying to divert some of his interest to herself, but this did not work. She joined him in reverent contemplation. Then he lowered his head and shut his eyes. Max burned. She fastened her steaming glance on the alluring turgidity, to draw him back into community with her, some state of love.

"Why don't you go through the thing about your father again," Hal said, without interest.

"If we could only make it once, I know . . ." Max began, anguished, futile. Hal pulled the sleep mask down over his closed eyes.

"It wouldn't be good for you, Max," he said, and began to hum his faraway tune, to do with his inner thoughts and state of physical tension. Max sat fading into sullenness and resolved not to confer upon his expectant member the erotic attentions it—if not Hal himself, who seemed now rather detached from it—always expected. His tune and his condition dwindled away, and Max swallowed against her desire to kiss and caress him.

"My father kept a cleaner's, but we all knew he had a little money put away, and he could have kept me from the juvenile detention home if he'd wanted to. But he really just wanted me out of the house," she began at last, and her voice wavered the way it always did, no matter how many times she told the story. "I was only eleven and a half, for Chrissake." Doctor Harris was no longer humming at all, but breathing deeply and regularly. She paused and sighed. "I may have been hostile, but I wasn't disturbed. Not then. Hal, are you asleep?" Deep breathing. Erection all gone and sweetly small. Max sighed again and pulled the sleep mask down over her eyes to shut out the distracting sight. Then she couldn't bear to hear any more of the story about the juvenile detention home, and Hal was asleep anyway, so after a while she got up and went outside. Max did not like to be alone. She walked up the bare hillside, stepping carefully between the baby ice plants recently set there, with some vague idea of talking to the new people, the Edwardses.

Barney and Bingo were startled by her appearance behind them in the kitchen. Max had done this before: suddenly appeared. Perhaps she never knocked or rang doorbells. Bingo wondered whether if you pretended not to or actually didn't notice her, she would go quietly away again. Barney, unused to her silent appearances, thought for a moment that an Indian was in his kitchen, though her thin and burning face had too much pain and passion for an Indian. Her eyebrows grew together over her nose. Her hair was thick and black and curly and lay over her shoulders like the pelt of a hirsute goat. She was wearing her habitual long black pants, black turtleneck, cheap nylon shirt, and rubber Zori sandals, and her feet were dirty. She had very wide feet, and she did not look like the wife of a prosperous Beverly Hills psychiatrist, though Barney realized this was who she must be: the neighbor Bingo had described. Bingo had asked her to sit down, and was introducing them.

"This is our neighbor Max. This is my husband, Barney. He has blood poisoning," Bingo said, returning her attention to her knitting, which seemed to Barney rather rude, but was apparently not disconcerting to this new woman, who sat down at the table between them and said, "Hi," in a wafting tone. She peered at Barney's slightly swollen, reddened leg.

"Get it from a needle?" she asked.

"A needle?" Barney didn't understand. "No, I cut my foot and got a little infection, which I neglected, obviously, and . . ."

"He cut his foot on an airplane window," Bingo explained, a statement she had had great success with that week: people never failed to react. But Max accepted it incuriously, gave no expected, mystified, curious coo.

"I was investigating an airplane wreck. I'm—temporarily —a flight surgeon," Barney explained. It made him feel funny to leave it unexplained, cutting your foot on an airplane window, just like that.

"Well, not really, of course. He's just doing his two years in the Air Force," Bingo explained. She couldn't bear anybody to think he might belong to the regular military. "He's stationed out at Palmdale, so we haven't had to move. It's hardly like being in the service at all. A lucky thing, except when we had to go to Texas for basic training. But then we were able to rent the house to some friends." Max's disapproval was tangible, disconcerting, understandable.

"I was investigating the super-mysterious F-117 that crashed. It was so super-mysterious I don't even know what it looked like. Just rubble."

"Oh!" Max said, turning upon him her very big bright eyes. "I saw you on television." She peered closer. "It was you eating the sandwich."

"That's right," said Barney, feeling famous. "I *was* on

television. We had to walk about two miles across the desert to get to the wreck, and it was lunch, so I took my sandwich. The television crew rode in very comfortably on a truck, but not the military, of course. Or the medics."

"How could you stand eating when you were fishing some poor guy's body out of a wreck?" Max asked.

"There wasn't anything left, just pieces," Barney said. "It was a terrible thing."

"But that makes it worse!"

"Doctors are absolutely disgusting," Bingo said. "Their stomachs are so strong it's indecent." She meant this defensively. She saw Max's point.

"Hal says you might like to come for a swim after a while," Max said, getting up to go. Barney and Bingo wondered if she was leaving in moral disgust, but her face was perfectly friendly. She must just have decided to go.

"I suppose it was—what?—insensitive to eat the sandwich," Barney said.

"Appalling, when you think about it," Bingo said.

"But it wasn't like that. I mean, there were no remains. There wasn't anything. Charred metal. But the idea of it, I see what she meant."

"Yes, I do too," Bingo said.

"I wish I would think of things like that. I worry sometimes, Bingo, that I'm not, well, a good human being."

Bingo looked at him with apparent surprise, and he felt piqued that she, who knew him so well, could look so astonished that he was capable of self-searching.

"Well," she said with a little start, *"I* like you," and then, sensing that this was unhelpful, "Goodness is like charm, I suppose. If you think you have it, you don't." It was kindly meant.

Bingo was good, he decided; though acerbic an essentially kind woman, as well as a useful one. Whereas he was, or thought of himself as, timid and self-involved. Whereas he wanted to be a worthwhile valuable human being.

"Good is kind of a quaint old-fashioned thing to want to be," Bingo remarked.

"I don't mean like a Boy Scout," Barney said. "I'm not explaining it, somehow." Bingo's nod signified that she agreed he wasn't succeeding in explaining it.

"Valuable," he began.

"I value you," she assured him kindly. Barney sighed.

three

Valued and valuing, they sat in silence. Presently Barney tried again, another subject. Bingo knitted.

"Pre-Columbian. Mrs. Harris looks pre-Columbian, like that little clay statue your mother brought us," Barney said. "Same color and shape."

"She has a certain earthy charm," Bingo said. "Kind of fertile and unwashed."

"She's the homeliest woman I ever saw."

"We could have *worse* neighbors," Bingo pointed out. "Silver-blond husband-swappers or John Birchers."

"If you would drive me to the lumberyard I could get some stuff and get started on the fence," Barney said.

Bingo, who had been feeling placid, suddenly felt irritated. It was a physical sensation that centered in her chest and caused her breasts to tingle a little, as if she were lactating. Barney had certainly pressed a button, and she was silent a moment, trying in her reasonable way to figure out what it must have been.

"You haven't even been outside to see how it is without the hedge, and here you are already planning to throw up some makeshift fence, as if it were something you could finish by tomorrow night. Wait till you get well and do it right," she temporized.

"Fences are perfectly simple," Barney said.

"Well, it just makes me nervous the way you always do everything so haphazardly. Just please wait and do it right for a change." She risked a look at Barney, who now seemed irritated, too, and, as always, appeared more attractive and manly in consequence. Wearing a cross expression, his face took on character. When he was happy it was one big shiny surface—two spectacle lenses and an expanse of teeth—but when he was provoked his mouth closed and tightened and lent some contour to the round blandness. She reminded herself now, as she often did, that Barney had a really nasty temper when he was finally angry. This was somehow satisfying. She wondered if Barney didn't secretly wish that he were taller.

"I just don't want a sordid fence, and if you do it the way you usually do things it will be sordid," she said.

"Sordid?" He sounded baffled.

"Inept. Slam-bang. I always have something lovely and right in mind, and what I get is hasty and inept."

"You really feel that way? Then why are you always after me to do things?"

"I keep hoping they will turn out," Bingo said.

Barney was now looking at her with a suspicious and hurt expression, in which there was no longer any sign of anger. His watery sensitive look was not one of his best. Bingo glanced away.

"*What* are you talking about?" he insisted.

"You know what I'm talking about. The fence," she said, realizing that she had not been talking about the fence, exactly. She tracked this realization no further, because it occurred to her she did not want a fence, not just yet, and she understood that she was angry at Barney for wanting to shut out the view of the Harrises' swimming pool. And now she *did* feel ashamed, finding herself with silly voyeuristic tendencies—probably natural, but sordid—and she could hardly blame Barney, who had only been trying to please, not thwart, her. Amid this confusion of insights she had the grace to say, "I guess I'm really worried about you hobbling out there and making yourself worse. You've been *sick*."

He was so easily cheered, became instantly all reflecting surfaces again. "There's no particular danger. The soreness is the only thing. I can work as long as it doesn't pain severely."

"Well, we will need a fence. To protect the children from strange sights, if nothing else." Guilt prompted her to add, "Like the Mulholland fireman swimming in the nude the way he did yesterday morning." Then she told him about it.

It was the day after the high-school boys had chopped down the hedge and hauled it away. She was still stung, and hung about in the yard glaring balefully at the Harrises' vulgar back yard, pool, *cabaña*, striped umbrella, hating the bare unguarded feeling of things and mourning the loss of her hedge and wondering what she could have seen in the Harrises, having supposed, because of Mrs. Harris's unwashed and interesting looks, that the Harrises must be interesting, when, with a vulgar pool like that, they must simply be unwashed. Then she found a tomato worm, which would have been fun to keep for Nelson and Caroline, but unfortunately it probably wouldn't live in a jar until they got back. She was a little annoyed to find a tomato worm in her careful garden, too, and when, glancing again down at the Harrises', she had seen three members of the Mulholland Fire Department, her particular enemies, she was conscious of feeling them somehow responsible for these affronts, which would not have taken place if she had had her hedge back. She watched with some interest to see what fire hazards they would discover in the Harrises' yard. As it was mainly succulents and cacti—surely the ugliest plants ever created, but fire-resistant—she supposed they would find nothing. She paused with her handful of tomatoes to watch.

In fact, the firemen did not seem to be inspecting the vegetation. They looked around them almost furtively. One flung himself down in a deck chair and dangled his fire helmet at his side in an attitude of fatigue. Another sat at the pool edge, coveralls hiked over pale hairy knees, dangled his knobby-calved legs in the water, and smoked. The principal fireman unzipped his coveralls and stepped out of them, peeled off a pair of knitted cotton shorts, stepped naked onto the diving board, walked to the end, paused, looked up, and nodded at Bingo, whom he observed staring in confusion. He sprang from the board and beautifully cleft the water, like a knife or other phallic symbol. Bingo, in the interest of understanding the ultimate Freudian significance of her fascination with the whole scene, thoughtfully watched for some time. He didn't seem to mind. He repeated his dives and disappearances and reappearances. It was a scene of peculiar charm. Skin white below the waist and on the legs, but brown chest and arms, strong neck, lean thighs: very manfully equipped in all respects, which she didn't mention to Barney when she told him about it.

Bingo had watched, fully aware that they knew she was watching, until the swimmer got out, climbed dripping wet back into his clothes and led the other firemen away again. Standing up there boldly looking down had been the most daring thing Bingo could remember doing, but she was interested. It was altogether a charming experience, and she thought it too bad that people in general were not wild and free and uninhibited enough to go around swimming in the nude in broad daylight. She knew she herself was too inhibited, but people in general. Though people in general, she had to admit, were not as presentable naked as this fireman. Of course, if they were obliged to go around naked they might keep themselves fitter. A fine-looking, virile man. It was odd how firemen and policemen were always handsome; you had to admit it, no matter how you personally felt about authority.

Barney didn't seem impressed. He heard the story with amusement and curiosity and had no inclination to probe her feelings or connect them with her attitude about the fence. He was fortunately rather insensitive to the female mind. Barney was a dear, really.

"But the first time Mrs. Harris goes swimming nude we put up the fence whether I'm well or not," he was saying. "Ten feet high. We came up here for the beautiful view."

"Do you suppose we're supposed to wear suits when we go over there this afternoon?" Bingo wondered.

"We'll just say we're too inhibited not to. He's a psychiatrist, after all."

"But he might want to *cure* us," Bingo said, "and we don't want to be cured."

"Psychiatrists never cure anybody," Barney reassured her.

"Hal Harris cures everybody," Bingo laughed. "Mrs. Harris says so."

four

Barney knew perfectly well that Bingo had not been talking about the fence. "Inept. Slam-bang. I keep . . . inept." It was obvious that she had been talking about their love-making. Unconsciously. Being devoted and tactful, she probably had not admitted her dissatisfaction to the forefront of her conscious mind, filled as that was with such a variety of information, trained as it was to the assimilation and generalization of facts and observable phenomena. But she meant their love-making all the same.

There was nothing observably unsatisfactory about their love-making. They were in fact fond of telling each other how good it was, and by any of the objective criteria by which these things are measured by those who measure them, it was good. "Like someone with sexual problems" was one of Bingo's most denigrating tag phrases, though, of course, she wouldn't apply it to anyone with really unfortunate "problems," like being gay, since that was not really a problem. She only meant people who didn't do it very often or, perhaps, very well.

It was perfectly possible that Bingo had not yet noticed the creeping ineptness and the psychological haste, even though she had just mentioned them. Barney shivered at his hypocrisy and deceitfulness. He had been having a guilty conscience for maybe a year. He did not feel guilty about, say, occasionally pretending that Bingo was someone else,

Miss Saunders or Alice Powell, because he knew such pretending was perfectly normal, and he wasn't really worried by the Disappearance of Romance, because you expected that after living with someone eleven years. But he was worried by the intrusion, with increasing frequency, of a particularly sinister and insistent fantasy, one which seemed aimed fiendishly at the very roots of his relationship with Bingo, and which had flourished the more vigorously the more he tried to think it, or drink it, away.

He found himself pretending, at a certain inevitable moment, when, after the more intricate toils of preliminary embracing, Bingo arrayed herself simply on her back beneath him, stretched out ready—he tried pretending that she was very, very stupid.

At first he saw this as a process, her becoming stupid before his mind's eye—all kinds of facts and gnomes of knowledge and angel ideas streamed from her head and wreathed it like an allegorical painting. He had worried, at first, looking at her real face beneath him, the eyes closed, the head wreathed by the embodied fruits of her intellect furnished by his fancy, that this was some sort of homicidal wish he had to deal with. But he soon got the real significance, and then, at that preliminary moment, he could cause all the thoughts to leave her head invisibly, like air escaping from a tire, in one simultaneous expiration; and eventually this became synchronized with his entrance into her body, as if he was using upon her some instrument for the expulsion of ideas. Take that! Leaving her blank, empty-headed, and beautifully, placidly, ineffably stupid.

If only Bingo had not been a somewhat verbal love-maker, given to elaborate descriptive metaphor ("Ah! Ooh! It's like a time capsule going off inside me, a kind of pleasure

Spansule. All the nerves in my legs have melted"). This testified that some sort of cerebration remained to her, and it blighted his fantasy awfully, and he couldn't say anything, because he knew she was only describing her sensations in order to show him how happy he made her.

So that was his problem. It was all right, occasionally, to wish the person you were making love to were someone else, but it seemed infinitely deceitful to be wishing all the time that she were different, and especially that she would lack the quality for which you loved her most. It was one thing to wish you were making love to a stupid woman and another to wish your loved one were stupid. And what he most hated was that he had such a poor command of his own psychology that he could not help this secret condition.

They had made love increasingly often over the past year in his hope that he would finally, somehow, poke the ideas right out of her for good. He did hope that she wasn't on to him now. He looked at her warily, but she was knitting with a happy expression and seemed to be thinking some private thought, having some charming memory.

five

Max walked home to Hal's house, hoping that he had waked up and would come out of his room before time for his next patient, and that he would scold her for having left without finishing their session, though she knew he would not because that would make him seem to express concern for her, which would be bad for her, otherwise he would do it. Hal, all-wise, all-knowing, she knew did really care for her and therefore always acted in her best interests. She was eager for him to see some plants she had stolen for him from the UCLA botanical garden. She was hoping he didn't have specimens of them already—they had looked quite odd and rare—but he had by now a large collection, and it was hard to remember the names of them all. The Harrises' house sat choking in tall succulents, in cymbidium, in unreal tropical foliage, which seemed, today, to be drawing strength from the parching heat while little garden flowers wilted.

The Harrises' living room was kept in semidarkness, blinds drawn, because otherwise the sun coming through the picture window at certain times of day made it unbearably hot. Also, the bright light was often unpleasant to the eyes of patients after they had taken any of the many mind-expanding, mind-relaxing, or mind-energizing drugs Doctor Harris used in his practice. The semigloom was just right for watching television, which Doctor Harris's cross but beautiful young wife, Irene, spent a lot of time doing. It kept her mind off the shabby rugs and furniture. She was slowly getting rid of them, but it would take a long time to have the whole place presentable.

Now she looked up from the television to snarl at Max in her Southern accent, "Can't you keep that cat outside? Look at mah chairs! The only decent things in the house and it puts its claws into them."

Max shrugged. "She's an expectant mother and she loves Hal. It'd be dangerous to upset her in her condition. We can't turn her out."

"Common, ugly cat," Irene said. "Horrible, shitting **kittens.**"

"Nice kitty, here, kitty," Max said, coaxing the cat nearer

to the good chair she was sitting on. Irene ignored this, and they all watched television. The cat purred as loud as it could, distractingly, which pleased Max.

Hal's next patient, Mrs. Fry, a hefty Mormon housewife and mother of eight, appeared early. She always wore the same dress, a polka-dotted silk, and the same expression Hal's other patients wore: of offhand eagerness, self-consciousness, friendliness, perfect devotion.

"Have some coffee, honey," Irene said, forgetting that Mormons don't drink it. The woman didn't seem to be offended. She just declined demurely and sat in the dining room, which was part of the living room raised three steps and separated by a little railing at one end. She looked vaguely majestic, sitting up there so big and polka-dotted, like Queen for a Day.

"How are the kids?" Max asked, as she always did. She always felt curious about this woman's many, many children. There was something sad about the idea of them. Even if they were well fed they probably didn't have toys or books or inner resources.

"Fine. Two have the mumps, but it's better for them to have them when they're young, so I'm not isolating them," Mrs. Fry said, staring meanwhile at the door of Hal's room and alternately at her watch.

"He was having a nap," Max explained, "but he knows you're coming." At this, like magic, Hal opened the bedroom door. He had put his trousers back on. The hair on his shaggy chest was whiter than the hair of his head, which was thick, too, but still sandy in streaks. The women looked adoringly.

"Max, did you water?" he asked. She leaped from the chair.

"Yes, I watered, and I brought you a present, Hal," she said, and flew past him to rummage on the dining-room table under newspapers for branches and leaves. "I got them from the UCLA botanical garden. The sign said '*Stapelia* something' on one."

Hal examined them and gratifyingly said, "Hmmm-mmmm."

"Hello, Doctor Harris," Mrs. Fry said, standing up, watching him and glaring jealously at Max's offering.

"Hello, Joan," he said. "Come along, if you're ready. I'll give you your injection in the bedroom. No, come with me. Max, get Joan some water to drink first." Joan waited in the bedroom doorway like a polite guest while Max brought water from the kitchen. She choked a little as she swallowed it, and Irene ostentatiously leaned forward and turned up the volume on the television.

Hal took Joan into the bedroom and closed the door. Max brought potatoes from the kitchen and began to peel them into Irene's fancy wastebasket, a new one made of turquoise straw with plastic flowers on the outside, very realistic except that they were dusted with gold paint. Dim strains of music streamed under the bedroom door and melted into fulsome violins from Irene's soap opera. The cat sharpened her claws on the sofa back. Irene pinched her lips and said nothing.

Lurking outside, thin and little, a young man, Noel Fish, nerved himself to walk in without knocking, for he had once been an intimate of this household. He stood among the succulents and tried to see in, but the bright sunshine glazed the windows and made the inside indistinct blackness. One shadow, a large one, might be Hal Harris's. A cat suddenly leaped up out of the interior gloom to the window sill and pushed her face among the houseplants to stare out at him through the glass, scaring him. He went quietly in through the kitchen door and walked into the dining room, following the sound of the TV. His body, standing in the light of the dining room, cast a pale shadow on the glass of the television set, so that Irene and Max turned around, startled. Irene turned back to her viewing again, a mixture of boredom and contempt making her face interesting. But Max was frightened and told him to go away.

"I came to see the beautiful father. Is he home?" Noel said quietly. His face was drawn, and parts of it twitched, now an eyelid, now the corner of his mouth.

In the semidarkness Max couldn't tell. "Are you high?" she asked.

"Am I high?" he repeated, which answered her question.

Max thought about him a moment. "Have you got anything I could have?" she asked. "Meth?"

"I'm no speed freak," he said. Max couldn't see his eyes. "Sorry, Max, poor little thing, no Meth."

"You'd better go, Noel, before he comes out and finds you here. He won't see you any more. He said so," Irene remarked loudly. She had not looked away from the television and was intently pressing the spot between her eyes where a wrinkle threatened, not very imminently, because she was only twenty-three.

Her voice affected Noel. It could take on the nasal imperiousness instinctive in Southern females cultivated on generations of darkies, although Irene was the daughter of an unmarried stenographer in Memphis and Noel Fish was white, even greenish. His pallor, from junk and incarceration, made him look strange and un-Californian, even in the dark living room. He was emaciated and waxy, rather beautiful, a former king's favorite newly out of a dungeon. His hands moved restlessly to his pockets, his fly, the back of his neck, as he stood there.

"Why won't he see me? I just want to talk to him. It won't kill him."

"He's on a session with a patient. They just started," Max said. "It'll take hours. He won't see you, anyway."

"I can wait. I have plenty of time. Oh, boy, do I have time."

Max leaned over her potatoes again, and Irene changed the station on the TV. Noel Fish stood where he had been standing, searched his pockets, sniffed, shifted his stance; but no one looked at him.

"Why don't you call Hal?" he asked presently. "Let Hal throw me out."

"He's with a patient," Max said. "This is an ugly wastebasket, Irene."

"You let me pick out mah own wastebaskets for mah own house," Irene said, suddenly furious. "How you all stood it the way it was ah don't know." Now the Southern voice worked on Max, too. She and Noel looked at each other.

"She's taken my painting down," he remarked after a time, as if Irene were not there.

"Hal took it down. He didn't want to be reminded of you," Max said. "You really hurt him. That's why you shouldn't be here, Noel, upsetting him."

"It was an ugly picture," Irene said loudly, her head still turned.

Now Noel sat on the floor, hunching his thin shoulders, his head drooping over his knees, nodding. Presently he lifted his head, returning from somewhere. It was ten minutes, then a half hour later.

"That'd be nice," he said suddenly. They looked at him. "That'd be nice if he'd get upset to see me, but he won't, the fact is. He won't give a damn and that's worse. It's me who would get upset to see him. 'Please, look at *me*, daddy.' Loaded down with everybody's love. The whole world just spreading its legs . . ."

"You took advantage of him, Noel, selling that stuff. He might have been sent to prison, or he might have lost his medical license. You don't seem to realize."

"Well, it was me who went to jail. And now I am a dangerous felon. Ladies! I am a dangerous felon!"

"Oh, go away, Noel," Irene said.

"How do you like being Mrs. Hal Harris, anyway, dolly? The wife of his bosom. The rest of us brothers and sisters hating you. You like that?"

"It needed a woman around here to clean things up, ah surely will say that," Irene said, with a sidelong look at Max.

"I bet you didn't notice that Irene is redecorating," Max said. Now Noel and Max seemed to sense Hal's coming at the same time, before he came and before his footsteps were audible. They both looked up. After a moment Hal's door opened, and he stepped out, very quiet in his bare feet. He was looking around, not at Noel particularly, but with that confused blankness that always made people think he was looking at something peculiar happening behind them. Noel drew his breath in and, with a sickened, panicky expression, stood up. Max put the potato peeler in her lap and folded her hands in an attitude of receptivity in case he should ask her to do something.

"Hello, Hal," Noel said.

"Hello, Noel. Max, are there any pots with leafmold in them? I thought I'd plant those things you brought." With the bedroom door open you could hear Mrs. Fry's voice droning on with things that didn't sound interesting. He must have used something quick-acting on her, to get away so fast. Max wondered if he could have put her on smack.

"I suppose you thought I didn't dare come around here any more, Hal," Noel said.

"Leafmold or redwood bark. How are you, Noel?"

"I filled some yesterday and put them outside the door," Max said.

Noel was edging forward toward the big, bland man, as if he were approaching a dangerous animal, and speaking in a soothing, taming voice, afraid underneath.

"Hal, I'm not well yet. I'm still sick. I can't kick it. I tried in prison, I keep trying, and I'm working, I earn the money and I give Sarah and the kid some, and I leave them alone, Hal. I'm trying, but I need help. Please?"

"I guess you probably do need help, Noel," Hal agreed, and was curiously echoed by the voice of Joan from his bedroom, crying, "Help! Help!" and more words, unintelligible. Hal shut the door and started for the patio.

"From *you,*" Noel said, his voice rising with anxiety at Hal's back.

"You know he can't help you any more," Max said.

But Noel had darted to the patio door after Hal and stopped, as if he were afraid to follow him outside.

"Out the door! He didn't even look at me. God, that crummy man. You stand up in front of him shaking and sweating and he doesn't even look you in the eye. Hal! I say I am sorry I did that, Hal. I was sick. You *know* I was sick. I wasn't responsible." A kind, muffled murmur could be heard from Hal. Noel slammed the door shut. His eyes were now streaming tears.

"I can't stand it. I'm going to do something to him. He's inhuman. I hate him."

"You could kill yourself," Max suggested.

"Hell, he wouldn't care," Noel said.

"He would care if I killed myself," Max said. "I know he would. I'm suicidal, but I wouldn't want to pain him like that. After all the time and patience he's invested in me. You can't kill yourself if you really love your psychiatrist."

"It's just a crime a man of Hal's ability and income can't have a peaceful life without all these *nuts* around," Irene said, looking more at Max than at Noel. Noel was simply sobbing in an addled, stupid way, so Max took the match she had been lighting her cigarette with and set fire to some envelopes in the bottom of Irene's plastic wastebasket.

six

Barney and Bingo were making their way down the newly bared hillside to the Harrises', slowly, so that Barney's leg wouldn't hurt him. They wore bathing suits and carried towels and had feelings of anxious neighborliness. Bingo, at Barney's insistence, had covered herself with a sun-screen cream, to block all the rays, even the tanning ones. Barney believed the evidence of responsible dermatologists that sunshine is primarily responsible for aging, wrinkling, and, in extreme cases, cancer of the skin. Bingo believed sunshine to be efficacious in relieving the symptoms, though of course not the underlying cause, of blood poisoning, and had insisted they come. They were hoping that someone, Maxine or

Doctor Harris himself, would hear them coming and greet them, because it was awkward just presenting yourself at someone's patio door, eagerly, with your little towel, saying "Here we are!" A tall, gray-haired man putting plants in pots beside the pool shed looked up at them briefly and then went back to his potting, and everything was curiously still. The big, empty pool lay invitingly before them like a warm turquoise. It was a hot day. The sun, which had been scorching at nine o'clock, was now subdued by a haze of brown smog, like a filter across the blue sky, filtering out frank sunlight but letting the heat stand.

As Bingo was putting her first foot on the patio a clamor of sounds arose, as if she had tripped an alarm. Shrieks in several voices erupted from the house, loud thumping, a crash, the sliding door, shouts. Bingo and Barney shrank and beheld a screaming woman, carrying a flaming wastebasket, burst from the house and rush to the edge of the pool. She flung the thing from her. It arched like a comet in the air and sank with a hiss and a sizzle. Within, now that she had stopped her screaming, some sounds of gleeful laughter continued and, barely discernible, from farther off, groans. The young woman, a beautiful, starlet-looking blonde, stared at Bingo and Barney as if they had caused the fire, glared all around until her gaze fell upon the man with the pots—who had indeed now laid down his trowel—and rested there.

"Hal, that damn Max did it on purpose. Ah simply cannot stand it," she said rapidly, with an air of considerable constraint. He turned his eyes to her, to them, to the entire patio.

It had taken Hal Harris a minute to understand that she meant the wastebasket. His mind was on the discovery of a large pot of assorted succulents he had found behind the pool shed half-buried in a shrub. He remembered throwing the cuttings, ragged odd bits pruned out, bruised and brown like old celery, into the pot, thinking to burn them. But they had grown! Nature's wonders. Or maybe Max had come along and rooted them properly. Now the pot was so thickly filled with vigorous green succulents that it was not possible to see the soil in which they had rooted. It was barely possible to insert a finger between the fat rubbery leaves of one plant and the next. He slid his forefinger between a crassula and a euphorbia and caressed the rough stalks beneath. The little pot was like an immigrant ship teeming with green life. There had been a boy's book—girl's book, maybe, but he'd liked it—*The Secret Garden,* in which a whole garden came to life. These succulents drew all their strength from one small hollow pot and an inch of soil, and they thrived apparently on struggle and neglect. He supposed he might feed them, a very little, for not even succulents could suck nourishment from nothing forever.

He saw that Irene or else Max had set something on fire and the women were shrieking. It must have been Max, because Irene didn't smoke. But it was Irene, as usual, doing the shrieking.

Some people had come to swim, one limping. They were probably wondering if it would be all right to jump in the same pool with a—what?—a drenched wastebasket. Or whether it would be polite to jump in and fish it out. It was hard to decide whether to thin before they burst the pot or see how long they could survive and how big they could grow on the scant soil, or maybe they lived off one another's roots; kind of an ugly idea, but feasible. If you broke away the pot maybe you could see their toils sapping food and moisture from each other. Plant symbiosis. Cannibalism? But it would damage the pot, which was a rather nice one, not valuable but serviceable. He wondered how long these creatures could live on an inch of soil and one another's desperate tentacles.

Irene was introducing him to some new people, the ones who had been wondering about the wastebasket, so he smiled at them and bade them welcome. The man smiled back flashingly—you knew what was meant by a flashing smile; it must have been the sun on his glasses or teeth. He limped around the pool edge, with his hand outstretched. Hal felt embarrassed that his own hand was dirty and stained with succulents, but he wiped it on his trousers and extended it. The new man was still smiling and said he was a doctor, an M.D., too. Hal felt the involuntary fearful constriction of his insides he always felt when he thought of M.D.'s, though he was one himself, and now here was one right next door.

"At least we won't have to worry about bugging each other for medical advice," the man was saying. "When we lived in Culver City when I was an intern some neighbor would come over about every night I was home. I pushed more pills around the neighborhood then than I have in all the time since." Hal couldn't think of any response but a smile, so the man added, "I'm an orthopedist," apologetically, as if he seemed to feel that orthopedists were not very important. They were not very worrisome. Hal was glad the new man was only an orthopedist and heartily asked them to swim. The new next-door wife—they had apparently come from next door—was not very pretty. "Barney Google with the goog-goog-googly eyes" was the song Hal had been trying to think of, because the new couple's name was Barney, they had said. He supposed he ought to go in and lend a hand to Joan, poor girl. Judging from her cries, she was having a fearful time of it.

Bingo and Barney forwent the temptation to cling closely together in the face of introductions and flaming wastebaskets and allowed themselves to be invited into teetery aluminum plastic-webbed chairs and to proceed with the teetery preliminaries of neighborly acquaintance-making, which somehow seemed to go more easily in bathing suits, as if, with so much of your skin showing—all the ignominious creases and missed hairy patches on legs—your secrets were revealed at once. With each other Bingo and Barney exchanged glances of secret rapport at finding themselves in a place that had looked relentlessly typical and was turning out odd. Who would have expected their neighbor the psychiatrist to turn out to be a large, gray vague man instead of a chubby, short, dark, intense one? Who was the starlet? These Harrises, of whom the starlet was apparently also one, seemed mostly incurious about Bingo's and Barney's secrets or, indeed, about even the most ordinary details of their lives, for instance, how many children they had. Bingo found herself contributing this information—two children, away for the summer visiting Granma—but no one had asked. "Their names are Nelson and Caroline." It was a one-sided conversation, yet the Harrises, smiling blankly in their chairs, seemed the most amiable sorts of neighbors to have. They were comfortable. The starlet, Irene, went for wine-and-soda for them all, and Bingo wondered where Maxine was. Barney's sore leg was extended in front of him in the healing sun.

Then sirens. The terrible sound jolted against the bright amenities and ricocheted from side to side on the hot patio.

Everyone leaped up, hearts beating, looked wildly around, hardly having time enough to realize that fire engines, dozens apparently, had sneaked up in front of the house and let loose their screams, before the firemen themselves, like armored automatons in their rubber clothes and black helmets, invaded over the shrubbery and through the house, giving rough shouts and warnings. They could see men coming at them and hear the heavy feet, could see the axes and other weapons, could hear the incredible, unreal loudness of the sirens still echoing in the pained ear. Bingo had snatched up her towel and was shaking absurdly even as she realized that the invaders were firemen and the shouts inquired about the fire—"Where's the fire?"—and everybody was sitting back down again except the blond starlet, who was affectedly laughing and pointing and explaining. Then the firemen stood around the edge of the pool and disappointedly regarded the watery shape of the wastebasket in the bottom of the pool, magnified by the blue water into a harmless sunken log hardly even charred. In the distance faint siren sounds over the hills suggested that the wastebasket had set up a chain reaction of lamenting wails.

Then Bingo's heart did not quiet, because *her* fireman was leading the pack. He stood back from the funereal remarks over the remains of the wastebasket to catch her eye, plainly recognized her, and was now approaching to speak to her, though she had retreated to the far corner of the patio by the foot of her own hill. His purposeful step seemed obscurely to suggest to her that they had all somehow come, sirens screaming, axes waving, because she had been so deceitful about telling Barney she had watched them, and so mean to him about the fence. She was aghast to see that he was going to speak to her now, though she knew with the top layer of her mind that he was just going to congratulate her on her compliance with his fire regulations. The baby ice plants sprouted bravely on the bank above them, Bingo stared at his approach, and the former scene returned in vivid and stimulating detail to mind, so that she felt funny and was obliged to look away.

His name was Geoffrey Nichols and he remembered that she was Mrs. Edwards from the time he had inspected her house, and he was pleased to see the hedge down, the ice plants in. If he remembered her watching him swim he didn't say anything about that. The firemen were plainly staying in the Harrises' patio now, scraping chairs and settling down, and Bingo found herself sitting beside Geoffrey Nichols. She wondered who would go if there was another fire somewhere; this was the critical fire season, and there were faint sirens in the distance everywhere. The firemen were given wine-and-soda. Doctor Harris had been roused from his preoccupation with a number of ugly plants by the *cabaña* to pronounce that wine-and-soda was very weak and could not count as drinking on duty. The firemen had their clothes on, of course, and, amazingly, Geoffrey Nichols now seemed to be telling Bingo about his sex life, really about the sex lives of Bel Air housewives.

He was the most beautiful man Bingo had ever seen, so she was surprised to find that he was intelligent. She had always secretly hoped the cliché, that people who were beautiful could not be intelligent, to be true. An irrational part of her reserved the privileges of intelligence to plain people like herself and perhaps prevented her from admitting, at first, that this beautiful man was not dumb. He was not dumb, exactly, her distracted mind perceived, but vain, and his vanity was even half-engaging. His subject was certainly interesting. How funny to be sitting in your neighbors' back yard listening to the sex life of a fireman.

"It was ridiculous in retrospect," he was saying. "I was literally working my way up Bellagio Road. Talk about community service." Bingo was suspicious, but his profile precluded wit.

"Basically I came to have a rather low opinion of women in general, or of American husbands. How do they let their wives get away with that sort of thing? When I get married my wife isn't going to fool around—she isn't going to need to. Basically I prefer a Latin-American type of wife, very passionate and dependent, and they know how to treat a man. American women are just bored and haven't got enough to do, especially in Bel Air. I used to be in Company 107 in the Valley, and the women out there didn't go in for it so much. More kids, more housework. These rich ones are kind of scary, almost. Well, I enjoy it, though. I'm not trying to make out like I get raped or anything."

"No, I was going to point that out," Bingo said, "that you wouldn't have to . . ."

"I've only had one bad experience," he said. Bingo widened her eyes, concentrating, interested, trying to keep her mind on what he was saying; he was so infinitely beautiful. It was depressing that he felt able to tell her all this, as if, because she was definitely exempt from his attentions, he could unburden his heart.

"I got emotionally involved," he said, and paused, as if he expected a sympathetic cry or that she would pat him. She managed a brittle expression of interest and felt her irritation and impatience grow. Not that she would want his attentions.

"To tell you the truth," he said, his face transfused

with an even more ennobling expression of authority and benignity—it seemed to produce brightness behind his profile, which, although it really came from reflection off the swimming pool, lighted him with an evangelically back-lit glow—"to tell you the truth, I like to awaken people. Teach the meaning of sexual joy. But to tell you the truth, there aren't that many people, women, I should say, that need sexual awakening. Most of them need sexual fulfillment, and that is a much more time-consuming and not so rewarding engagement. You see the difference."

"Of course," said Bingo, who did not and was, at the same time, wondering which category, in other circumstances, he would put her into.

"Take a few years ago. There were a lot of women, it seemed like, who couldn't"—he leaned forward—"well, come. They had never been taught. And they were always so surprised and pleased, it was very rewarding. But now they are very reproachful if they don't, and the question is not if it's good; it's if it's the best. Are you being fulfilled to your utmost potential?"

"No, of course not," Bingo said.

"I meant . . ."

"I mean, nobody is ever fulfilled to their utmost, no doubt," Bingo said. "It seems rather demanding of people to expect it of you." Her face felt reddened.

"Yes. But I was telling you about this time I got emotionally involved. It started like that, with awakening. Her husband was a brute—you wouldn't think, in this day and age. . . . She was nothing special, when you think of it. She looked like, I don't know, a Girl Scout leader by Norman Rockwell."

Bingo's apprehensions rose at this fancy simile, but she

didn't know what she was suspicious of. He had not paused for effect, anyway. "You know, pretty but a little busty, a little overweight, a little crowsfooty, but so sweet and loving. And I think when you've awakened a woman she means something special to you just on account of that. Well, I don't know how it was, but I was suddenly really involved. I mean I loved her."

"I guess it didn't work out . . ." Bingo asked politely.

"Well, she was married, kids—these things don't ever work out," he said positively. "That's why you mustn't get emotionally involved."

"I'm sorry," Bingo said ambiguously. Feeling ambiguous. Then she felt panicked, having an odd revelation, only she couldn't for the moment think what it was.

seven

The sun seemed to grow, or actually grew, hotter now, and the groans that had never ceased to be heard faintly became louder, as if everything had been turned up. Even the Southern voice of the starlet seemed louder, asking them if they wanted more wine. Nobody made any move to swim, although that was what they had been invited for. The groans merged oddly with the increasing volume of a drone, a roar, a din in the sky, which must have been growing there for some minutes but which Bingo, in her fascination, had not noticed, and now it passed the threshold of bearability, so that they all looked up and threw their arms over their eyes against the sun. The flattening drone was accompanied by a looming shadow, like a giant bat or roc come to snatch them up. Bingo experienced another shock of momentary fear before she saw that it was just a helicopter, one of those helicopters that seemed always to be circling high above their house, keeping watch, she supposed, on the water tank or for fire. One had never come so low before, as if it would land in the pool, and its shadow was monstrous. Doctor Harris pushed back his chair, tipping it over, and dashed off toward the house, his arm raised above his head as if to protect himself against its droppings.

The noise was insupportable. "Sons of bitches," Geoffrey Nichols shouted, and waved his fists at them with mock pugnacity. A head, arms, appeared out the windows of the hovering machine and waved down at them. "Out for an eyeful. They like the sights down here. Sorry, buddy!" he shouted at them. On the side of the helicopter, as it passed and dropped lower, Bingo could read "L.A.P.D." and see the barrels of rifles stuck like bars across the bubble of glass at the back. And she felt the same anxiety as when she was driving and saw the letters L.A.P.D. on black-and-white cars, even when she hadn't done anything. The other firemen, like Geoffrey Nichols, were jeering, and then their jeers turned to cheers and laughter. Bingo, looking around at them, saw that Max (who she understood by now was not really Mrs. Harris) had taken off her bathing-suit top and was jiggling huge, low, bare breasts contemptuously at the helicopter, her face not laughing. Beyond Max, Bingo could see Barney's rigid surprised face, though she could not see his eyes behind the sun-reflecting glasses. Knowing him so well, she knew their expression: horror and amazement. She smiled reassuringly, and the police helicopter, as if embarrassed at being caught in a nasty act, flew furtively away. It was hard to say, Bingo could not say, exactly how a large hovering machine that filled the whole sky with its blades and guns and noise could manage to seem embarrassed and creep furtively away, but it did, with a sudden lift, a graceful forward leap, and vanished over the water tower. Max walked unconcernedly into the Harrises' house, and Mrs. Harris— Irene—said to Doctor Harris, who, however, was not even there, "Hal, ah simply cannot stand it," and Bingo agreed, even without knowing exactly what she was talking about, that it, something, was not to be stood.

They all sat down and again began their conversations. Bingo was aware with part of her attention that Barney was wiggling frantically in his deck chair, signifying his wish to go home so violently as once to scrape his chair with a horrible and embarrassing screech across the concrete. One of the firemen was swimming, in his underdrawers, and Mrs. Harris, Irene, was swimming in a pretty bikini. Bingo wished Barney would swim, or something, and stop that reproachful squirming. She had all she could deal with trying not to look at Geoffrey Nichols's knees. He had taken off his shirt and rolled up the legs of his baggy fireman's uniform, vainly browning his legs, like a girl. Nothing in her past experience had quite prepared Bingo for the way it affected her. She knew that men liked to look at women's legs, though she had never analyzed why, but she had not noticed, either from literature or personal experience, that men's legs had any erotic effect. And yet the effect of those legs sticking out of the rolled-up blue pants was certainly erotic. They were long, large, broad legs, with strong knees and calves thickly covered with fair hair, thrust out in front of him as he talked and lounged like incredibly immense and virile extensions of himself. She could almost feel them, not in a spe-

cific and embarrassing way, but as a tumult of internal confusion entering her body somewhere in the area of her upper
inner thighs and filling her upward progressively to stick
finally in her throat, temporarily preventing the pleasantries
and witty remarks with which she had been encouraging his
confidences. She sat there dumbly and tried to look neither
at the gesticulating Barney nor at the knees. There was almost no place to look.

Barney now swayed to his feet in an infirm but stout-
hearted manner and went limping to the poolside, in effect
turning his back on Bingo and the fatuous fireman with
whom she pretended to be so enthralled and who could not
have worried him less. He supposed she was still sore about
the fence, which was what she thought the fence discussion
had been about. But he was mildly surprised, having all this
time assumed that such a tired gambit, flirting, was beneath
Bingo's dignity. He was even surprised that a girl with such
a lofty mind could conceive of it. He smiled winningly at the
doctor's wife, Irene, who was paddling around the pool with
her nose pointing up at the sky, like a puppy. Cute, thin little
nose, very aristocratic. But she did not paddle over to be
petted or exert herself beyond saying, "Come on in; the
water's fine," possibly not to him only but to everyone.

Something rather touching, however, happened to Barney at the edge of the pool. The Harrises' cat, a calico he had
noticed around the yard, came over to him, threading its way
in and out among the bare legs of people and chairs with
austere agility so that it never touched any of them; he
watched the whole time as it came toward him, aware that it
was approaching water, cautiously sniffing but purposeful,
intending to sit on Barney. It had singled him out. This cat
was a she. Barney gathered her up and could feel hard lumps

of kitten in her belly. He held her carefully and stroked, and the creature purred smugly, feeling clever, Barney supposed, to have found the one man there—very likely the only one— who really loved cats.

His rapport with the cat was interrupted—it was the third such interruption, and his nerves were definitely shot—by more shouts and shrieks, a wail of infinitely serious timbre from within the house. The cat sank her claws into his sore leg fearfully. The ugly neighbor, Max, came running onto the patio, her breasts now covered, her face somber with frantic eyes. She stopped still and looked around.

She had such an air of real trouble about her that everyone shut up. In her black bathing suit, with her black hair and black eyes and unmoving stance, she looked, in the bright mediterranean Los Angeles sun, like someone from timeless Greece; even Barney, who was not of a classical turn of mind, caught a glimpse of the Eumenidean presences behind her and wreathing her head. The firemen shut up; Irene, splashing in the pool, shut up. Max saw her and darted to the poolside.

"Guess what's happened! You've got to help me." She was trembling. "They're coming to take away the kids."

Irene looked at her and submerged, making her toes re-emerge first. She shook water off her pretty head. "Who is?"

"The Child Welfare people, I don't know. And I've called my house, and the kids aren't there. They were supposed to stay home till I got home, and now nobody's there at all. Maybe they've got them already! We've got to go down there and *do* something!"

"Who does?" Irene asked.

"Please, Irene. You know I haven't got a car any more, and anyway, my license is suspended—what if they checked it when I came driving up? And we could take a note from Hal. And we have to hunt for the kids."

"Really, Maxine, if you ask me it isn't all that bad an idea, the Child Welfare Department. Ronda and Derek would be better off someplace where they'd get some attention, some love."

"I *love* my children," Max shouted.

Irene touched bottom and stood, submerged to the chin, to smirk ironically. "That's why you leave them down there all day, sure 'nough, loving Mama. If you ask me, they need a good home."

"Irene, are you going to take me down there?"

"Ah don't reckon ah am," Irene said. "We got company."

"Irene, look, come on, it's the kids. You know where they take them? Juvenile Hall. This dump prison; little kids. Don't you know what happens? They sit in prison while all these hearings and, and sittings and—in jail, and then they put them in some dumpy home with pictures of Jesus on the walls and plastic tablecloths and a nice mummy with an I.Q. of ninety and American flags in the window and—Irene! Shit, come on and take me down there!"

"It's better to live in a filthy motel room with junkies, ah surely do agree," Irene said.

"My children are fine. They have books, and they know things, and they have parents who love them, and they always go to the best schools, where teachers are that can appreciate them, and, oh, well, you dumb bitch. Somebody else will take me." Barney was horrified to see her turn to Bingo. "They may have got them already—I told them to stay home and they aren't there. Could you . . . ?"

Bingo, looking compassionate but reluctant, opened her mouth and sought Barney's glance.

"Couldn't you just drive me down to my house so I can find out what's going on? I can't let this happen. Fucking social workers. What do they know about my kids? I can't *stand* this! Between cops and social workers, oh, I just—will you?"

"Of course, sure," Bingo assured her. "Just down the hill?"

"Santa Monica Boulevard. I'll change and then I can tell you on the way." Bingo agreed and got up. Max was disappearing into the Harrises' house, stripping off the bathing suit as she ran.

The firemen were all on their feet now, too, shaking their heads and muttering a variety of opinions and gathering their axes and shovels. A distant siren made them cock their heads like hungry sparrows. Irene was bidding everyone good-bye in a malicious tone, and then Barney found himself resting on Bingo's arm as they climbed the hill to their own house, holding onto her so he wouldn't slip on the bare earth where the young ice plants had not yet proliferated, furious at her and with great pains shooting in his foot.

"What do you mean getting mixed up in something like that?" he complained.

"A wild adventure, driving my neighbor down to Santa Monica Boulevard. Fraught with thrills and danger."

"No, I mean you'll end up having to swear to her character and go to a hearing—you'll see. I've had some experience with county welfare agencies, with patients. It's a pain in the ass."

"Imagine hearing that someone was going to take your children! Can they just do that so casually, Barney—just appear with writs and whatever and take them?"

"No, of course not. There's probably an elaborate history to all this that we don't know about. She may have a record of child neglect—who knows? Have you ever seen the kids? Ow, careful. It hurts to climb."

"Sorry. No, only once. I guess they're always in school when she's up here. Well, I thought she *lived* up here. But I don't follow the poor woman's movements, after all. She may have them with her constantly. How would I know?"

"It really pisses me off, them just coming up here and arbitrarily saying we have to chop down our hedge. I wish to hell I'd checked with the lawyer. Talk about letting the world in," Barney snarled as they reached their own house. Their kitchen seemed blank and cavernous after sitting in the sun; they entered into darkness. He was angry at his own feeling of apprehension, his reluctance to let Bingo go off on an errand of helpful kindness; he felt shabby and obstructionist. Yet he did have fear. Silly, because Bingo was always sensible about these things and would handle them, and it was he himself that got tears at the idea of sad little children. Now he had only a vicious conviction that they should go to a foster home. Whoever they were.

He lay in their darkened bedroom, on top of the Navaho-Indian-blanket bedspread, which was scratchy. He was puzzling over his emotional distress until he heard Bingo drive off. It was unlike her to go on quixotic errands of mercy, was his first thought, but then he realized it was utterly like her. She had a sharp tongue, Bingo, but a dependably kind heart, more like her mother than she would have liked to believe. This thought raised the depressing specter of Bingo's mother —the horse face, the incongruous mass of gray curls—and his immediate, gratified recollection that Bingo at least didn't look like her mother. Bingo's father (divorced from her mother) had seen to it: had subsidized contact lenses for Bingo when Barney was still a penniless intern. Other in-

terns with plain wives had thought it self-indulgent, he supposed; all of them were so poor. But Bingo's father was an
understanding man, and he also paid for a hairdresser with
money that was, under no circumstances, to be used on anything else. Bingo would never have gone to a beauty parlor
every week otherwise. Barney fell asleep feeling obscurely
proud of her for this, and grateful for a father-in-law who
allowed her to have moral scruples *and* a nice hairdo, and
proud of her, too, for not feeling subtly denigrated by her
father's thoughtfulness. If he had more character, Barney
supposed, he would tell the old son of a bitch off.

eight

In the garage Doctor Harris took a handful of Eagergro
from the big plastic sack and threw it into a bucket. He supposed he ought to go inside and attend to Mrs. Fry, whose
groans were audible at the corner of his conscious mind.
There were advantages and disadvantages to having your
office at home. Her mind had probably expanded to its op-
timum now. But he carried the bucket back to the patio and
half filled it from the hose, stirring carefully, making sure
the fertilizer was completely dissolved. You cannot be too
careful with chemicals where a delicately balanced plant environment is concerned. He poured the solution on the succulents, following with a very little water to rinse the leaves
against any possible damage. The tender, smooth leaves
under his fingers, the sucking, hungry noise the soil in the
pot made as it drank, the notion of frail roots, communicated

through his fingertips to his throat a sudden painful swallow of emotion. He could, for an instant, see himself as a plant would stretch up to see or sense him, as a benign shadow cast above it, loving hands appearing from some invisible height to provide water and caresses, to move it to the sunshine, to pour upon it solutions of strengthening minerals, knowing what it needed. He was touched, moved. The plant would think of him as a pair of disembodied caring hands. He would never have to speak to his plants. With the utmost delicacy he moved a leaf to look at a tiny swelling on the stalk beneath, a new shoot. It would be nice if thoughts were truly energy and could, like chemical fertilizer, galvanize the very cells of this plant with his pride and love. The miracle of life. Then he got up, with an awful crack of the knee, and went in to see about Joan Fry.

He found her on his big bed, where he had put her, lying sweatily with her sleep mask askew, revealing her tightly closed eyes. Good virtuous woman to observe both the letter and the spirit of his insistence on sleep masks. She was panting, gripped by memories and giving them forth in tormented gasps, rumpling the red bedspread. Her dress had crept above her stocking tops, disclosing hefty thighs; she looked like the cover of a pornographic paperback. He went to his bathroom, which adjoined, and lathered his face. The bathroom was done in mirrors and gold-speckled Formica, no doubt by the original Beverly Hills builder; not to his taste, but Formica is the sort of thing that is a nuisance to change, and his wife, Irene, liked it. As he shaved he made soothing grunts through his lather in reply to Joan's cries and revelations.

"I have such a terrible conflict about leftovers," she was saying. "Leftovers! I can't help it. I always give him the leftovers. I'll cook something nice for the children and then make up some casserole or something for him. They taste all right, but fattening, but somehow I can't bring myself to give him anything nice, so he just gets fatter. I get fatter too. But he gets fatter. I suppose he'll have a heart attack."

"Mmmmmmm," Doctor Harris encouraged from the bathroom.

"I wanted to play the piano!" she shrieked. "They always told me I could. 'Joanie has talent.' And I went to college and studied music, and they always said, 'Joanie has talent.' I can't even play the piano. I never play it now. I played 'My Country 'Tis of Thee' in a recital when I was little, but I played it an octave too low." She cried at this. "Nobody knew the difference, and everybody said it was just fine."

"I like a low tune," Doctor Harris said in the bathroom. He wiped his face pink and walked into Joan's tormented presence. He laid a soothing hand across her eyes.

"Open up now. There are lovely things to see. That's enough thinking about things." Her eyes opened obediently.

Doctor Harris put on Holst's *The Planets* and adjusted for her better view a glass bottle on the dresser, which was lighted inside and contained colored water in which a globular semisolid mass continually changed form, bits breaking off, floating, readhering, the whole mass heaving as if in labor with itself in this chartreuse amniotic fluid inside the bottle. Joan's eyes seemed duly fascinated with it, and she smiled and sat up a little, breathing deeply.

"We want to come down in a positive way," Doctor Harris said. "Reorient ourselves to positive life-pleasure attitudes, sight, sound, love." But she gave a cry at this, and began clutching at her chest and whimpering. Alarmed, he uttered soothing sounds and her name: Joanie, Joan. He could not for an instant quite remember what he had given her or what dosage.

"I have this awful feeling in my chest. I had it last night. I'm afraid I've got something. It's a, an in—I forget, but I've got it now." Her eyes on him were focused and imploring, and he guessed that she must be coming off the acid. He had forgotten what time she went up.

"Last night?" he prompted, sitting in his chair, leaning forward doctorially.

"Last night I woke up in the night. I had been dreaming. Not a scary dream, but I woke up, and I just felt this incredible pressure of fear, and also pressure on my chest, and pain. It was as if I was being drained of happy thoughts, drained like a basin of water, and filled up with poison. My heart was pounding. Feel my heart!" He put his large hand over her large breast, through which, of course, he could feel no pounding heart. But she was shivering. Bad trip.

"It was as if my stomach was dissolving. That was from the fear, I knew, but then I understood what I was afraid of. I had read in the paper, oh, last week, about a young woman who died from one, a pulmonary embolus, and she was taking the pill, too." She was shaking and clammy.

"Very rare," Doctor Harris said reassuringly. "And anyway, surgery . . ."

"But if you have them at home in the night you just die. They find you dead. It was silly—I looked at myself to see if my nightgown was decent, and all the time I thought I was dying. But I didn't really know what an embolus feels like; that's what's so odd—that you can know you've got one and not know what it feels like. I'll tell you, it's this crushing feeling in the chest. I have it now. Hospital," she whimpered.

"You're all right now. Your medicine is giving you a little fright. Better to work it through," Doctor Harris said gently. "Tell me about last night. Let's get that fear out before you come down. We want a beautiful trip down." If she came down quickly he could go finish transplanting the cymbidiums. With a start of panic he tried to remember whether maybe he hadn't read that September was the worst, a fatal, time to transplant. And yet they were clearly dormant.

"Dying, Hal! I was afraid of dying. That is so frightening, the fear of dying. I was afraid." She shrieked but quieted to his little pats and soothing words.

"I wanted to wake up my husband. I thought maybe he would have heard about emboluses or he would know how they felt, or just to have somebody to talk to would be reassuring. I knew I could say, 'How does it feel to have a pulmonary embolus? Was that one?' and he would tell me it didn't feel like I was feeling, and I would feel better, but I couldn't wake him; I mean, I couldn't make myself try. I remembered you get them from clots or from bumping your toes or from bruises, and look." Her fine broad thigh was bruised, and Doctor Harris stroked it. In the light from the bottle it was a green thigh, like a smooth orchid leaf.

"I kept thinking, Would it do any good to pray? If God has decided you are going to die in the next few minutes and you catch Him in time, will it do any good to pray to avert it? I tried, but I got more frightened, because preordained or not preordained, God wasn't listening then or He could have at least let me die easily, not so dreadfully, dreadfully afraid. The clot could keep coming, but He could give me some moments to think about my life, about my children. It could just come through my veins—arteries?—unnoticed. But, of course, why does God kill you at all if not to punish you, and it wouldn't be a punishment if it were easy, I could see that. But couldn't He just punish you with fear? Wouldn't that serve the purpose? And not kill you, after all?"

"You are punishing yourself," Doctor Harris said. "Turn your thoughts now." His own thoughts turned as usual, but sternly he returned them to Joan.

"I know," Joan was gasping, running on. "You think it will happen if you think you deserve it. But I don't; I don't really think I do. I'm not so bad, not compared to some people, even people I know, who are much wickeder, or think of the monsters of history. But, of course, the wicked prosper. I know that. I got up to go to the bathroom, and I got dizzy and shivered and tried to find the paper, where it gave the statistical evidence, but I know, I've heard; my brother-in-law is a surgeon. They see these women. I kept going over it, crazy, thinking of all the women I knew who took the pill and are alive."

"The pill won't hurt you, Joan," he said.

"But there was incredible pain, and I kept wondering if they could tell at the autopsy if I was taking the pill, because, of course, my husband has had himself fixed, so why would I be taking it? And then at the autopsy they would know, and I thought of writing him a note about how I was trying to achieve menstrual regularity, which is why my sister-in-law takes it. Can't you see how I felt? I was so frightened. And now this pain . . ."

"You're working out the guilt; you're reliving it. It is very healthy, but you can stop now, Joan. We need to have our bitter experiences only twice—once when they happen and once when we work them through. Twice only, not hundreds of times. Haven't I told you that?"

"Oh, yes . . ." A smile of relief and pleasure began to replace the contortions of anxiety on her pleasant, broad, unhappy face.

"When we come off a mind-expanding drug—haven't I told you?—we have to come down into a better mental and emotional environment than we left ourselves in, full of love, at peace with ourselves, love and pleasure, like growing plants."

"Love and pleasure," Joan repeated, as if it were a hard discipline. She straightened resolutely. Doctor Harris left off stroking her big breasts to go fix the record, which had been turning on the silent whisper of the last groove, a not unsoothing sound, and then rejoined his patient, who was now stretching voluptuously with new thoughts. He prodded himself into performing the penultimate professional attention of this session, the rest of the improving lecture. He had a number, by now, of routine improving lectures, which did not make them any the less effective; people seemed to be able to listen to them over and over. There was one for each motif in the concert of human problems, very few motifs at that, too, though there were a seemingly infinite number of variations. He picked up Joan's.

"You were feeling guilty about love-making with men besides your husband—you thought you should be punished, don't you see? And your body sent you pains and fears to punish you. But that's over, and now you need to think how silly it was to feel bad about something as lovely and necessary as love. Adultery taboos, you know, are just leftovers from the old primitive property laws, when men began to feel concerned that they really were leaving their herds of sheep and tents to their own children and not to some other man's. There's nothing natural about staying with one person all the time, and when you don't love him or don't want to sleep with someone, say, your husband, it's unnatural to sleep with him, because then there's no love or pleasure. It wouldn't be moral."

"That's true. How true," Joan said, snuggling up to him.

"Your mind is reforming itself right now, reorganizing attitudes that were formerly fixed, breaking up the old bad attitudes and opening itself to the new attitudes of love and pleasure, forming new ways of looking at things. That's the chemical action of the drug as well as the work of your mind. Your conscious thoughts and the biochemistry of your brain work together in this critical phase of the drug experience, and it's important now to exclude all thoughts of guilt and fear. Each time we have the drug experience we encroach a little on the old cell patterns, reorient ourselves to healthier growth. . . ."

"Orient me, Doctor," Joan sighed, so Doctor Harris gratefully left off talking and began to gather up the round, semi-solid masses of Joan's breasts and buttocks unto himself, divesting them of the impeding silk polka-dotted thing, at which she assisted, writhing happily under his hands. He turned his mind from thoughts to love and pleasure, which he was a lot better at than speaking and had once believed in more, too. He undid his belt buckle and stepped out of his pants. Her eyes were still on the green electric bottle. Her legs parted at the suggestion of his finger. She had a succulent body, green, even, in the light reflected from the bottle, and wrapped him in her smooth leaves to receive his moisture and his restorative, nourishing care.

nine

Max climbed around inside the car as they drove, looking under the seats, twisting to look behind, as if the Child Welfare Department might be coming after them with war planes or motorcycles. She was like someone on diet pills; she twitched and jumped, and her eyes slewed around. When she spoke she tried to make her voice light, offhand, but it came in fearful gasps.

"We'll just go find the kids and get them out of there. I'll find someplace else to stay with them. They can't get them if they can't find them. Maybe Hal would let them stay a few days, only he doesn't like kids around there, but this is an emergency. Or I have a friend named Nellie, or . . . If only they'll realize, I'm *trying* to handle my drug problem. It's just a matter of time."

"Barney says they can't just come, just like that, and take a person's children," Bingo said, trying to reassure the agitated woman. Although Barney hadn't said that, Bingo was sure such must be the case.

"The hell they can't," said Max, who seemed to know better anyway. "Especially if you have a felony conviction. Or if the father signs—there're a lot of ways. They've tried this before."

"*Do* you have a felony conviction?" Bingo asked, interested.

"Possession. That was about five years ago. Just pot, but they took it more seriously then. They thought it really led to heroin. And then a couple of years ago I was arrested for shoplifting, and the Child Welfare people were hovering around the whole time just ready to pounce. But the charges were dropped. Ronda was out in the parking lot chasing her balloon, and I convinced them I had rushed out in my anxiety not noticing that I was still wearing the coat. Well, that was true, in fact, but if they hadn't come out I wouldn't have gone back, I don't suppose. And then they were going to make an example of me, but Hal and my lawyer talked them out of it. But the Child Welfare people said then that if I got into any more trouble they'd . . ."

"What kind of trouble are you in now? I mean, why do you think . . ." It all became more interesting. It was odd to think of Max as a *felon*.

"I don't know. Nothing. *I* haven't done anything except the usual traffic things. They took my license because I was driving without it. Weird. You mustn't drive without your license, so now we're going to take your license. Logical."

"Surely there was more to it than that?"

"Oh, an accumulation of things. The problem is that ever since Hal's little trouble they watch us like hawks—witness the helicopter. And the minute you run a red or—or anything—pam, a pig is on you. And the big search for drugs and the car is impounded and, and, and. Harassment, this is known as. Oh, they let Hal alone—he has money and can scream—but they hope the rest of us will incriminate him. He's who they're after."

"But what *was* his little trouble?"

"Pot. You might have read it in the papers a couple of years ago. Beverly Hills psychiatrist grows marijuana in yard. This was back before everyone did."

"Does he use these things in his medical practice or . . ."

began Bingo, ashamed of feeling shocked and defensive on behalf of the medical profession, of which her husband was, after all, a member. Of which Doctor Harris was not representative, she hoped.

"Oh, yes, he's a pioneer in the use of drug therapy. One year he got the sort of Academy Award of psychiatrists—this was back before everybody got so hysterical about drugs. He's done some important work. He's really helped my drug problem."

"Where on Santa Monica Boulevard?" Bingo asked as they turned onto it. The radiance Max's face had acquired as she talked about Doctor Harris now faded as she remembered their errand.

"If the kids still aren't home that'll mean they just went someplace without leaving word. We'll just, oh, turn here, that's the place. You can park behind."

It was a small motel that probably had gotten more for its rooms before Santa Monica Boulevard had become so busy. Now an impromptu, home-painted sign appended to that which read "The Monica" said "Fair Weekly Rates, Clean Rooms." Bingo followed Max as she looked in the mailbox and pounded on the door. No one came, but there were no notes from Child Welfare officials, either. Max got a key from the landlady and some information that made her face brighter.

"She says they went out. They probably went to the store or the park. Look, you stay here in case they come back, and I'll go hunt for them."

As they went into the unit the phone was ringing, so Max ran to answer it. Bingo stood in the doorway, staring at the most disorderly room she had ever seen, reluctant to step into a hot, dark place that reeked of cat sand; but the heat and stench came out at her. Max knocked over a pile of boxes to get to the telephone. "Yes, of course I'm here. Where would I be? They're out playing." Silence, and the expression of concern increasing on her face. "Why should I do that? Look, my kids are fine. Nice, bright, self-reliant children. I don't see . . ." Someone was obviously reading her a stern lecture on the other end, and her face trembled like a child's, but when she hung up she was all resolution again. Bingo stepped into the living room.

"So they're coming, on account of me being this junkie kleptomaniac unfit mother. Somebody called them—I think it's Hal, frankly. Oh, God, it's so ridiculous. I'd con them if I could think of something, only I can't. I really need a shot, I think."

"Was that . . . ?" Bingo asked.

"Sure, the guy from the Department of Child Welfare. Oh, God, I know. I'll go find the kids and keep them away from here, and you stay here and be me."

"What's the good of that?"

"Well, they can't take them if they can't find them. And you're obviously so straight," Max explained, and Bingo felt this, oddly, as a reproof. "Nice and clean, with short hair and shoes on. You can talk to this guy in ladylike tones or screw him or, you know, whatever it takes to get him off us, and I'll keep the kids away. You can say they're at the park or whatever. It wouldn't do to just leave here now, because they'd issue a warrant, but if you could convince him . . ."

"But," Bingo said, feeling herself drawn by the concavity of Max's cheeks and by her tone and depth of feeling and by an attraction toward the idea she could not entirely explain, toward the idea as she came to understand it.

"Be me for a while. It's all arbitrary, anyhow."

"For how long, do you think? I told Barney . . ."

"Not long. The Department is just down on Pico, and he said he'd be right over. I'll beat it now—listen, if the kids do come back here explain the thing to them, and send them to the park. I'll watch for them there. Oh, the car keys."

Bingo mechanically handed them over and watched Max out the door and didn't remember until she had driven away that Max had no license. If you let somebody drive your car who has no license you are no doubt responsible. It was the sort of thing Barney would worry about frantically if he knew. Criminal charges, your house taken away. She concentrated instead on the business of becoming Max, mother of—what were the children's names? Yes, like little hopeful movie stars, Ronda and Derek. It was sad.

She stepped from spot to smudge across the dirty carpet, like crossing some turbulent brook on little secure stones, where real hamburgers had left real ketchup on the floor of this unreal room. Outdoor plants were growing all around inside, palely in the lath-house shadows of the drawn Venetian blinds, and a Kitty Litter box was underneath the card table, where the remains of a meal withered on dry plates, and all the walls were banked with boxes out of which spilled toys and clothes. All implements—forks, spoons—were turned to other, frivolous, purposes. A chapel of Gothic-tined forks had been erected over the figures of a wooden soldier and his pipe-cleaner bride. The broom, straw end up, wearing a disagreeable expression cut from magazines, frowned out a window where the blind was askew. A toy telescope on a tripod stared at the ceiling. The smell was of broom straw, dried food, rancid ketchup, cat dung, and gasping plants. In one corner a litter of books was especially shocking to Bingo: books heaped, thrown, backs broken, covers off—desecration. A room owned by villainous children making little monuments to the wreck of Western culture. The records were broken; the tone-arm on the portable phonograph had sprung from its socket and swayed in the stillness on its unwound spring, like a satirical snake, very poisonous, guarding the Naugahyde sofa-bed. The part of Bingo that despised tidiness and housekeeping fetishes warmed, appropriated this really defiant mess. Her reaction was almost admiration, or admiration and revulsion combined. The broken books and unwatered plants were going *too* far, maybe, but she began, in response to Max's housekeeping, to feel a little like Max. Perhaps personality *was* arbitrary, along with names; she could as easily be Max as Bingo, and when it came to that, why had she spent all this time being Bingo, anyway? Her real name was Marilyn. Either was absurd, though the "Edwards" part seemed natural, representing a voluntary identity that was instantly symbolized in her mind by two images: an anchor and a sort of wastebasket receptacle appended to Barney. These served as vivid reminders that she had decided to give up being Bingo for a while, and she somehow weighed anchor and, with a distinct floating feeling—induced by, as much as anything, the now-overpowering stench from the Kitty Litter in the corner—became Max, just a little. The creaking and rusty anchor hauled aboard a captain-free, gently rolling ship. She stood uncertainly, wondering if she should pick things up before the social worker got there, when the front door opened and a man, who she first thought was Doctor Harris, came in carrying a torn sack of groceries, holding together the contents—lemons, avocados, milk cartons—with an expression that suggested they were bulging and spilling from a wound in his stomach. He hurried by her into the kitchen. When he returned, Bingo confirmed that he did, indeed, look like Hal Harris—tall, meaty, and white-haired—but was not.

"I'm Hal Gartman," he said. "Do I know you?"

"No, I'm, uh," Bingo faltered, wondering who she was supposed to be. *Was* this the social worker? "Uh, we haven't met." Perhaps social workers brought food. But then he asked her, in a hostlike voice, if she'd like a cup of coffee.

"Where's Max?" he asked.

"She went to look for her children and left me here in case they came home meantime," Bingo explained.

"What a sense of responsibility. Terrific. It's her psychotherapy, probably, that's doing it. In fact, I saw the kids and told them to stay out so I could get some cleaning done."

He did not clean but instead drew Bingo into the kitchen, where he made coffee by boiling it in a saucepan and occupied himself putting away the groceries while Bingo sipped. She found it was not necessary to talk to him, because he maintained a cheerful monologue about household products and grocery prices, familiar subjects which, with the coffee, made her feel at home; that is, helped her to develop a comfortable feeling of superiority to such subjects and to those who talk about them, enabling her to talk about them back.

It was therefore possible to regard him, not with the mixture of fear and predatory interest she usually felt toward men, but like one of the girls. He wore crumpled corduroy pants and peeling yellow shoes, and his face under its heavy brows was almost excessively genial, with the lines and furrows all oriented upward, as if by a sharp tug on his hair. His smile was boyish, this effect enhanced by one broken tooth in front, and he was about fifty-five. Bingo still did not know who he was, but since she did not in the least feel that this man was someone who was going to rape her or anything, she didn't mind being there with him. And there is something about a very messy house that makes you feel that if you *did* get raped it wouldn't be the end of the world. The idea had flickered in her mind for a second, because his body was large and more youthful than his shaggy face; he stepped around the kitchen in his yellow shoes with the loose-kneed spring of a basketball star.

"I don't understand exactly who you *are*," Bingo complained.

"Hal Gartman. Max's husband," he said, "though those are not my usual terms of self-designation. Actually I am her father. Or, actually, I used to be her father. Now I'm her husband."

"She talks about you all the time—'Hal this, Hal that,'" Bingo told him politely, hoping this would please him, whatever his role was at present. She had not understood him.

"She was talking about Hal Harris, no doubt, her present father. Don't pay attention to much that she says. Although she's very truthful, she sees things differently from you or me."

"We all think of ourselves as individualists," Bingo said, jealous of her own eccentricities.

"Some of us *are* individualists, even," Hal Gartman said, laughing.

"What is it you do?" asked Bingo.

"I'm not an individualist; I'm an engineer."

"Oh, how n—"

"Even employed, at present. Unemployed whenever I can manage it. Well, contrive to have a few little things going."

"What is it you, uh, engineer? Is that the verb?"

"At the moment I am engineering a helicopter. That isn't quite the verb, is it? I'm building one for two eccentric guys who live on top of a hill and want a helicopter. I'm more of a mechanic at the moment."

"From scratch? You're just building it from nothing?"

"Yes. Kind of fun, and they're paying me well."

"Barney would like to see it, I imagine," she said. He did not ask who Barney was. He had now finished scouring the sink and was drying his hands on a tea towel, at the same time peering at her in a new way, as if she had a smudge on her nose.

"You're a cute little rascal. I hadn't noticed that before."

This surprised and somehow pleased Bingo, together with alarming her. It was quite untrue that she was either cute or little, as she well knew, but his voice did not strive to be unctuously convincing. This suggested that he was not trying to flatter her untruthfully but had just discovered, instead, that her particular combination of shape and features appealed to some special taste of his; was his though not necessarily anybody else's cup of tea. Then she was alarmed, because she knew that compliments from men you were alone with probably meant advances, and sure enough, his did. He hugged her—awkwardly, owing to their positions, hers on a chair by the kitchen table and his leaning sideways from the sink. Bingo smiled politely, feeling partly complimented and partly horrified. People who made advances to her were always too old or too short or something; and the implications of this depressed her.

"When I am unfaithful to you it will have to be with some Adonis; otherwise, what's the point?" she had occasionally remarked to Barney, and he had, in consequence, never been much worried about her. Now she assumed an expression of unnoticing vacancy, as if Mr. Gartman had belched, but he was not one to let his impulse pass without comment.

"Very cute. We could go in there right now and make it," he suggested.

"That would be very nice, of course, but Max . . ." said Bingo, trying to think of an impersonal excuse. Her limited experience had at least taught her that finding impersonal excuses not to sleep with people usually shortened the discussion.

"Oh, Max would be relieved," he said. "In the several senses of the word. However." And he gave her a friendly smile to show that there were no hard feelings, that his admiration remained undiminished, and that he had plenty of tact of his own.

Bingo felt a little disappointed, as when someone accepts too readily your offer to pay the check. Some importunity, at least, would have been reassuring.

"Anyhow, the social worker is coming," she said, "to get the children."

"Oh?"

"Max's gone to find them. She's going to hide them. I'm going to put off the social worker some way."

"Oh, shit," he said, and although his amiable expression barely changed, Bingo saw that he was angry. "I'd better see if I can find them before she does. Do you really think Max *should* be in charge of her children? This sentimental motherhood slop . . ." He was drying his hands.

"I—I assume so. I've never even seen the children. But she seems very fond of them, and very worried. A mother . . ."

"Sure, sure she is," Hal Gartman said. "You see the cozy home she has made for them here. The attentiveness with which she watches over them. You noticed the bulging larder? The closetful of clean clothes all so washed, so ironed? There is in this motel a nineteen-year-old virgin from

Iron Mountain, Minnesota, who takes better care of them than their own mother does."

"Well—there are a lot of toys and things. You can see she loves them."

"She loves them," Hal Gartman agreed. "I suppose you're right." And he left abruptly in his peeling yellow shoes, with Bingo wondering if she was doing the right thing.

There was nothing to do but wait for the social worker, and Bingo saw that whether or not she pretended to be Max —a question she did not debate but simply lodged in her mind for it to solve itself—she ought to clean up the place a little. But it was too staggering. There was nowhere to start. Strangely, it affected her like her own messy house, with the same defeated and incongruous sense of personal unworthiness. If she could not keep order in an array of material objects, how could she keep her mind in order? Her life? These objects could not move themselves. When you found them in a mess did that not mean that the guiding principle by which they had been arranged (you) was a mess? Or else was chaos an inherent property of things and life, too, against which some people are fitter than others to mobilize? Bingo sagged onto the Naugahyde sofa-bed and considered at least piling the books properly. She understood librarians and had a passion for classification.

But, of course, this was not really her personal disorder. She kept reminding herself of that. She considered lighting a match to the place, except for the danger to others. Could this place possibly be within the province of the Mulholland Fire Department to come and quench? No. Too far away. Otherwise Geoffrey Nichols (!!) would come and quench it. Bingo occupied her mind with wondering about the etymology of "quench," applying as it did to both fire and thirst, and both of which—it struck her as curious—are employed as metaphors for the same thing. Geoffrey Nichols, quench my fire.

ten

Presently the doorbell rang, and Bingo got herself into a Max frame of mind. A man stood outside.

"Mrs. Maxine Gartman?" the man asked, eyes meanwhile busy around the room, dwelling on spots, a crease of revulsion beginning between his brows. He was black. His white collar shone badgelike against his skin, but his tone was kind and unbureaucratic. Bingo as Bingo felt a liberal gratification at seeing a Negro professional man. You see how we progress, she was thinking, though she did not forget that it was she, Maxine, who was now the target of his professionalism.

"Yes?" she replied in her best Radcliffe tone.

"If I may come in. We spoke a while ago on the phone— I'm Mr. Brown, Trugood Brown, from the Department of Child Welfare." There was just a bit, in his voice, of "Ha! You didn't expect me to be black." Or maybe Bingo was imagining that.

"Certainly. How are you, Mr. Brown," she said, extending her hand. They shook hands gravely, and on the basis of her composure Mr. Brown evidently decided she was emotionally able to take the news.

"You probably have guessed that there's been another complaint, and we really have to take action now about the children. You knew that, if there was another complaint. Where are the children, by the way?"

"At the park, playing. At a supervised city park, Mr. Brown. This is all really annoying." A high tone, she thought; indeed, it came naturally. "Whose complaint, by the way?"

"The landlady's. And of course we corroborated her allegations. The children are alone here most of the time, often not fed or fed irregularly, terrible attendance record at school, really unfit household conditions—do you call this a *home,* Maxine?" He waved his hands at the mess, and the new note in his voice of real emotional upset made Bingo almost want to protest that she hadn't done it.

"I'm *not* a good housekeeper, admittedly, Mr. Brown," Bingo said. "But that seems a trivial consideration next to the fact that I love my children and am, I believe, essential to their emotional development. A not unusual relationship for a mother and her children. There are such things as emotional reality, which may override appearances. And, anyway, a landlady is obviously not the most informed person in the world."

"Well, you'll get a chance to talk about this at the hearing. I've just come to get the kids. You haven't been home here since yesterday. Those kids were here alone all night, all day today. Got themselves to school—late. Came home, no food in the place."

"They, um, had pocket money," Bingo said, guessing. "And I called to check on them. It's just that I couldn't get here, was held up unavoidably. I was in constant touch."

"Day after day! I've been checking into it, Maxine. And in view of that, I must tell you, I wasn't prepared for a woman of education and poise. I know, it says in our files college graduate, but a lot of those go downhill, get on drugs or funny religions, or they can't cope for one reason or another, but you don't find nicely dressed women sitting in squalor defending their behavior in this calm way."

Bingo, thinking that he was suspicious of her identity, tried to look subtly disarranged and illiterate.

"Frankly, it makes me sick." His voice increased and then subsided. "But it isn't my business to approve or disapprove. I'm concerned about the children; the State of California is concerned about the children. We think their welfare is our concern now."

"But, Mr. Brown, I'm telling you there's no reason to be concerned."

"Why haven't you gotten a job, Maxine? An educated woman. You say there's no money for a decent apartment, but you could work. You could afford a decent place, baby-sitters. This is the fourth dump of a motel in six months. You could afford an apartment. You should see what other people have to live in! A woman like you could get a good job."

"I—the children are still so young."

"You say your husband won't give you any money. There are a lot of women in the same fix—most of them have a lot more kids than you—but they don't just abandon the kids; they try to make a home. Against a lot steeper odds than yours."

"Mr. Brown, are you here to lecture me or to take away my children? It seems to me you could do either thing without the other," Bingo said, realizing, however, that it was no time to be logical. Mr. Brown was impassive.

"We need to talk about the possibilities, Maxine. The State of California believes, as a general rule, that children should live with a parent or parents in a natural home. I'm always trying to give a mother every benefit, every chance. I'm happy to suggest avenues by which things can be worked out."

"Benefits!" Bingo said. "Other people get financial help when their husbands don't support them. Welfare . . ."

"It's hard to see how you can be considered for Aid when you own that Facel-Vega—a seven-thousand-dollar car, or was, new—and anyway, Mr. Gartman, according to his testimony, gives you adequate support, even though you are separated. He spends more time here than you do! I know women with seven, eight, nine children, who work all day long six days a week, sometimes at night, too, scrubbing floors—one woman who cleans people's houses and works nights cleaning an office building—who keep a neater house than this. The kids are decent and clean and fed. I know poor stupid women who don't even know why they keep having babies, let alone how to prevent it, but when they come they love them and get along somehow. *You* have a college education!" he was shouting.

"Mr. Brown!" cried Bingo, feeling afraid. His voice dropped.

"I'm sorry. I get depressed. Look, maybe you could just level with me now, just *entre nous,* okay? How much of a habit have you got?"

Bingo was blank for a minute. "I don't have a habit," she said when she understood.

"Oh, come on."

"No, really." *Did* Max have a habit now?

"I don't care about the junk; I do care about the kids. I'm simply asking. It must be pretty expensive if he gives you all the money he says he does. Or do you get the stuff from that doctor where you spend all your time?"

"Look, I just, I smoke a little pot, is all," said Bingo, feeling very clever and convincing. "I'm afraid of needles, besides," she explained.

"We could slap a child-neglect charge on you, remember," he said. "That's a little tougher, and you have a record already. I'm being a pretty nice guy."

The door behind them opened. Mr. Brown turned around, and Bingo started. A small, dirty, blond child, with curls so tangled they would have to be cut and teeth decayed along the gum line though she was no more than six or so, smiled at her and said, "Hi, Mommy."

"Hi, Mommy," said Mr. Gartman, coming through the door after the little girl and followed by a boy who said nothing. Bingo stared, realizing that they were speaking to her. Mr. Brown swayed uncertainly, as if he were tempted to snatch up the children and be off with them. But Mr. Gartman's presence was reassuring.

"They were just down the street at the candy store. Of course, I keep telling them that they shouldn't eat candy instead of square meals, but kids are so forgetful."

"How long has it been since you cooked them a meal, I wonder," Mr. Brown said.

"The issue surely is whether they get food or not, not who cooks it."

"Often when Max is out I come home and take them to a friend's house, the Miss Hart I told you about, who gives them a decent balanced dinner from time to time," Hal Gartman explained. His face was creased with fatherly concern. Mr. Brown was leaning forward inspecting them intensely, like the witch inspecting Hansel and Gretel for fatness or signs of malnourishment. The children, Bingo noticed, were quite robustly plump. The little boy had a neat

English haircut with bangs, an expensive department-store-salon haircut. It was puzzling. Bingo struggled with the impulse to gather the children defiantly to her and throw the men out. But, of course, in the end she agreed to go with the social worker to the Department of Child Welfare and be interviewed and there straighten the matter out.

While Mr. Brown was getting the car Bingo thought of something obvious that had not struck her before.

"Where do you come in in all this?" she asked Mr. Gartman. Nice, sane face, sacks of groceries, concern. "Why are you letting this happen?"

"Ah, well." He seemed surprised that she should bring him into it. "Some of the values to which I tenaciously cling are not exactly approved of by this society," he said. "Matters of life style. I believe a certain amount of time should be spent in meditation, for example, and this affects my employability. A sad comment on our—however. Also, my forte lies in the conception of devices for which there has not yet been a widely recognized need. Also, my wife, you will have noticed, is a dope addict, and she isn't home much. What can a man do in the face of all this, except cope in his modest way and hope that way will be good enough for the Department of Child Welfare? Who, however, will be impressed by such a reliable-looking woman as yourself. Swami Venandeyami says . . ."

"There's Mr. Brown," Bingo said nervously. "I think we'd better go."

"Good luck," he said, with a pleasant smile. He had sat down at a table and appeared to be wrapping himself up with innumerable lengths of insulated wire. Outside, Mr. Brown honked, and the children jumped up and down as if they were off to a party.

eleven

Barney awoke slowly in the darkened bedroom, slowly became aware of outdoor, daytime noises and his hurting leg. His mind focused on the details of his presence in bed at one o'clock in the afternoon. He listened for Bingo but could hear nothing, nobody, in the house. The first seconds of this realization were accompanied by the intensest anguish: who will take care of me? This was followed by the recognition that he was neither a child nor bedridden now. But the feeling, momentary terror because Bingo wasn't home, had been undeniable. He raised himself on his elbows, feeling chagrined; coughed, snuffled, cleared his throat, made other loud noises asserting his presence, his awakeness. His leg really did hurt excruciatingly. Things were so often like that when they were healing; they itched and tingled, exacting pain for not having killed you. Barney's tingling proceeded reliably into his groin, where it felt nice, and whence, there being no immediate prospect of relief, he drove it with a thought of Bingo. Then he was aghast. Just one thought of Bingo, summoned up to encourage the warm, nice sensation, had been enough to send it instantly away instead, and what the hell did *that* mean?

He got up, stepping carefully across the room on his sore leg and wondering what had kept Bingo so long: almost an hour. But he himself had warned her it would take all afternoon; it always does when you get mixed up in other people's affairs. He got some leftover *blanquette de veau* from the refrigerator to heat for his lunch, but it tasted good cold, so he sat down at the kitchen table and ate it that way.

Now he was conscious, as of a growing stomach-ache, of a growing yearning for Bingo. Was he worried about her, thus to be attacked by a husbandly feeling in the middle of a sunny afternoon? No, not really. But it was extraordinary, he thought, how a feeling of need to see somebody suddenly took you over like that, as you were eating cold *blanquette de veau*. And she had been gone only an hour on an innocuous errand. Perhaps she was in trouble and sending him a tele-pathic communication that very second. Possibly he was, while placidly sitting there eating, ignoring Bingo's an-guished cries for help. He continued to eat. It was reassuring to realize how badly he wanted Bingo home. They had known each other since childhood. It seemed quite possible in that length of time for people to build up the ability to communicate telepathically; also to develop a funny kind of dependence. Probably they needed to spend more time apart, but they would hate it so. Barney recollected the six weeks he had been away at flight surgeons' school. Hell, simply hell, and he felt like a child at the very memory of their separa-tion. They should try the trick with ESP cards, the ones espe-cially designed by Duke University, to test the extent of their special rapport.

Suddenly, because he was rapt in his thoughts and hadn't seen or heard her enter, Maxine seemed to appear before him and was laughing at his half-awake amazement.

"I thought I'd come take care of you," she said, and began by looking in the refrigerator. "Could I have some of this?" She held up an opened tin of pineapple rings. "My mouth is dry."

"Where is my wife?"

"Holding off the fuzz. And baby-sitting, and, oh, helping. Saving my kids, I hope. But I knew you were up here bedridden, practically, and I thought I ought to come. Though I'll have to go make Hal's snack pretty soon. He eats nothing but cream. He has a lot of character. He's beautiful. Your wife is pretty nice. I used to be like that, sort of sensible and motherly, when my kids were little. Oh, well."

"It's very kind of you to come," said Barney, with some irony and some relief that someone would be there to feed him if it did get to be too painful hobbling around on the leg. He had to admit she didn't exactly exude comfortable womanly neighborliness; in his frame of mind he would have preferred someone more Ma Perkinsish. But any female cooking your supper is better than cooking it yourself. Barney's mother had been County Recorder and not very domestic, so he had in fact learned to cook well, somewhere around the seventh grade. But he didn't like to have to.

"If you don't mind, what's your phone number? I think I'll call Bingo," he suggested.

"Let's. I ought to check on what's happening, I guess," Max said, and dialed. Whatever Bingo told her appeared to reassure her. The children were with Bingo, and Bingo had talked to the social worker. Barney listened while Max gave Bingo odd facts—children's names and ages, other names, dates, places, random details of life that puzzled him. Then Max handed the phone to Barney.

"What do you think you're doing? When are you coming home?" he said, though not in a mean voice for fear too much irritation would hurt Max's feelings.

"I don't know," Bingo said. "I think it will be better if I stick it out for a while. I'm going to his headquarters and talk to some people. I'm sure I can straighten things out. I, I can't talk just now, though. I'll call you back."

"What do you mean, you can't talk now? What have you gotten yourself into? Who is there?"

"Call you back, babeee," she said placatingly. "Fix yourself some lunch. I'll talk to you in a little while."

Barney hung up and glared at Max. "I hope all this helps. I don't mean to be unsympathetic, but I don't understand."

"Eat some of this pineapple. I'll do my best to entertain you. Want to screw?"

"No, thank you!" Barney blurted, and then felt embarrassed at this involuntary, heartfelt, and unnecessary response to what had no doubt been no more than a jocular remark. She didn't seem offended or anything. But he found it odd that any woman so outrageously unattractive—more downright homely than Bingo by a long shot, and with no apparent redeeming features of domestic accomplishment or wit—could have got herself laid even enough times to have a couple of children. He had just been wondering what on earth her poor husband could be like and had conjured up appalling pictures of dwarves or a blind man.

"You're a medical doctor—you write prescriptions and things?" Max asked.

"Yes, why?"

"Oh, no reason. I was thinking, you could write a prescription for the most incredible things. So can Hal, but he won't; they watch him too carefully. I wish somebody would write me a prescription for cannabis extract. It's supposed to be the distilled essence of pot. You just take a spoonful, like cough syrup. I don't know what it's used for medically, but doctors can get it."

"Never heard of it," Barney said. "I can't think of any medical use."

"Do you have a pharmacopoeia?" Max asked.

"Somewhere around," Barney said, uncomfortable.

"Oh, well," Max said casually, with watching eyes. They sat silently on either side of the kitchen table, the way he and Bingo had done earlier in the day—the coincidence struck him. Max elongated herself from time to time, stretching to look out the kitchen window toward the Harrises', but she didn't seem to see what she was looking for; her face remained unlit.

"Why is it all women, including my wife, gaze down on that rooftop with such manifest devotion? My wife doesn't even know your psychiatrist," Barney said.

"She can probably sense him. Everyone can. He has an aura. We are his slaves, literally. He finds it embarrassing sometimes. Even little old ladies. Even men. His most devoted patients are the men. He's real."

"He exists, obviously," Barney conceded, "but to me he seems like a big vague guy who hums to himself while you are talking and never looks directly at you."

"Well, some people bore him, I think," Max said, "but he has a lot of compassion, so he can't help but help them, and once you are his patient he'll always take care of you. And we have to take care of *him,* in a way. He's not very practical and forgets to send bills, and he'd be busted except we get stuff for him in Mexico and around, the stuff he uses for his therapy. He really helps addicts most—that's his main interest—but straight people, too. But mostly you can't get the right stuff here without freaking out the fuzz or the AMA, so he takes a lot of chances. But his mind is so above it I don't think he realizes."

"No one is ever passionately devoted to his orthopedist," Barney said. "I suppose in some ways it's an advantage."

"What do you do around here?" Max asked.

"Do?"

"Watch television? Another good American home. How many televisions do you have?"

"I work in my darkroom," Barney said huffily, "and I paint in my studio. And I build things in my shop. I do a lot of things." He wasn't sure whether this woman was being hostile or following some dimly recollected social prescription: asking people about their hobbies. Her voice had a rhetorical empty ring, and her eyes, oddly bright, wandered the room.

"Oh, well, I'm not much better," she said. "I let my kids have TV. They ought to have more music. In the old days there was always somebody with a guitar or some records, and we would just listen or sometimes dance."

Barney was not listening, because he was formulating a polite way of suggesting that he really could get along beautifully after all, and it would be all right if she left. Then someone knocked on the door, and she ran to answer it.

Leaning against it, so that she was caught by surprise when Max opened it and lurched slightly into the room, still wearing a conspiratorial merry smile and carrying an evidently heavy package, was a lady Barney had never seen. Plainly a lady, the phrase that occurred to him in description, for her clothes were elegant, and so was her bone structure, and so were her manifestly expensive shoes. Barney was always very noticing of shoes and bags and other leather goods.

"Good heavens! I'd propped myself up. This weighs a ton! Two tons! And I carted it all the way from Doctor Harris's driveway, because they said you were up here, Maxie. Help!"

Max assisted with the box and looked in it. "What is *that*?"

The new woman began to giggle engagingly. She was in her thirties, a monochromatic blonde whose skin and hair and good tweed suit all matched, a pleasant wheat shade, and her face was alight with pleasure at the astonished puzzlement on Max's.

"*That* is a Jacuzzi pump," she announced. Max lugged it over to the table and set it down.

"It weighs tons," explained the new woman, and together they hauled it out of the box. It was, from the look of it, some sort of physiotherapy apparatus, a two-foot-tall chromium affair, with many dials and valves and an electrical cord.

"I'm, um, Barney Edwards," Barney said. "I'm afraid we haven't met."

"How do you do? What a magnificent name: *Barney*," the woman said. "You should have beautiful long shaggy hair and heavy brows, and pipes."

"I'm sorry," Barney said, and she laughed and patted him. A lady, but maybe a trifle too self-composed. Why *was* she here with this Jacuzzi pump, anyhow?

"I'd always wanted one, really," she was saying. "They cost a lot, though. But I was in the Jacuzzi-pump place in Beverly Hills and—is he all right?" She looked at Barney.

"I don't know," Max said, "but you can always deny everything."

The woman laughed. "I suddenly realized that no one was looking. No one was even *around*—imagine! The thing costs five hundred dollars. So I just picked it up and walked out. I suppose I wouldn't have gotten very far, it being so heavy, but the funny part was, as I came out I ran into a friend of my husband's, a very important producer, and he most gallantly said to me, 'Dear lady, let me help you,' so I handed it to him—my unwitting accomplice—and we strolled along most unconcernedly to my car. All the time they could have gotten the man for grand larceny, I suppose. It would have been so funny to see his face if he had known he was carrying stolen goods. Anyhow, I brought it to you, because I knew you'd love it."

"We must try it right away," Max said. "It'd be good for his leg."

"Has he a sore leg? The very thing! Something must have made me come up here like this. These things can't be coincidence. Someone with a sore leg and I appear with a Jacuzzi pump. What does your horoscope say today?"

"I don't know," Barney said, astonished at everything.

"Have you got a book?" Barney hadn't. "We'll have to use the newspaper, though it isn't very good."

The paper said, "Express your fine ideas now, and others will realize you are a person of real character. Your plan, through the auspices of friends, can now be put into operation. Encourage all to work more efficiently for the future. Plan some amusement that can be mutually enjoyed this evening."

"That's it!" cried the ladies. "The Jacuzzi pump."

The problem was to make it work. Barney declined to help—his leg, he said—but he told them where the bathroom was, and they bore it off, laughing, and he could hear the water running in the tub. It occurred to him that he hadn't really been very gracious or spirited.

"Tell me when you have it going," he called out to them, and felt better. Bingo would never forgive him if he did not at least have a detailed report of all exciting happenings. It was seldom that two women appeared at your door with a stolen physiotherapy unit and threatened to give you a bath.

When he thought of it that way, as an adventure or rare occurrence, the whole thing began, to Barney's mind, to take on a new and more favorable aspect. It was, he thought a bit sadly, the only sort of adventure he was ever likely to have: in the privacy of his home; practically with Bingo's sanction. He wondered how many responsible, respectable, normal, nice, liberal citizens—the sort of person one knew—would in fact turn in, or at least turn out, the thief of a five-hundred-dollar machine.

Probably most people would not turn her in, but they would disassociate themselves by asking her to leave. Odd how one's notions of rectitude are complicated by sanctions against tattling. Very odd, too, that such a prosperous-looking woman would run such a risk. Perhaps she had a compulsion, was perhaps a patient of Doctor Harris's, in treatment for kleptomania.

He had painfully hobbled to the liquor cabinet and arranged a little tray with glasses, sherry, and whiskey, and was moving down the hall to the bathroom with it, when they called to him that they couldn't make their machine work.

"Serves you right. Ill-gotten gains," he said, going into the bathroom.

He had not been at all prepared for the sight: the two ladies, stark naked, leaning over the bathtub fiddling with the machine, their two round bottoms the first thing he saw. Bare female bottoms of people he didn't know. "I brought sherry," he said, with a hospitable smile and a private feeling approximating dismay, but not unmixed with pleasure at being trusted or accepted by these strange people to the extent that they assumed he wouldn't be shocked or outraged or made unduly lewd by their nakedness. They thought him more adventurous than he was, or perhaps—it flashed disconsolately through his mind—perhaps they thought that, being a doctor, he wouldn't think anything about it. One of those foolish doctor untruths everybody seemed to believe.

They straightened up and greeted him, a strange pair: the one, pale and thin and breastless; Max, squat and dark, with broad thighs and pendulous breasts. They were like two goddesses of opposing principles about to celebrate a reconciliation rite. Barney tried not to look too particularly at certain parts of them. The one had a small patch of pale brown fuzz, and Max a black thatch; great dark nipples and little dainty ones barely marking the bony chests. The old stories about not knowing where to look in nudist camps, and looking resolutely at people's eyes, conjured up for Barney another picture: of nude people wandering around with frozen, lifted eyes, the perfect pictorial metaphor for piety. Surely he had seen some old picture like that.

He forced himself more or less to regard them casually, balanced the tray on the wash basin, and asked them what they would have to drink.

"I'll do this," said the lady, taking the tray. "You fix the pump. We want our bath."

"Whiskey for me," Barney said, trying to remember what time it was. Somewhat early for drinking, but never mind. He manfully leaned over the tub and felt around in the water for some kind of switch or some way to turn the silly thing on, vaguely fearing electrocution. The nude lady, like a topless, bottomless waitress with her tray, poured whiskey and sherry, with sociable humming sounds.

Fixing the pump was simple, because they had plugged it in but they hadn't turned on the switch on the wall. It was that sort of switch, he explained, as though they might need to know for another time. The water in the bathtub was immediately convulsed and foamy, an alluring turbulence that invited a plunge into it in a mood of desperation, as you might fling yourself into a fatal whirlpool, but with the underlying promise here of soothing and solving. Barney and the naked ladies looked at it with the respectful silence due a five-hundred-dollar appliance functioning in your bathtub. There arose in the bathroom a warm and steamy cloud, which drew pleasing female odors from the skins of his companions: lavender from the elegant blonde and perspiration and chlorine from Max. The chlorine must have come from the Harrises' swimming pool. The admixture was agreeable and stimulating. He regarded their buttocks more boldly now.

"Your turn first," Max said to him. "Take your bath. His leg is sore," she reminded her friend.

"Off with your clothes," the friend cried, in the voice of the Queen of Hearts. Threatened, Barney withdrew himself inside his clothes and knew that it was out of the question. He protested jovially that he really didn't care to, bad for his leg, really, not feeling inclined after his swim today. Max did not remember that he hadn't gone in the water.

"Come, come, come," they teased, with mocking tones that were especially sinister to the ears of one who was ashamed of being ashamed to take his clothes off.

"Have some sherry or whiskey," he said to distract them. The water rushed and bubbled and sounded like a very distant waterfall you nonetheless had to raise your voice to be heard over. Or it seemed as if they were talking too loudly in the small, steamy bathroom. Barney shivered, and his leg hurt. He sat down on the toilet and held the tray primly on his knees, like a visitor.

"Oh, all right," the women said, and clambered into the tub together, splashing and laughing loudly. Bathtubs are really not built for two adult human females, Barney reflected. Two human beings of any sort, though he and Bingo had taken playful baths together when first married. Or had they? In retrospect he had perhaps only wished to, for it was hard to imagine Bingo cavorting in the erotic intimacy of a bathtub the way these two ladies were now doing. Bingo was not modest, but neither was she good at cavorting.

Well, this *was* a bit shocking. He smiled at them encouragingly and made jolly-sounding noises—"Whoops!" and "Look at that!"—as they slid around the limited extent of the tub and indulged in what you had to admit was erotic play. The blonde sat in back and Max sat between her legs—how else could they have fitted?—and she rubbed Max's back with soap and Max rubbed against her legs, and their laughter was knowing. And all the time the pump thing was blowing bubbles at them, and the water was getting soapier and foamier. Finally, the new woman climbed out looking notably rosier, leaving Max to scoot around in the tub by herself.

"Towels!" she cried, and, "You must try it, Barney. Take off your clothes!" so insistently that Barney found himself unbuttoning his shirt and wondering if he was expected to get in with Max. At the same time, knowing himself to be a creature of volition, he recognized that he was not going to undress in front of these strange women. Another compartment of his mind, whose ruminations became more insistent, told him that he had the makings of an adventure here, very possibly an orgy, a rare and unduplicable experience which, although he wouldn't seek it out, he oughtn't to miss if it offered itself. He had only to make some gesture, perhaps stroke the long wet flank of Max's friend. Or perhaps that would disgust them, disappoint them that he turned out to be just like other men: mind on sex, incapable of appreciating the wild, free, childlike pleasures of the Jacuzzi pump.

In the tub Max was innocently and with giggles of childlike pleasure aiming the jet of water between her legs.

"They never say anything about this in the ads," she said. "Ooh!"

Her friend peered at this encouragingly and said, "I thought everyone knew it. That's what people use the things for. Come with it, can you?"

"I never come," Max said, snapped her knees together, and began to scrub her elbows.

In case this was a touchy subject, Barney quickly interjected an offer of another drink to Max's friend. She had wrapped herself in a big towel, which she held together with one arm. The other reached around with a snaky gesture and took a glass of sherry after tapping him coquettishly on the chin. Possibilities crept back into Barney's mind.

"Why don't you take your clothes off, Barney? It's beautiful. The freedom of the body—why do you let yourself be constrained, afraid?"

"I'm not afraid," Barney protested.

"How can the mind be free when it cloaks and covers its temple?" the woman protested.

"My mind *is* free," Barney said. "I just don't feel like taking off my clothes."

"Fear! Liberate yourself. The wild freedom of the naked body, hiding nothing. With that the mind changes. Good body feelings . . ."

She divested herself of her towel and stood, naked and comfortably dry, in demonstration. Barney tentatively put out his hand and patted one rather skinny buttock, expecting a rebuke, and was confounded to find her on his lap in seconds, encouraging such gestures of spontaneous feeling.

"That's good. Take off your shirt, now, and see if it isn't nice, touching each other." Barney was willing to go this far, but he could not dispel a sensation of unreality. He felt as if he were in a line-drawing cartoon, say out of *Playboy,* or in an episode from an old Topper novel: naked goddesses capering in the bath and egging on the foolish, grinning, normative American dope to join them in their bacchanalian orgies, which would probably not, in fact, materialize; would vanish into smoke—foam—the minute his normative middle-class, middle-aged, middle-income inhibitions broke down and he revealed himself to be the libidinous beast they imagined he liked to imagine he really was inside. It got complicated. Was he a raging beast? No. Capable of becoming a . . . ? No. Sorry about his incapacity to become a . . . ? Harder to decide on this point, but probably not really sorry. And the ladies, unlike the ladies in *Playboy* cartoons, were ugly. He jiggled the blond lady up and down on his knees amiably, like a grandfather; patted her; and at length gave in to her teasing and acceded to her demands for what, it became clear, was not really to be a sexual orgy at all but a Jacuzzi bath.

He was just getting out of his trousers, which he had pulled on over his dry bathing-suit trunks, and was thinking that he could perhaps Jacuzzi in the trunks, and he was thinking simultaneously that he was being stupid and provincial, like sheepish travelers to Japan who return with wry stories about what happened to them in country inns there, when Bingo called on the telephone. The timing was strategic, Max's friend's hands on his waistband as they were. Bingo's instinct for when he needed her was miraculous.

twelve

With the children safely away at the Department of Child Welfare until perhaps five o'clock, Hal Gartman could count on a peaceful afternoon—"at play," as Max would have said. He had learned not to notice the orange peels and clutter in the motel room and was happily bent over his own work. He looked like the kindly toymaker in a children's book, snowy hair and eyebrows, wrinkles of purest benignity, tie spotted with polka dots and egg. He was making a gadget that hooked onto the radio and then onto you to enable you, by means of minute electrical impulses, to *feel* music. It was projected to be an instrument of infinite refinement and possibility, capable of producing pleasurable sensations distinct for every note in the audible range—possibly beyond—but as yet, in its crude form, it produced only three distinct sensations, bass, middle, and high, by means of electrodes adhesive-taped to critical areas of the wrist. Hal was a little afraid the perfected instrument was going to require in its user some sort of permanent socket or other inlet directly to the brain stem, which was probably not yet widely feasible. Also he would need the collaboration, eventually, of a competent neurophysiologist for this and some other fine points.

Now he was intently evaluating whether the bass feeling he got (apparently triggered only by a bass G, an encouraging sign) was qualitatively much different from mere vibration. Merely producing good vibrations was nothing at all;

what he was after—call it psycho-aural pleasure—required a different sensation altogether. He had read accounts of finding on the brain stem a center that, when electrically stimulated, produced an intense feeling of "pleasure," which was otherwise indescribable but for which rats would repeatedly press a bar, even if given the alternative of eating. It might be possible to correlate that feeling to one specific sound, which would occur only a few times in any given piece of music, introducing the element of suspense and surprise. Perhaps Max would choose to hook herself up to it and stay home.

Hal was philosophic about his troubles with Max. If you married people in their cradles you must expect they would grow up and bite your hand; only, it did seem that Max went to a lot of trouble biting when she couldn't possibly be hungry. She was always filling her body with drugs and ice cream and other people's bodies. He had been very scrupulous about her, too: waiting until she was eighteen before taking her virginity and then being capable of amusement—genuine, not feigned—when he discovered she had lost it already. His hands were scarred now, but he bore her no malice, because the poor girl was so disturbed. He was too old, he felt, for malice.

He tuned a guitar to the mid-range note that appeared to stimulate a sensation. It was the B below middle C, ever so slightly flattened. He had absolute pitch. It would, with the guitar, be possible to discover whether the same note struck a number of times would reproduce the sensation each time. This involved setting up a microphone to play through the radio. He was annoyed to realize he had no data on the fidelity of the microphone, but that could be checked later and he could tune compensatorily now.

He was surprised but not alarmed to realize that Noel

Fish had come in without knocking. Noel must have learned his furtive, haunted, futile slink from movies about the Mafia. His collar was turned up, even, and he breathed rapidly, with stagy passion. But there was no mistaking the serious menace—to society, some other day—in the yellow, sick eyes. It would be very easy to hook him up to an electrode and put him out of his misery. Probably just turning up the radio would do it, he was so ruined by heroin. He was so ruined, unfortunately, that he probably didn't have sufficient synapses to convey a fatal charge to the heart; but this was an interesting question.

"Hullo, Noel, would you like to try a new very heavy thing?" he asked.

"I have a very heavy thing on. Where's Maxie? Still up at the Great Doctor's?"

"Our Maxine is up at the Great Doctor's neighbor's, baby-sitting for some fellow with a sore leg, at the request of his wife, who is doing a favor for us. Give me your wrist."

"Huh?" Noel was already not paying attention or was unable to, and his thin neck swayed under the weight of his head. "Oh. Here. You mean she's *not* at the Harrises'?"

"As I said." Hal Gartman held onto Noel's skinny wrist with one hand and tried with the other to unpeel the roll of adhesive tape. Noel was now trying, with feeble irritable jabs, to pull his wrist away. Hal pulled the tape with his teeth. Noel was a little ratlike, an experimental animal.

"Hold still; I won't hurt you. It's nothing. I do it to myself, but it's so awkward to work the controls, too. You'll love it." He showed Noel his own taped wrist, and Noel's hand went submissively limp. As Hal began to tape it he had another idea.

"Look here, Noel, lie down on the couch. I'm going to

attach the thing to your spine, something I *can't* do to my-self."

Noel was glad enough of the chance to lie down, anyway. He scurried, ratlike, to the couch. "Just brush that stuff off. The kids leave their things around," Hal told him. Noel arranged himself like a patient on the Naugahyde slab and, by the look of his eyes, promptly began reeling off into a drug dream. Hal dragged his apparatus closer on the wobbly card table, brought over a chair, and sat down. When he pulled Noel's shirt up Noel made an outraged rustle but didn't move. Now his eyes were closed. He smelled of some kind of men's cologne and, beneath that, of dirt. His shoulder blades were keen under his waxy skin. Hal turned on the radio very low and began to touch the electrode to various points on Noel's spinal column. Noel lay stuck to the Naugahyde and apparently felt nothing. His back, soft and wasted, was not unlike Max's. Noel's was so feminine; Max's so dark and hairy—hairier than Noel's. It was dismal to have a hairy wife.

Finding the location of correlated nerve groups along the spine, assuming Noel had any, was a painstaking task requiring great patience. Hal talked to Noel as the tip of the wire progressed from pore to pore. Junkies were, in their way, very pleasant people, very accepting and good at listening, Hal thought; though being married to one had its disadvantages. Who would have thought she would end up a junkie? An occasional joint never hurt anyone. He had given them to her himself.

"Poor old fellow. You didn't gain any weight in prison, did you? A plate of fishbones. Ha-ha." Extra jabs with the wire for emphasis, and Noel's leg twitched languidly. "I could use a stretch in prison. I grow too old and paunchy.

My wife won't even sleep with me—though it's not because of my paunch. It must be quiet in prison, too, I suppose, but on the whole no place for the intellectual life. Did they take you off junk?"

"Threw me off, dragged, pushed me off. Christ, was I sick!"

"Poor thing. You're better now, right? Yellow and smelly and right back on it, right? You remind me of my wife. Your hairy back. The faint chemical odor. I have the same wish to heap you with warm blankets so the blood can thaw and move more freely through your blighted veins. My wife's arms are made of blue knots."

"Oh, my troubles are over. And they never would of begun if they hadn't sent me up in the first place. You know they couldn't have except that I confessed to Hal Harris's crime. I wouldn't of had to do that. And now he won't help me or have nothing to do with me. I did a noble thing for that son-of-a-bitch shrink."

"If you call it a noble thing planting grass in his yard and then showing the police. Even if you did take the rap for it later. Handsome. Noble Noel. I've always been a little sorry you didn't get away with it, but I suppose husbands never like their wives' psychiatrists. Not that Doctor Harris isn't a very fine man."

"I swear he knew it was there. He told me one day that hill was a perfect place to grow, and I . . ."

"Another knight who takes the monarch seriously. You nearly did King Henry in, Noble Noel. You landed him in a real mess, not that he doesn't with impunity perpetrate much grosser crimes upon the sensibilities of society. But if they had sent him up think how our poor Max would have languished. And think how he has helped her cope with the realities of her life situation. Hold still, my dear punk; don't you feel *anything?"* He turned the radio up.

"Do you know why I said my troubles are over?" Noel murmured.

"No. A premonition? A bird flew into your house. A black cat—what?"

"Listen. I have enough stuff laid away for myself for the rest of my life. I never have to worry, I don't have to buy no more, I'm set. After tonight. I make two simple connections with the stuff on me, and then I can relax for the rest of my life. No buying, no selling."

"Capital," Hal Gartman said. "Ha-ha. Just don't give Max any."

"Don't you care? When I say I have some on me? Why don't you call the police, you're so straight? I have fifty thousand dollars' worth of magic white powder on me. Why don't you call them?"

"Why? Why would I do that? Hold still."

"I wish you would. Just pick up the phone. I could get out of here before they came, anyhow."

"Noel Fish with fifty thousand worth of H. What a hero! Your picture in all the papers. Fame, interest. Poor fellow. It all happened to you because your name was Fish, I suppose. That fixed things for you before you were ever born."

"My kid is named Devil," Noel said, "but I don't go to see them. I promised not to ruin their lives. Funny how I go around ruining lives."

"Don't be pretentious, poor Fishy. I doubt it, unless you want to take credit for ruining all those people who are going to shoot up all the stuff you're peddling."

"No, I'm not going to sell any more after tonight. Well, I'm going to sell something. I have a job, Hal, selling swimming pools. Beverly-Air pools. And I won't have to worry about the other thing any more. That's what I was trying to tell Doctor Harris, the bastard; he wouldn't even listen." Hal Gartman realized, with sorrowful detachment, that this little sick fellow wanted very much for him to like and approve of him. He had only to make an approving remark and the little fellow would smile and glow. Sourly he did not speak but applied the electrode to Noel's spine instead.

"Ah. I felt that. Felt good."

"Good. You have some nervous system left evidently. And you're going to work. That's fine, Noel. Beverly-Air pools. For the housewives of Beverlywoodland. You'll have a business card and a suit on, and how will they know you for a thin, sick junkie who is going to rape and strangle them in their kitchens? Well, your suit will be ill-fitting; they can tell from that. Why should you not have a well-fitting suit, though, Fish? Why shouldn't I? The garments of the poor. Surely they must fit someone? Or are they artfully constructed to fit no human shape extant so that anyone wearing one will be instantly visible as a poor sick criminal? Sad . . . A badge of one's social culpability: cheap suits. A bill in Congress: the Cheap Suit Cutting Act, a Safeguard to Society. Can you still feel it? Every time that same note comes on?"

"Yeah. Is it therapeutic?"

"No, pleasurable. This is just a little thing I invented to turn our Max on. Give her a little pleasure in life. What more could we want, after all, than Pleasure? Capital P. I sometimes think we do want something more, but this is my age showing. A certain amount of metaphysical yearning, normal enough as our balls cool, I guess. Or I would settle for the satisfactions of my physical yearnings and a few basic emotional needs: a hot breakfast, say, and dutiful children and a loving wife. Are those emotional or physical needs? What boring needs. I greatly regret having the same needs as everyone else, Fish. I find that offensive. Do you have the same number of vertebrae as I, Fish? I forget. There is a girl in this motel, a virgin from Iron Mountain, Minnesota, with lovely red hair, who asks me questions, and I explain things to her. I think she loves me. She has just come to Los Angeles to find a job and has never been away from home before and is staying at this motel. She could become either my housekeeper or my mistress or both, I have no doubt. Have you felt it again?"

"Every time it goes oom-*pah* on the radio. Great feeling. Tingles. You know, Hal, you have no more reason than me to love Doctor Harris."

"I'm very grateful for his many kindnesses to my poor, sick wife."

"You should help me do something to him. I'm going to do something to him."

Gartman felt a start, an unreasonable sensation of fear, for, though he had no reason, any more than poor Fish here, to love Harris, he did not want to harm him. His hand, holding a bared wire, hovered ambivalently over a protuberance in the pale, lumpy spine. "What an idea!" he objected. "Hal Harris is my friend. He has said—and it's obviously true—that there are very few people, straight, independent, that he can consider friends instead of patients. This was said in a confidential way, and he seemed almost embarrassed afterward. It was the longest speech I have ever heard him make." This was indeed something to be proud of. But, of course, poor Noel had not been so fortunate as to win the esteem of Doctor Harris.

"And think how kind he has been to my hairy wife." He looked down at Noel's unmoving, pale back, the blue-scarred forearm folded under the flaky cheek, the closed lid, faintly granular. Perhaps Noel was allergic to heroin. "Do you sneeze a lot?" he asked. The poor ruin—was it the fifty thousand worth of heroin that bulged from the back pocket? —barely moved. A hum emitted from him, generated from his singing veins and ringing ears, he was so high. His hum conflicted in a high-frequency way with Hal's machine. It could probably be obliterated by turning up the radio, a good idea, though it might also kill him. A good idea, and you could wash the fifty thousand dollars' worth of magic white powder down the drain or perhaps devise some kind of patent cough medicine, a better idea.

Then something about Hal's own volume increased. He would just kill this poor little fellow. He became noisy inside himself, taking deep breaths, the good idea making him heedless and joyful. Here, then, was the moment hunters hunted for, killers killed for—bullfights, moments of truth. Interesting moments. You could feel every separate particle of your body, every power of your brain. You were utterly present, utterly concentrated. Very interesting. Hal could feel himself sway on the thin edge of decision, knowing what he would do, yet postponing the action because of the exquisite corporeal awareness. Then, as in diving, a minute failure somewhere inside him, the inability of some component part to sustain the tension, triggered motion. With a lunge he placed his full weight on Noel's back to hold him fast and tugged to pull the baggy trousers down, shouting threateningly for Noel to hold still, while he pasted the electrode at the base of Noel's spine between the damp, hairy buttocks, chill, bony ones. Noel flattened in terror, like a cat in heat. Hal leaped off and toward the radio. Now Noel was sitting up, outraged, tearing at his behind and shaking with fear, trying to find and understand. He was clumsy. Hal rotated the volume knob, and at three-quarters' turn Noel was interrupted in the act of peeling the painful tape, was jolted; his mouth and eyes went wide open, as if his life had been routed from his body, and he sagged onto the Naugahyde. Hal, stifled with excitement, stared, shook. He was an old man. Grinning. But Noel's life returned after a few seconds. Hal felt both relieved and disappointed.

"How did that feel?" he asked.

"The hell. It was *too* much. Not pleasant. What are you trying to do, anyhow? I had enough of that in prison. Leave my ass alone," Noel said, pulling the electronic tail off.

"Poor fellow," Hal sighed. He was resigned. Little sparks died; a hopeful spurt subsided. "Let me offer you a sandwich in order to preserve your life past the great events of tonight."

thirteen

They had been sitting for fifteen minutes in the small waiting room of a brick building on Pico, where Mr. Brown had left them. Bingo was restless, anxious to get this over with. She fidgeted in her chair, while Ronda and Derek sat solemnly still. Bingo gave them sneaky, assessing, sideways looks. Bingo did not greatly care for children. This was another secret sore, or sin, at the bottom of her mind. She liked her own children. She cried at pictures of sad little crippled starved ones, and she sent money to Care. She never could manage Barney's doctorish detachment. She felt passionately about the lives of little children; she did not greatly care for their company, was all, and so now felt some mixture of irritation and compassion, in disconcerting conflict, some impulse to kiss them and comb their hair, much apprehension that they would want attention and love and conversation. They did at once begin to talk, their legs dangling from tall waiting-room chairs, as soon as Mr. Brown had gone.

"Why are you pretending to be my mother?" the little girl, Ronda, asked.

"She's busy. I told her I would help her out with all this silly business, that's all," Bingo said.

"My mother has black hair," Ronda said.

"How is it you have such pretty blond curls?" Bingo tried.

"I take after my dad. Derek takes after Mom. We have very smart parents. My mom isn't home very much."

"Don't say anything like that around here," Bingo said. "Your father explained it, I suppose."

"He said we were supposed to act like you were our mom so we wouldn't have to go to a foster home, right?"

"Right," Bingo said sadly.

"What's your name?" Derek asked, and when Bingo whispered, "Mrs. Edwards," he sniffed and found a magazine to read.

"You look like a teacher, if you don't mind me saying so," Ronda observed, perhaps interpreting her brother's disapproval. Bingo found this insulting, though she couldn't say why; found herself on the point of saying, in the spirit in which one might mention a bogeyman, that she would turn him over to the foster home. But, of course, she did not say this.

When they had sat another ten minutes and none of the

people ahead of them had been taken away by the officials, Bingo got a dime from her purse and went to the telephone in the foyer. She would let Barney know he had been right: this was going to take a while. She was always pleased when Barney was right about things, more pleased than he, and also she didn't want him to worry.

"I'm in the waiting room of the Bureau of Public Assistance. They have to check my finances and things to see if I should be getting public assistance, and what they should do about my children—I mean, Max's—and about my life. They have to decide whether I live in unsuitable conditions and neglect my children because I am poor or because I am vicious, these things being so hard to separate in the official mind."

Her voice had an edge, but Barney didn't feel inclined to probe after its origin, and she was her usual controlled and ironic self otherwise.

"Is it amusing?" Barney asked, hoping it was at least that.

"No. I have to wait here, about two dozen people ahead of me, and the children are along. Fortunately they are resourceful and quiet. Not bad kids, actually. A great argument for child neglect. I'm hungry and have about a dollar in my purse. What else—let me see. Do you think I'm liable to be criminally prosecuted if I tell them I'm not Maxine Gartman and just walk out of here?"

"Of course not, unless you took money or swore to something. But why don't you leave? She's up here just doing nothing. She could at least come and speak for herself." Barney heard the absence of conviction in his own voice and recognized that now that it was settled he didn't quite want to relinquish his Jacuzzi-pump bath.

"Oh, I just about did, but I felt embarrassed finally, because—well, because the social worker is black. Somehow you mind deceiving a black social worker. I mean, though you don't mind deceiving him, you mind flaunting your deception at him, as if to say, 'Ha-ha, do we all look alike to you?' "

"Well," Barney said, "I can understand that. But come home as soon as you can."

"I will," Bingo said. "Hold on to Max, and I'll call about whatever the next step is to be. Tell her the kids are fine and not yet in the hands of the State of California. You should see the waiting room here, Barney; the magazines they have here. Three back copies of *Arizona Highways* and two old *Newsweeks*. So everyone just sits looking miserable and apprehensive or else bored and accustomed, and no one reads anything. Or maybe no one ever reads, and that's why they don't put magazines out. Maybe if you read you look too resourceful and then you can't get any money. Or maybe they can't read. Well, it's fairly depressing."

"I imagine," Barney agreed. "Be sure you get something to eat."

"Okay. I'll keep you posted," Bingo said.

They sat and waited. Ronda moved unexpectedly against Bingo's knees. Bingo looked up from the old *U.S. News & World Report* she had been holding to screen her reverie, a sort of disgusted calm into which she was sinking.

"Would you like to be our mother?"

"I—why?"

"I just wondered if you'd like to be our mother."

"Why, I, of course," Bingo said. She had been going to say that she already had a little girl and boy of her own. And she would not like to be Ronda's mother. "Of course I would. Why?"

"Instead of our play mother?"

"Sure. You and Derek are good kids," Bingo said.

"Derek hits me sometimes," Ronda revealed, but Bingo did not qualify her praise.

"You're a little brat sometimes, Ronda," Derek said, from his chair.

"Sometimes he buys Chicken Delight. He gets to decide where we get dinner. Most of the time we have to get pizza, because he likes it."

"Don't you like pizza?"

"Not too much. Especially not with pepperoni." A secretary walked through the waiting room, carrying large files in ring binders. Ronda hopped back up on her chair and shrugged conspiratorially at Bingo. They sat some more and waited.

Presently Bingo, becoming aware of one very wrong thing, went up to a person whose desk was nearest the little masonite half-wall that had been built between the personnel and the waiting room, as if to protect the people sitting at typewriters from the onslaughts of frantic public dependents. These, however, sat apathetically on chrome chairs among the *Arizona Highways* and ash trays on stands and evidently could be depended upon to sit quietly, because the girl behind the desk stared at Bingo with a kind of uneasy mistrust at having anyone at all approach.

"Excuse me," Bingo said, "but do you have any change?"

"What for?" the girl asked.

"I want to get something to eat out of that machine in the hall, and all I have is a dollar."

"No, I don't have change for a dollar," she said.

"Well, could you ask someone else, maybe? Or I could go across the street to that little sandwich shop and bring food back if it would be all right to leave."

"You'll lose your appointment if you leave."

"Would you mind if I ask some of those other people? I've already asked the other clients, and nobody has . . ."

"Clients cannot go beyond the reception area until the preliminary interview," the girl said.

"The children haven't had lunch," Bingo persisted in an equable tone. "Is there a place in the building where . . ."

"I'm *sorry*," said the girl. "There is no place."

"Mrs. Gorman," a black woman, coming in at the rear of the room, announced loudly, "Mrs. Gorman?"

No one moved. Bingo suggested herself—"Gartman?"— and the woman, rechecking her paper, agreed.

"Will you come back here for your informational interview, please, Mrs. Gartman?"

This consisted in being given forms and filling them out under the woman's watchful eye, so that she had to try to do it from memory, with only a covert peek into her purse at where she had jotted down Max's birthplace and her financial assets. Max had pretty well known (it was lucky) what they would ask.

"I think I've answered just about everything," Bingo said, briskly handing over the papers and closing her purse. "Do you, by any chance, have change for a dollar?"

"No, I'm sorry," the woman said, expertly riffling the papers for signs of blank spaces. "You can go sit back down now. Heah—you belong to any organization?"

"The Sierra Club and . . ." Bingo began, momentarily forgetful. But then she decided it would be a good thing for Maxine to belong to. The woman filled it in but did not look up at her any more, so Bingo went back and took her seat. It seemed impossible but was the case: that they had been there forty-five minutes and this was all that had happened. Bingo stared long and disbelieving at her watch.

"I'm hungry," Ronda complained. She was picking her nose, which gave her an unsupervised air, so that Bingo admonished her.

"Only in private," she said. "Around here you must mind your manners. They will think you don't know any better." This is what she would have told Nelson and Caroline, too.

"She's hungry." Derek giggled.

"What revolting children," Bingo said, but kindly. "Derek, why don't you take the dollar and go across to that sandwich shop . . ." Derek seemed a bit more resourceful than Nelson. Not so sheltered.

"Mrs. Gartman, will you and the children step this way?" the black woman called to them. She led them beyond her desk to another desk, empty, around which chairs for waiting were arrayed, and told them to sit down. "Your preliminary interview. Mrs. MacNary, the In-House Casework Supervisor, will be here in a minute. Were you applying for welfare?"

This extraordinary assumption affected Bingo like a kind of challenge. She stared. All tales of all bureaucracies recalled themselves to her.

"No, I am not here for welfare. I am here because I was made to come so that you can see whether I am a fit or an unfit person."

The woman made a noise in her nose and smartly re-evaluted Bingo with a roll of the eye. Bingo felt her face grow defiantly down-turned and disdainful in reply. She felt subtly less fit, and stiffened to resist this feeling.

They sat arrayed in front of the empty desk for nearly twenty minutes. Bingo's stomach growled. She did not try to keep Ronda and Derek from scrambling on their chairs and hopping off and even, once, crawling into the fine cave of the kneehole of the desk. She was aware of disapproving looks everywhere. She resisted them.

"Now, then, Mrs. Gartman"—a fat, blond woman appeared, bulging in a gabardine dress, her hair piled two feet high, like Marie Antoinette's, and batted her cold, purple-lidded eyes at them—"and these are the children?"

"Yes."

"Yes, could you have them sit . . . ?"

"Ronda and Derek." The children scrambled back onto their chairs.

"Yes. How old are they? How old are you, children?" The children told her.

"Mrs. Gartman, what is your approximate weekly income?" Bingo told her.

"And the amount of your debts? How much money do you have to pay each month? Payments, rent, everything, but not counting food, if you can tell me?"

"I'm not applying for welfare," Bingo said. "You are to see whether or not I am fit to take care of my children."

"I *know* why you are here, Mrs. Gartman. I'm just going to ask you a few routine questions now."

"I feel most unfit, most derelict, in my duty at the moment," Bingo said watchfully, "because the children haven't had lunch, and nobody has change for a dollar, or else we would have gotten something out of the food machine in the hall. Do you . . ."

"You will agree to medical and psychological examinations? I know this seems odd to you, but it is strictly routine and nothing at all to be afraid of. Sign here. This is just a permission slip saying you are being tested of your own free will."

"Would you by any chance have change for a dollar?" Bingo asked more loudly, assuming she had not been heard.

The woman shook her head, smiling, and tapped impatiently for Bingo's signature on a blank line on a half-sheet of paper. Bingo signed. Perhaps the woman was deaf and only lip-read.

"How long have you and Mr. Gartman been separated?

"Are both your parents still living and in good health?

"What employment have you had?

"Do you operate a motor vehicle?

"Were your pregnancies normal?

"Have you ever had fits or fainting?"

Bingo gave up trying to imagine what Max's actual circumstances might be and began to answer truthfully, deciding that this at least had the merit of making her seem convincing. Normal pregnancies, no fits or fainting. The woman wrote in a slow backhand and then, when the questionnaire was finished, appeared to be going to do the whole thing over on her typewriter. Bingo rose.

"Do you . . ." she began.

"I'm sorry, Mrs. Gartman, we can't give cash from this office. Any check will have to come through Sacramento and takes ten days to two weeks," replied the woman, without looking at them again. And nobody told them what to do, so they went back and sat down in chairs.

fourteen

Barney went back to the bathroom, not too quickly, which would have made him seem eager for their baths and their strictures, and not so slowly as to seem to be trying to hide. Casually he limped in. Max's friend sat now on the edge of the tub, drinking her sherry, and Max, with a sly and startled look, closed the medicine cabinet and muttered something about aspirin. As he opened the door and stepped in, Barney was newly aware of the steam and bubbling geyser noises; it was like stepping into the sinful sort of Turkish bath you read about in Tennessee Williams. He had nerved himself up to taking his bathing suit off very coolly, and he now did.

His audience cheered, with only the faintest derision. Barney hoped the derision was not for his anatomy but only for his reticence. Max inspected him, but more for signs of reticence than for physical details. Barney found he did not mind, and it even seemed perfectly natural after the first few seconds of exposure to be standing there without his clothes: not bad at all. He climbed into the tub, squatted in the froth, then lowered himself onto his backside, extending his sore leg carefully until it encountered the vigorous current from the pump. It was a pleasant feeling, like the one you get standing in front of the place where the water comes into the swimming pool, a strong, warm current. Momentary alarm when Max appeared to consider climbing back in with him. He expanded, filled the tub, sloshed around in a proprietary fashion, and she just fished her underpants from where they had fallen in the clothes hamper and pulled them on. They were black and had holes, through which little bristles protruded. If only women would understand the bad effect of ugly underwear. Bingo didn't understand it very well, either, Barney had to admit. But he couldn't feel aggrieved about that, for once, because it was really awfully pleasant to lie in this seething tub. He felt successful. This was his first success in a long time, he thought.

He leaned back. Currents and bubbles caressed him. His

ladies mercifully or disappointingly seemed to lose interest in him now that he had acceded to their wishes. Max's friend was pinning up her hair where tendrils had escaped and lay wetly on her shoulders. Her face, which Barney could see in the mirror, was pink and clean. She was really a rather attractive woman.

"Now, isn't that better?" she asked. "Now you can relax and be yourself."

"I feel less myself. More anonymous, like a comfortable blob," he assured her, meaning to compliment her recipe for nakedness and soothing baths. Her face in the mirror turned disapproving.

"I don't think you are in touch with yourself at *all,*" she said.

"I know as much about myself as I care to know," he said cheerfully.

"Is there much to know?" Max suggested.

"Do you have a self?" said her friend at the same time, both very rudely, and Barney felt more annoyed than he would have thought possible at such irrelevant speculations by unknown ladies.

"I *do* have a self," he said, "and it has nothing to do with baths or my bare skin."

"It's your cock, I bet," said the blond lady, coming over to sit on the edge of the tub. "It always is with men. It must be nice to have a self you can see right out there in front of you."

"That's not myself either. It's only part of me, which is different," Barney insisted. "Sometimes I think it isn't part of me, actually. You get so you think of them as quite autonomous."

Max's friend peered solicitously into the tub, but Barney's

second self was modestly obscured by the churning bubbles. Max, Barney observed, had surreptitiously opened the medicine cabinet again and sat quietly contemplating the contents, and seemed to be interested only from time to time in Barney's self.

"My self is what I do!" he said suddenly, as if no one had ever thought of this before. The ladies, who had turned away, looked at him, more surprised that he was still thinking about it than at his explanation. The blonde was pulling stockings on her long, damp legs.

"I make things, then I can see them, and then when I understand their form better I understand me!" He was most pleased with this explanation. He lay back. The bubbles caressed him; it was like bathing in Alka-Seltzer. The force of the water massaged him, and some center of himself seemed to be dissolving outward through his skin, like a dissolving tablet; he could strangely feel himself effervesce.

"This isn't bad," he said. "You know, I prescribe these things to people, but I never tried one."

The blond lady dangled her hand and wrist in the swirl, in the general neighborhood of Barney's autonomous member, which washed against her like seaweed, and she laughed. Max was still staring trancelike before the medicine cabinet, like a cat before a fish bowl. Barney, in the fish bowl, felt worried.

"Can I get you anything? What are you looking for?"

"Oh, nothing. I was more or less wondering what kind of stuff a doctor would keep in his own medicine chest."

"Just one or two doses of things," Barney said, seized by a realistic apprehensiveness. "Not a full dose of anything, but just enough to hold somebody in an emergency until they can see their own physician. A few Gantrisin tablets for a sudden flare-up of bladder infection, an initial dosage of oral penicillin—that sort of thing. We used to have neighbors who descended in droves with sundry complaints, regularly in rotation at dinnertime, the whole blockful of neighbors. So I got in the habit of being prepared."

"You are what you eat!" remarked Max's friend, inconsequentially, it seemed.

"You are what you *drop,*" Max corrected.

"No," Barney said, remembering his idea, "you are what you do," and this, too, seemed to displease his female guests, because they glared and sniffed.

"You are a healer, I suppose, in your very essence?" the blond woman inquired. And Barney had to admit that was not true.

"That is my work but not my essence." He wondered if he had been right to be a doctor. "I'm a maker of things," he said. "I once built a house with my own hands, when I was seventeen. I once commanded my own ship for two years."

"Really?" they said.

"I am—I think of myself as being more interesting than I look," Barney said.

"Indeed?" said the blonde, crossing her long legs and shifting slightly. Barney could have inserted a finger at the tiny indentation where her coccyx met the hard porcelain tub and thought to himself that it must be uncomfortable as hell to be so skinny. But it was a splendid orthopedic display. He admired the various protuberances of her backbone.

"For instance, I know all the names of all the bones in your body, of which there are two hundred and six; and I can put them back together properly or even in new combinations. And I can, oh, build you fences and do celestial navigation, and I can skin a bear. I can develop my own pictures. I can paint a little, nothing much. I can cook."

"Indeed?" said the friend.

"Gee, wow," said Max.

"Do you have a *darkroom?*" the friend said, in what might have been meaningful tones. She had stood up and was fastening her stockings to the straps of a garter belt, but she wore no pants, presenting an alluring triangle. Barney thought of getting her in the darkroom like that, and underneath the water he began to grow autonomously, so that it was necessary to sit there and think pious, husbandly thoughts until it was safe to surface. He climbed out of the tub and offered to show them his studio darkroom. He wrapped himself in a towel, and the ladies came along after him down the hall, undressed; but he did not, firmly did not, let himself lay libidinous plans.

Bingo, Ronda, and Derek had now been waiting for about half an hour in the anteroom, which had probably once been the living room, of an old green bungalow on the other side of the street, to which they had been sent. On the way over they had met someone with change for a dollar, but this other building had no machines. Bingo was in conflict about whether to dash next door to the sandwich shop or not; on the whole she was afraid to. Anyway, her own hunger had been replaced by a headache. An elderly man had offered Ronda and Derek some gum, which they took, without saying thank you; had never been told not to accept things from strangers or to say thank you. Bingo suppressed a fearful fantasy about a psychopath with candy and little Ronda.

A sort of fence had been erected between them and two ladies at large desks, who answered telephones and put papers on various shelves of the bookshelf stacked with papers behind them. On the desk of each was a little tower of deep trays, like a miniature parking garage, and each bin was filled with papers. The women wore tired expressions of extreme boredom and irritation to match the one Bingo supposed she, being tired and irritated, must also be wearing. Ronda and Derek, her ostensible children, sat like good little things on too-big chairs, legs dangling, reading *Life* and *Sports Illustrated*.

Bingo now found that her irritation and indignation were available to her only in flashes: pricks of developing hatred for this green room, and homesickness, a wish to be in her house. But her mind slid off onto other things. She tried to apply it to things she meant to do: address some envelopes for the Ecology Center, call the Bus-a-Child theater-party chairman, make curtains for the children's rooms, paint shelves; but she could not even sustain purposeful thoughts of this kind. It was as if her thoughts were being vacuumed off and her head filled with a docility-producing vapor, rendering her able to sit still for long minutes, quarter hours, hours. Everyone else in the room sat breathing the same gas, still except for a crone, a crone with a plastic purse, who gave loud exclamations to herself—"My Lord! Hum!"—at intervals without change of expression, as if she did not know she was speaking. A young black girl, pregnant and stolid, with rollers in her straightened hair, slept in the corner chair. A black social worker, with a cloud of natural fuzz, stared contemptuously at her as she slept. Someone ought—drifted through Bingo's mind—to do something . . . Quiver of indignation. Good little children to sit so still so long. You would rather be somewhere else, lying by a warm swimming pool, and you would have a good tan, Barney rubbing your back. A fireman giving you artificial respiration, pushing against your brown back, and your cheek lying against the hot cement. Bingo felt tired and wanted to press her hot cheek against the fireman's strong, brown back.

Something must have buzzed in the ear of one of the women, who looked up suddenly and said, "Mrs. Kitano will see you now."

Bingo looked up. "You," the woman said, and pointed to a door. A sign on it told Bingo that Mrs. Kitano, a tiny, wrinkled Oriental person, was the Case Study Screening and Placement Officer. Bingo was invited to enter the cubicle office, and to sit, and to answer questions about how old she was and where she was born and other matters on which she had no information. She made up things, with a fine abandoned and philosophical air. She was determined about this, committed.

"Sometimes in these cases," the Case Study Screening and Placement Officer was saying to her, "we feel it is to the advantage of all to give Help rather than to interfere with the Family Unit. Have you ever had Help, Maxine?"

Had she, Bingo wondered, but the woman didn't wait for an answer anyway.

"We're going to give you several tests to indicate something about what might Help you best. Emotional tests, to show how you feel about things and to show us the areas in which we can be most helpful. Perhaps later some vocational-interest tests. Aptitude tests. Tolerance tests. Stability tests. . . . Nothing to be afraid of. Just fill out the answers as honestly as you can, and if nothing comes to mind just put the first thing that does, even if it doesn't seem to apply." And she provided pencil and printed form and separate paper for marking answers, and left.

Bingo stared resentfully at the papers and pencil. "You have one hour," came the woman's voice, from the hall.

When her first irritation subsided a little Bingo decided to take the test; it could only improve Max's case, assuming she, Bingo, was in fact the more stable of the two. The opposite possibility did not seem a probability. And also Bingo was not entirely unwilling to experience the fascination of having a disinterested official person analyze her character, maybe even tell her something helpful; it was a chance worth taking the trouble for.

Most people are honest.	True	False
Sometimes I feel a tight band around my head.	True	False
Sometimes I think people are following me.	True	False
I have never gotten in trouble because of my sex impulses.	True	False
I generally get the raw end of the deal.	True	False
I am a happy person.	True	False
Some days life scarcely seems worth living.	True	False
I sometimes have feelings of hate.	True	False
I sometimes have feelings of fear.	True	False

True False. True False. True False. Bingo worked quickly and as truthfully as she could, resisting temptations either to answer as she thought Max would or to try to outwit the examiners in their painfully apparent attempts to prove her a manic-depressive paranoiac schizophrenic. She put the pathological answer, faithfully, where it was the true answer.

I get headaches a lot.	True	False
My sex life is satisfactory.	True	False
I sometimes have thoughts of suicide.	True	False

You would have had to be a very slow reader to take a whole hour with it. Bingo sat aimlessly staring at the green wall, wondering if Ronda and Derek were all right, inspecting the dismal aspects of the old structure, the slanting doorjambs, the sloping floors. Surprising that a state agency was allowed in such a firetrap. Bingo thought about fire, about being in a fire. Sometimes I want to burn everything down. True False. The house would be burning down, and the firemen would come rushing in; into her chamber surrounded by flames and forbidding smoke. And no one dared come in but Geoffrey Nichols, who discovered her there. Still tied to the bedpost, where the villain had been going to work his will on her but the fire had scared him away. She would be naked, her body very beautiful. Unable to restrain his passion, Geoffrey Nichols would take her himself, several times, amid shouts from outside to hurry, the danger, the flames, to which they in their ecstasy were mostly oblivious. But then afterward and at the last possible moment he had flung a blanket around her and carried her in strong arms down the ladder to safety. Barney in after years always saying, "I was so terrified; I thought they'd never get you out of there!" and she giving a secret, dreamlike smile.

fifteen

They had made the darkroom and painting studio out of the laundry, a small room between the kitchen and the garage. The washer and dryer were in the garage so that Barney could have the whole place to himself except when

Bingo had to go through to do the wash. Barney had constructed folding shutters that fitted tightly over the window and opened to daylight—north light at that—when he wanted to use it as a painting studio. Max and her friend were earnestly and politely inspecting his work. Barney had gotten quite used to their breasts and things and realized that he was far more concerned with whether they would like his paintings. There were a lot of paintings. Against the wall around the room, on shelves, stacked, hung, were all Barney's paintings, canvas faces staring from every surface, gazing up from the tabletop, from behind the laundry sink, from the easel. The room swam with faces, eyes. The faces wore funny hats, robes, masks. Some were green and contorted with malice; some melted into pastel beauties of irresolution. The face of a jester in his belled cap made mocking grimaces at the viewer. A Venetian gondolier regarded the ladies with tender, dark eyes and a musical, desirous smile.

"But all these pictures are of you!" Max said.

"Well, I'm the only person in here," Barney said. "There's a dearth of models. The kids won't sit still, and Bingo . . ."

"There must be a hundred oil paintings here of you! Look, Nellie, all of him!"

"Why—all of him!" said the friend.

"Do you really get dressed up like this to paint yourself?" Max asked, looking at the picture of Barney wearing a tall bishop's miter, his face solemnly composed in an expression of ecclesiastical anger or maybe pain.

"No, of course not. Where would I get a hat like that? I look at photos, or I make them up. Obviously I have to make most of them up," he said, meaning in particular one picture where his face was green and seemed to be melting.

"Do you look at yourself in the mirror or what?" Max asked.

"No, I just paint what's in my mind's eye, if you'll pardon the expression," Barney admitted. The ladies looked with renewed curiosity at the pictures, a hundred of them, all of Barney.

"There are many sides to my character," he said.

"You paint rather well," said the blond lady.

"Nellie's a painter, too," Max said.

"Oh, not really. I'm not very . . ."

"Of course, I just dabble . . ." Barney said. But they shushed him and seemed really interested in the pictures, turning them over, stacking seen ones against the wall, walking backward for better looks. Barney watched it all with increasing anxiety, proprietary artistic pride.

Suddenly Max said, "Which one is you?" And Barney, standing in his towel, bare-legged among all these canvases, which were now propped around like so many fun-house mirrors distorting and misreading his countenance, suffered a momentary confusion, a feeling of panicky unreality. He reached out as if to steady himself. For the briefest moment he didn't know the answer to Max's question.

"Which one is the most you?"

"They're all me, obviously," he said after an instant, but the instant had shown him something unpleasant.

"Some are more me than others," he qualified.

"*Guess* which one is me," he said in another second, fighting down the sensation of panic. Perhaps none of them was him. Perhaps the real corporeal Barney was insufficiently apparent, unpaintable; he had always suspected this. His anguish and anticipation increased. Would they guess? Did he himself know? He felt, or began to feel, quite sure that one of the pictures was more peculiarly him, and that he didn't know which one, and that he was quite strangely desperate that the ladies find him. He felt like a little boy in agonies behind the curtain while his mother pretended to hunt everywhere. The exquisite suspense, the anxiety to be hidden, to be found, to surprise. To learn which one was him. He didn't know and caught his breath while they capered irreverently among the strange faces and never once looked at him standing there naked except for his towel.

But nothing at all happened. Max soon appeared to tire of the whole thing and went into the kitchen, where her clatter alarmed Barney, who followed. He was getting chilly, besides, in spite of the hot Santa Ana weather, and wanted to put his clothes back on. He wished Bingo would come and somehow dispatch his odd guests and feed him something decent and substantial.

In fact, Barney realized, Max had not even mentioned Bingo, or the children, either. She seemed to have forgotten them; perhaps she was suppressing her anxiety, but she didn't appear very anxious, except when she would look down toward Doctor Harris's. Then her longing gaze, the pained gaze of the cruelly exiled down upon his terrestrial dwelling, transformed her into a swarthy Blessed Damozel. It was sad to see the poor woman's face transfixed with love; it was so unlikely that she would ever receive any. Fortunately she seemed continuously hungry in the ordinary way, too, which allowed Barney to fill one of her manifold and manifest needs by suggesting at intervals, as they sat rather dully around the kitchen, that they have something to eat. Then Barney had an excuse to eat with her. And there is no denying the relation of full bellies to happiness. If Bingo were gone all the time he would get quite fat, he recognized.

He also noticed that Max put food in her pockets. She asked if she could take the cream to Doctor Harris for his supper, a ridiculous suggestion, which Barney vetoed.

"I was supposed to stop and pick some up," she explained. "It's all he eats, and orange juice." Which, no doubt, meant that Doctor Harris was supremely happy, too happy even to eat. They looked down at Doctor Harris moving in his garden for a short time, but he did not look especially happy, just somnambulistic. His hands worked slowly among the fleshy succulents; his face was expressionless. Max could be heard to pant, actually to pant at the sight; and even the calm friend, who was coming in from the darkroom with two of Barney's pictures under her arm, apparently forgot what she wanted with them at the sight of Doctor Harris's hairy, bare torso among the succulents. Barney was frustrated at her failure to say anything about the pictures. Had she found the real him? But she just put them down on the dishwasher and said she had to go over to the Harrises' to see about her appointment. The expression in her eyes was identical to Max's; they were like witnesses to a supernatural event, people who would never be the same again.

"How old would you guess she is?" asked Max, when her friend had left. "Only thirty-two, and she has already had her eyelids lifted. She dreads growing old, and she thought they were puckering. She had to lie with cloths on her eyes for four days, and we held her hands and played music for her. She has a terror of growing old, but Hal is helping her."

Inside the Harrises' it was quiet, the ordinary banal quiet of places without conversation. The television was on so that Irene, sitting under the beauty-parlor-sized hair dryer in her dressing room, could come in to peek at it from time to time. The pregnant cat prowled restlessly, looking for a nest or perhaps for Max, and exchanged contemptuous glances with Irene each time they found themselves in the same room. Hal Harris's next patient napped by the edge of the swimming pool, and the present patient, a poet, was raving and writhing on the red-bedspread-covered bed. Doctor Harris drowsed on the straight chair in the corner of the bedroom, replying in grunts to the patient, soothing him. He was blinded by the sleep mask: a blind poet, like Milton.

"Are you there, Hal? Hal, are you there?"

"Mmmmmmm."

"Stay with me, Hal. Help me through this."

"Mmmmm." Hal had been thinking, until his thoughts became too blurry, how all the ravings people raved came out the same. It was funny that a poet didn't rave, somehow, more poetically. But not surprising.

"Mmmmmm," he said, returning to semiconsciousness in response to a question. He was there. He was listening.

"Your mother," he said. "Mmmmmm." It was a lovely, warm day. He would have a swim after a while. Then he fully awoke, chilled by the unasked-for recollection of those plants Max had brought and which were—where? Had he planted them? It didn't do to let the roots remain exposed to direct sun; never mind that succulents were hardy. He couldn't quite remember, and this was an agony, like not quite sneezing. The poor little things might well be out there shriveling—was it when the firemen came? Or when he had found the pot of prunings?

"How was I to know she would die? It was just a simple operation—varicose veins. Why should she die? But she said she would. She was afraid. She died from the ether, or maybe it was chloroform. Is that what they use? She wanted me to visit her in the hospital the night before, and I didn't go. My own mother. Too much to do. No, I was sore at her for crying and being afraid to go to the damn hospital. No, I was sore at her for being a whiny bitch, and she never loved me, anyhow. You know, I walked outside the hospital and looked up and didn't go in. She didn't love me, but I could have gone to the damn hospital, and at least I wouldn't feel so guilty now. I mean, when somebody is dead how can you tell her you're sorry? How is she to know? Maybe she died in grief wondering why Billy hadn't come to see her in the hospital or something like that. Oh, God." His sobbing was fortunately loud enough to allow Doctor Harris to tiptoe from the room.

sixteen

After another wait, invested with a certain portentousness by the clerical personnel who scrutinized her in deep-breathed silence, Bingo had been sent in to see a Mr. Peguez. She was apprehensive, but he was only a tired, paternal man, whose shirt collar stuck out from his neck like a hoop, as if he had lost weight or was wearing someone else's clothes, or—it crossed Bingo's newly cautious mind—perhaps he *was* someone else. He had a yokel haircut and a kind expression, though he peered intently at Bingo as if trying to decide if she was quite clean in a way she would have resented from a bank president but now tamely and acceptingly sat for, trying to look clean. She stuck her shoes out. Clean tennis shoes. Her dress was old and ugly.

"So, we meet again, Maxine. I was hoping our little talk last year might have helped you straighten things out." Bingo raised her eyes and looked directly at him, but there was no sign of irony. He did not remember Max. Or perhaps it did not matter to them if your face changed into someone else's.

"Everything is fine. I don't know why we're going through all this. The kids are fine; I'm fine. I could use some money, is all. I have trouble making ends meet."

"How about getting a job?"

"There isn't anything I can do," she said. It was true enough. "And the kids get home from school at two-thirty, and so where would I get a baby-sitter?" All true. She had thought about getting a job. These statements flowed from her as if rehearsed. Mr. Peguez sighed. Baby-sitters. No skills. The usual woman's problems.

"So you give up. A little reality problem—where to get a baby-sitter—and you give up. Instead of trying to lead a normal life . . ." He stopped, watched her, changed his tone. "I expect you think I'm awfully square, people like me," he said sadly. Bingo politely protested. She did think him awfully square: yokel haircut and earnest, reforming tones. She could not conceal it altogether.

"Yes, yes, I know," he said, staring at her high-bridged nose. "But let me tell you something about us squares." Bingo shrugged. "We live in our mortgaged houses, make payments on the car, worry how to pay for the kids' braces. Our wives nag; our wives are unhappy. We watch TV, we go to the baseball games—we go to church, for that matter. We read the books that everyone is talking about and forget to write letters to our congressmen and have just begun to dare to let our sideburns grow a little. I know. We do the same things day in and day out. We don't know the meaning of life."

I am just like him, Bingo thought dismally. Barney and I. An ugly man, with a dull life. She was embarrassed for them both. His office was air-conditioned, but she sweated unattractively.

"Our wives want a built-in kitchen. Hell, our wives have a built-in kitchen. We live in the Valley, and all the houses have built-in kitchens."

Bingo thought of her built-in kitchen and tears unaccountably sprang to her eyes. We don't know the meaning of life. We do the same thing day in and day out. We are not beautiful.

"All those things satirists satirize, we do! The Boy Scouts, Little League. Still, you can't just pin a label on us squares and say that everything we do is wrong. Because we do some good with ourselves and for each other. We have love and security—maybe not excitement—but we know somebody's going to be there, and our kids have a sense of security, right?"

"Well, why are you making it sound so bad, then?" Bingo asked. "Surely it's better to pretend it's all just—I don't know—just swell, even if it isn't. More gallant."

"I didn't want to gloss over the bad part, the part people like you usually dwell on. Because the point is that maybe it's bad, but it still isn't as bad as living in dumps with social workers after you and putting out all the time to support a habit and living in fear of the fuzz." Bingo found his familiarity with words like fuzz offensive, but she could agree with his idea. It was even some consolation.

"Well, why don't you see this in your own life? A woman with your psychological profile—you're intelligent and not that unstable—you could probably, if you got some help, cope with things pretty well. Your depression, it would probably clear up if you just changed your life," he said. "A normal life . . ." Bingo recognized simultaneously that he was now talking about her, Bingo's, psychological profile, as recorded, True False, and, moreover, that she led what he meant by a normal life, which seemed elaborately tragic. She had tried to avoid a normal life.

"I have box turtles and hens," she said. She had a momentary fancy, the dull life proceeding at box-turtle pace, the aging woman in the smoggy back yard with turtle food, she and the turtle glaring undeceivedly at each other with their fixed and lidless eyes, the weight of the shell on her back. She began quite openly to cry. Mr. Peguez, accustomed, reached with a fluid gesture to the box of Kleenex in the bottom of his desk drawer and extended her a handful of tissues. He did not understand her reference to box turtles, but his expression confided that he did not need to know; he understood. With practiced eye he watched and, eaglelike, leaned forward at the correct moment, as Bingo, with embarrassment, was wiping her eyes, and said shockingly, "I wouldn't be surprised if you wanted us to take your kids, basically. All your actions seem designed to force our hand."

"We aren't going to have braces and all that stuff and Little League. I wouldn't subject my children to it," Bingo sniffed, irritated and baffled at herself. *Did* she want him to take Nelson and Caroline? "I didn't mean for the kitchen to be built in. . . . Should I have had them rip it out?" she said.

"Max, if I may say so, your pose of a superannuated hippie is nothing if not undignified." Mr. Peguez had apparently lost the train of her thought and began in a speechmaking voice again. "Kids nowadays are pathetic enough, but when social deviance gets carried too far—people in their thirties—it's sad. It's sad and it's silly. We have your Martini drinkers on the one hand, these Beverly Hills types, just as bad for my money, and we have the dropouts, like you. How does it happen? How can we help prevent this?"

"Mr. Peguez," Bingo began, pulling herself together, "I disapprove of the social norms this social-welfare system is based on. They are very bourgeois, and they leave no room for, well, joy. I'm very glad to be getting into this, finding out about it."

"Ah, your philosophy is what I question. Now, if you want to talk about joy . . ." he began, but then a secretary came in and pointed out that their ten minutes were up and Mr. Hopkins was waiting outside. Bingo realized in a second or two that they were waiting for her to get up and leave the office. She did. She stood outside the door, rather dazed, and watched the secretary help in an old weak man with watery, runny blue eyes and a straggle of hair.

"Mr. Hopkins, you told me once that you believe in Jesus Christ Our Lord," Mr. Peguez could be heard to say through the door.

"Yes," came the thin old man's voice.

"So do I, Mr. Hopkins, so do I, and we both know that Our Lord has promised that we should meet our loved ones again, isn't that so?"

So. "But, Mr. Hopkins, the Bible tells us, doesn't it, that we must not murder ourselves; you know that." Murmur of response.

"You haven't eaten, Mr. Hopkins. You just sit there wait-ing to die, and if that isn't self-murder . . . Our Lord giveth and taketh away, now, isn't that right?" Bingo could hear the old man begin to cry and then Mr. Peguez going on,

"How, then, can you expect to meet her again in heaven if you don't eat?" and then some secretary walking by told her to sit down.

seventeen

Barney found Max in his bedroom, cast across his bed in an attitude more limp and motionless than that of sleep. He leaped forward, for a second thinking of death. But she blinked. Her eyes, always unnaturally bright, were now as bright as glass and as unmoving, seeming to emanate tangible rays, like heat off a pavement. Something similar seemed to emanate from her whole body. She lay stiff and brown and staring, like an old dead Indian, and whatever it was about her, Barney could identify it no more precisely than as the smell of something heated and cooling off; and the color of her skin had changed and yellowed in the same process. She was as solid as ever; but now that she was lying on her back her breasts looked less pendulous. Her legs were spread apart in the torn underpants uninvitingly. Her smile, as she raised her head a little to look at him, was distant and silly.

"Wow," she said, "what a high!"

"What's the matter? What have you taken? Are you all right?" From the medicine cabinet, obviously. His mind raced over the toxic stuff in there.

Max's head lolled, and her mouth stretched foolishly. Barney's irritation increased with his anxiety: what if she had taken some impossible mortal combination of things? What had she taken it for, moreover? Was she wretched? Of course, yes, you knew to look at Max that she was wretched, but because she was gallant and because her desperation was self-contained, you tended to think she had it under control. Barney was angry with himself for having misjudged her. He was angry at her, also, for being wretched.

"It must be great to be a doctor. You could just stay stoned all the time, legally stoned the whole time," she sighed. "Would you like to screw?"

"What did you take?" Barney insisted, mind tormented with concern and intermittent thoughts of malpractice suits, for which he despised himself.

"I don't know, but Bennies, I think. Six or eight. A pretty good high!"

Barney started to run, hurt himself, went more slowly into the bathroom. The medicine cabinet was slyly shut, nothing inside disarranged. He had no Benzedrine, so what had she mistaken for it? There. It was Propadrine, in fact. A vasoconstrictor. No wonder she looked high and dry.

"At least your nasal passages must be clear," he said to her disgustedly, coming back.

"Why are we here?"

Barney understood this to be a rhetorical metaphysical question, and ignored it.

"Let's go down to Hal's. I have to take him his cream; he must be starving. His bitch of a wife never feeds him. It's funny how he married her: he just went to this psychiatrist convention in Louisville, Kentucky, and came back with a wife. She used to be married to a man who made her watch him doing it with men. I forget which part he did with men, the woman's part or the man's part, but anyhow it hung her up. At first we figured her hang-ups interested him. Now she doesn't interest him at all. She doesn't mind, because she's redecorating. I think she's having an affair with her decorator, but of course Hal isn't jealous, so what's the point? He screws everybody except me."

"Why not you?" Barney asked, fascinated, though the reason seemed clear enough. He held her limp arm and took her pulse.

"He says he doesn't like to screw people who don't come." She now raised herself on her elbow to look beseechingly at Barney and then flopped back. "With him I would, which he also knows. He's a monster, really, even though everyone loves him. They don't see his infinitely incalculable pure patient hate and malice and goodness and love. He is a monster of comprehension. He is real but spiritually removed—I don't know. He doesn't mind a blow job, but he just won't fuck. We have a love-hate relationship, I think. I think he loves me, in a way. At least he doesn't love Irene. He . . ."

"Maybe you should drink something. We need to keep our fluids up when we take too much antihistamine," Barney interrupted in a droning doctor voice.

"If he didn't love me in a way he wouldn't keep me around; anybody could water the plants and vacuum. I'm a child to him, I think. He hasn't got any kids. Doesn't like them."

"You hang around being *his* child, while *your* children . . ." Barney began severely, but then the doorbell rang.

It was a policeman. "I'm sorry to bother you, sir," the policeman began most politely, in a different voice from the one they use when they come up fiercely to the car window after pulling you off the road. He was large, with an anonymous, orderly face and a short military haircut, and he wore an American-flag tie clasp. Barney, who had no fear of police, was nonetheless curious.

"Well! Not at all!" he said, smiling, jovial. He had learned how to talk to police when he was an intern working in an emergency room and they were always bringing in drunks. You talk to them confidentially, knowingly, showing that you share their concern for human frailty.

The policeman's face reflected just a trace of concern for the fact that this apparently able-bodied man was home at an hour when you usually find only mothers. An artist, maybe, or some other suspicious type. Barney, sensing this, drooped convalescently and limped backward a step.

"Have you been troubled with anybody—a suspicious-looking guy around here?"

Barney uneasily tried to understand. Was the cop hinting that *he* was a suspicious-looking character?

"What sort of— Come in, Officer." He limped into the front hall and started suddenly with the recollection of the grand-larcenous Jacuzzi pump in the bathroom. And the stoned lady in his bed. The cop extended a photograph of someone who did not look at all like Barney as he followed Barney into the hall. It was a photo of a suspicious-looking character, in fact.

"Wanted for questioning. A dope addict out on parole and likely associated with a couple of robberies. We know he hangs out, or used to, with your neighbor, that loony—uh—that psychiatrist."

"We just moved here a couple of months ago," Barney said, studying the picture, an unknown face, a weaselly face. This must be what is meant by weaselliness in the face. Barney could not remember ever having seen a weasel. He was good on faces because of experience with his own (chipmunk) face. He knew how to narrow the distance between the eyes, cast a gray shadow, view askance from the sly eye, elongate the nose to make himself a bishop or a judge.

"Haven't seen him around?"

"No, no one like that," Barney assured him. While he looked at the photo the policeman, he knew, looked at him. "Loony psychiatrist, you say?"

"No, that's your neighbor. Has a lot of dangerous people as patients, because he specializes in junkies, but then he's probably a junkie, too. He doesn't prescribe anything we can get him on, though. I don't mean to allege anything."

"This isn't Doctor Harris," Barney said.

"No, I know," the policeman said disgustedly, taking back the picture. "It's a robbery suspect."

"I'll have to meet Doctor Harris," Barney said, prompted by some undefined impulse of loyalty. "I'm an M.D. myself," he added, partly to embellish a fellow M.D. with the luster of his own rectitude and partly, perhaps, to convince this policeman he was not the sort of person who stole Jacuzzi pumps. He was alarmed that the policeman had not briskly pocketed his photo and badge and gone about his business. The law-enforcing eyes were restless and scrutinizing, which is bound to make you feel about to be caught whether you have done anything or not, because, of course, you have.

He was a perfectly benign-looking policeman. Except for the American-flag tie clasp. Did this mean he was the sort who would turn savage and beat you if you were not neat, or were black at the wrong place or time? Barney looked at the policeman's face to see if it was bulldog or bore signs of concealed paranoia. But it was Wheaties, and you couldn't tell how it would distort in rage or fear. There were no lines on it as clues. Perhaps he would beat you with no change of expression.

"You look like an understanding guy," the cop suddenly

said, in a lower voice, stepping close. "This is irregular, but—could I use the rest room?"

"Right there," Barney said, certainty concentrating all his wariness, all his powers. It was evidently the Jacuzzi pump he was after, after all. He showed the cop to the powder room behind them. If getting into the bathroom was his game he was going to have to ask, directly, for a search. Barney swallowed. The cop made peeing noises inside the powder room—perhaps was actually peeing!—and flushed the toilet. Washing-hands noises. In a minute he came out, told Barney to keep his eyes open, and left. Barney shivered and was oddly conscious that his head had been aching. Cops, robbery suspects, loony psychiatrists, nude firemen, unfit mothers. Tomorrow he would build a colossal, eight-foot-high fence.

He went back to see to his patient. She was sitting up on the bed, curled like a sow bug, into herself, head between her knees, covered over by her arms, and motionless. If you pushed her she would roll.

"Well, let's get you some orange juice now!" Barney said, in a therapeutic voice. "Before you wither up like a raisin."

"What did that cop want?" she asked weakly, and he saw that she was really shaking.

"Looking for some guy. He showed me a picture. A robbery-suspect patient of Harris's. *Not* the Jacuzzi pump."

"Oh, I knew not the Jacuzzi pump," she said, lifting her face. "The suspect, I suppose, is Noel, who's supposed to show up here, as a matter of fact. The cops are smart in an uncanny, lucky, dumb way."

"You really were scared, weren't you?" Barney said, as he saw her face. In fright it was hideous, drawn in and pinched, strained.

"I ought to be getting used to them, but I always get scared. I have this neurotic fear of going back to jail. That's what Hal says. I mean, I'm not so sure it's neurotic."

"Have you been to jail?" Barney asked. Like most people who have never been to jail, he thought it would be disagreeable but interesting, if you weren't there too long. Two or three days, to get the feel of it.

"I was in jail for three days once. I'd rather die than go back. Hal says my anxiety is intensified by having had these bad experiences as a child, when I was in the Juvenile Female Correction Home, which is this kind of practice jail for children, when I was eleven."

"Well, why?" Barney asked, indignant for her. "What happened?"

"Nothing. It wasn't so bad," she said, putting her head down again.

"I mean, why were you in a juvenile home?"

"I ran away a lot," she said. "I'll tell you how jail is. It's the feeling, when they put you in there, like the man from underground, or Kafka. You think you're an insect, an indescribably horrible but particular sensation consisting of your skin hardening and bumps coming out on you like stumps of new appendages, feelers and legs and things, and your eyes becoming flat or migrating into your fingertips. And then you get an insect brain capable of receiving only the crudest sensations; for instance, you would feel it only if someone stepped on you and squashed you, which you constantly expect them to do. Later you have a kind of amnesia about it except for feeling that you'd rather die than go back."

"Well, but *why*? What did you do? Why were you in?"

"It was my own fault, I suppose. I had committed myself to the funny farm at Camarillo, and you have to go before a judge, and somehow they found pot on me. Hal says that was self-destructive; I must have kept a joint or two in my pocket on purpose. So I was in while they figured what to do, which was to send me to Camarillo for drug rehabilitation. That was back when they thought you needed rehabilitating when you used marijuana, and they put me on probation for that, but meantime I was in jail for three days total."

"When you were *eleven?*"

"No, no, this was a few years ago, after I had been married to Hal. I was a mother, even."

"I'll go get you some orange juice," Barney said, agonized for her; she was clearly so agonized. He stroked her shoulder, to comfort her. Her skin, hot and dry, was not comfortable.

"And I had to go to a clinic until they thought I could function. I don't function, though." She laughed. "I stopped functioning. Can't cope. Mind blown, you see. Oh, sometimes I connect, for instance, at birthdays. I give the kids great birthday parties, wild fantasy parties, things hung all around, popcorn streamers, rented cotton-candy machine, grass for the mothers if they smoke. Nice Westwood mothers. Something turns me on about birthdays."

"That sounds nice, Max," Barney said. "Sometimes things like that mean more to a kid than whether, oh, whether you go to the P.-T.A. or not."

"I *go* to the P.-T.A.," Max said, shutting her eyes.

eighteen

Bingo, sitting in a waiting room, almost without warning and certainly without knowing why, was seized by a powerful constriction of the heart and a burning of the eyes: the inner and outer manifestations of tears of unknown origin; a feeling of powerful sadness drawn from the smell of the dog-eared magazines and institutional dust, from the teased bouffant hairdos of the dark Mexican girls with too-high heels and passing civil-service scores sitting at typewriters all around, and from people's names on doors, painted right on with terrifying hubris. Her feeling was, perhaps, not so much sadness now as terror and the consuming desire to be enfolded in a protective embrace, anybody's. Such was this need, and the terror, that if someone had come in and taken her on his lap and embraced her and unbuttoned her blouse, she would not have minded, despite the other people sitting around patiently in chrome chairs. The idea was comforting. Bingo could almost imagine the pleasure of warm, consoling hands inside her blouse enfolding her breasts. Perhaps, as she was sitting on the person's lap, she would feel a pleasant, hard lump under her as he became excited, and then, perhaps, kisses on her neck and breast, and perhaps the people would all go out or get called to their appointments. Then she could unzip his pants and put him inside her, and then the people could even come back and they wouldn't necessarily even notice what they were doing, and they could make love the whole time they were sitting there, him in his fireman's suit, with her dress pulled respectably down over her knees in front, without anyone even noticing that they were having wild pleasure.

Someone came in and called for Maxine Gartman, and Bingo was unnerved to realize that she was sitting entranced, a rapt and, no doubt, foolish smile on her face, staring into nowhere, and that her pants were quite wet. As she rose, her eyes darted around furtively and swiftly at the other people waiting. It was so: their eyes were all vacant, seeing afar off, and some of them had foolish smiles, others little frowns of concentration beneath the surface blankness as they stared and rocked, all driven by the waiting and the flat air and the hum of the air conditioner into the recesses of their however subtle or simple minds. Bingo tried to regain for the next interview whatever subtlety her mind might have once possessed, but only simplicity remained, and the need for love and a feeling of fear.

Doctor Harris went into his kitchen, looking fit, relaxed; he was having a mostly good day, but he was thirsty and he hadn't had his cream. He had had his orange juice.

"Where is my cream? Where's Max?" he asked Irene, who was opening a Coke and told him with satisfaction that Max had to go see about her children, who were being taken away from her.

"Which ah must say is not a bad idea," she added.

It seemed to Hal Harris that this was true. Max's children were a nuisance; he was always having to write letters for her, and, for instance, where was his cream? You couldn't seriously wish people to lose their children, especially smart ones like Derek and the little girl, but it was annoying not to find your cream when Max had promised to bring some in.

Confusing. He hummed and wandered away. Irene made a face after him.

"Ah'm going to be out tonight. With Gregson. We're going to, um, look at some wallpaper." She loaded her voice with innuendo, with the sliding sounds of the transparent lie, but Hal had wandered out of earshot and wouldn't have minded, anyway. Her pretty teeth clenched in disappointment. She had a headache. That cat dragged by; it looked as if it was going to have nineteen kittens—just what they needed around there in addition to the dangerous criminals and crazy housewives and pimps and such. Just then the four-o'clock patient, who had been doing some weeding for Hal in the front, came darting through the door, sweating and fearful, to say there was a cop car in the driveway. Irene couldn't have cared less.

Hal Harris—to whom this was announced on his patio, the four-o'clock patient trembling with the importance of his message and with the hope that Doctor Harris, the great man, would tremble also, would exhibit some human alarm —just walked around to the front drive, tightening his belt over his white-haired stomach, looking fit and relaxed, humming. He admitted without apparent hesitation that the dangerous ex-patient had been there but had been sent away, and that everything was indeed regrettable. This he had certainly discovered, but he did not feel keenly about it, since, apparently, the policeman did not either. A man has to make a living; they had their livings to make. The psychiatrist and the policeman did not, however, look at one another with rapport. Doctor Harris walked away, the warm sun on his belly, toward the dark house. In the police car, as the first officer climbed behind the wheel, the younger one, who had sat the whole time with his hand on his gun peering through the glass at what manner of man this crazy nut psychiatrist was, was just as mystified as ever; he was a new policeman and had not yet learned the art of making up his mind about a man just by the look of him.

It was easier to make up his mind about the hippies that came up the hill, with their greasy clouds of curls and shabby Civil War uniforms and buckskin pants and bare feet and beaded bands around their brows. One was a Union soldier, one a Confederate soldier, and another uniform, harder to decide about, may have come down from either the Spanish-American or the First World War: this was a young cop. His hand went to his gun again, but, of course, the filthy creatures hadn't done anything, and they couldn't see him; it was a gesture of self-indulgence. The hippies had come to talk to the psychiatrist, who had stopped in his driveway and was answering them, nodding, that same blank expression in his eyes. Then the radio came on and sped the young cop and his partner off somewhere down the hill, where there was a wreck.

Hal, whose mind was on a tall spray of *Bletilla striata* behind them, which he noticed had come into bloom, nodded pleasantly enough at these nice kids, who were always coming to see him and in whom he had formerly, when he had had more faith in the personal and social benefits of a drug culture, taken more of a prophet's interest. Now they seemed too full of thoughts, expressed in jargon, but were kind of cute, especially the girls. He saw an occasional kid as a patient; friends would bring up somebody on a bad trip who didn't want to be seen in the emergency room, where it gets on police records, hospital records, county health-statistic records, U.S. Public Health Service records—he forgot all the different ones. All you did was give them Thorazine and a little attention, after all.

"Of course acid was different in those days, right? Purer. I heard you had to destroy three pounds of peyote during the bust."

"And that one of the sisters ate three ounces of it and was up for a month on it, but on account of her they never found it, right?"

"Hal, do you really think the drug experience will be a normal part of life in the future?"

"It already is," Doctor Harris said, thinking of Irene, for example, who lived on aspirin. This was a funny time of year, he was thinking, for *Bletilla* to be blooming, or maybe it was just terribly early. With the dryness he may have been overwatering in compensation, forcing it to bloom.

"How about governmental use of mind-affecting drugs on civil populations?"

"Probably. I'm expecting it," Hal assured them, noticing with alarm, as he turned to go inside, how the rare blue bishop's blood he grew in the living room was burning. He could see brown foliage against the window where the blind was partly raised, and he was anxious to go inside and move it back from the glass.

"I have to go," he said. "I'm with a patient. Just came out to chat with the officers." Catching this beautiful irony, they laughed and stepped back reverently, then diffidently forward to ask whether now that the pigs were gone they could bring in their friend, who was having a bad trip.

"Sure, bring her in," Doctor Harris kindly said, as he always did.

nineteen

Bingo was now directed to cross a cement parking lot to a temporary-looking building made of tarpaper and open wooden steps for climbing up into it. It was set on what appeared to be sawhorses. A sign at the side of the door said, "State of California Department of Mental Hygiene." Bingo did not know why she and Ronda and Derek walked toward it, climbed its steps, and pushed open its door with such docility. Go there, someone had said, and they had gone. Bingo's despondency, to which she was always susceptible, had numbed her resistance somehow, but this had made her, in turn, more comfortable, belonging here. Ronda and Derek, glad to leave the last waiting room, skipped and jumped across the cement parking lot, making rude remarks about the lady that had just been talking to them. But at the door they ordered themselves into cross, starved, quiet-looking children, and Bingo could think of nothing to bestir them into robustness.

Inside, the first things they saw were desks standing about on a brown linoleum floor. There was a water cooler. The walls were a chipped, equivocal pink, one hung with a calendar representing a tropical paradise, presumably the collective aspiration of the employees and clients of the State of California Department of Mental Hygiene. Another was studded with coat hooks, on which hung dirty Orlon sweaters and a doctor's coat. Someone was remodeling the ceiling, now half-covered in acoustical tile, and a tall ladder lay against the third wall, with some fluorescent light boxes.

Wires hung down dangerously from the ceiling. The whole seemed to present a confused attempt to disguise in modern perforated squares the peeling and badly plastered system of social welfare the building contained, or perhaps to streamline the lives of humans by absorbing their voices. Bingo wondered whether, if she raised it, her voice would be heard, but she had no voice. She also had no thoughts, except to ask herself, as she sat waiting, if she was a person who could get along inside her own mind for an hour or two of sitting on chairs, if she could make up thoughts of sufficient interest and distinction to convey her through one miserable hour; if not, what good was she? And she had a supposedly superior brain. What manner of infinite blankness did the minds contain that were not, officially, so good, so educated, so resourceful? Much of existence, when you came to consider it, consisted of not having anything worthwhile to think about, and thinking, in consequence, disagreeable, sour, angry, unimportant little half-thoughts. And everybody's brain at this task emitting electrical energy: negative charges. The world negatively charged by stupid, paranoid, ill-natured half-thoughts. She wondered if she should get her ears pierced.

Ronda and Derek, invigorated by the run outside, were talkative again.

"Are you fond of children?" Ronda asked. It seemed to Bingo they had asked this before. She was about to explain her position, liking individual children though not children in general, but she stopped. This individual child was looking at her with fierce concern.

"Yes," she said.

"Then you can't be all good," Derek said, and they laughed at luring her in to their joke, but Ronda took her hand.

"He likes W. C. Fields, but I like Charlie Chaplin."

"How do you spell Xenophon?" Derek asked, and looked disappointed when Bingo spelled it.

Bingo sat, figuratively huddled, ungainly in her chair, fortifying her mind against foolish, erotic fantasies with a well-thought-out plan to blow up the entire place. She would have to be sure all the people were out but all the social workers in, and when would that be? Her posture had assumed a chairlike curve. Why had she cried in the office of the man with the built-in kitchen? She wished she could understand that one thing.

She wished she could have been more beautiful and bold, or had, even now, some attractive glitter of reckless charm. Panache. You could have that, or style, without being beautiful, if you only knew how. But how? Inside your mouse face you were a desperate and passionate woman. Bingo watched a person she had seen in the other building enter this one with the air of being on a mysterious mission, and pass to the girl behind the desk a thick folder, Manila, which Bingo supposed, from the direction of the receptionist's covert glance, pertained to them. Another woman got up and hurried out of the room with it and, in a few moments, returned to tell them the doctor would see them, and to follow her. They did, silently. Bingo had a strange feeling of misgiving, the way she always did when going to see a doctor. He was a seedy, fat little man surrounded in whiteness and respectful silence. Many chrome pincers lay on his white table.

"Your mention of joy," began the doctor, "naturally suggests your concern with acid, and take a little tip from me: don't go talking about acid around here. We see too many horrible sights, people blinded from staring at the sun, smashed from walking out windows, slashed wrists, carved faces, horrors, let me tell you. I'm only here to make a medical report on the physical condition of the children, but the joy business is bound to get into Peguez's report, so it would be better if you let me make a blood test cooperatively. If you're clean, swell. If not—it depends."

"What mention of joy?" Bingo asked. She couldn't remember any joy.

"Your remark to Mr. Peguez, that our social norms are bourgeois and leave no room for joy."

"Oh," Bingo said, apprehensive. Did they record what you said? "Well, you can't make a blood test in any case, because I have a horror of needles."

The doctor, assuming this to be a witticism, laughed ironically. "I tell you what," he said, in a confidential way. "If I find anything, well, awkward, I promise not to report it. I don't want to see them slap a drug felony on you. Child neglect is one thing, but narcotics is another. If everything is okay it would look better on the record if I could put down a negative blood test."

"No, really, I get sick at the sight of blood," Bingo said, though she knew she ought to give Max the benefit of her own narcotics-free blood stream. "Can't I spit in anything, or something like that?"

"Well, you can pee in a jar," the doctor allowed, and got her a jar and showed her a cubicle of a bathroom. If she had been a paying patient somewhere, she wondered, would he have said "urinate"? The humiliations of the poor, was this? Or was it "communication"? Anyway, she peed—a decorous amount into the jar and the rest into the toilet.

They have taken my inner thoughts and now my urine, she was thinking. Perhaps by some delicate technique of assay they could tell everything about you from your urine. She could imagine someone bent over her psychological-attitude test sheets staining for the delicate organisms of social maladjustment, or dropping urine from a dropper, to bring forth from between the lines the answer to her character. All you would have to do would be to get everybody to pee in jars, and in this manner you could determine the problems of the entire society.

She handed her warm jar to the doctor, with the vague disassociated expression normally affected during this transaction, and felt curiously imperiled, as if he might indeed discover dangerous drugs there or a disease she didn't know she had. Or perhaps the uneasiness was rooted in an innate reluctance to give away a part of herself, related to those superstitions about keeping your fingernail clippings from your enemies. These apprehensions were no doubt shared by the bored but inwardly apprehensive stolid sitters on the plastic waiting-room chairs, bladders treasonably storing up evidence, to be extracted by this doctor, of malfunction, malcontentedness, malnutrition, maladjustment, malformation, malice. Malice.

"We can tell as much from the urine as from the blood stream," the doctor said, "and people don't mind it as much, naturally. Your children apparently get enough to eat."

"Of course," Bingo snapped. Max's children were plumper than her own. She in fact disapproved of overfeeding children.

"Whether the right foods is another matter," he said.

"The 'right foods' attitude is greatly exaggerated, Doctor," she said, regaining her habitual superior tone, quoting from Barney, who, like most doctors, thought vitamins and balanced diets mostly nonsense. The doctor looked intently, noncommittally, at her.

"One can tell from the advanced tooth decay. Baby teeth

have to be looked after as well as any others, you know. See here, Ronda's gum line, completely decayed." He lifted Ronda's upper lip, so that the little girl appeared to grin like a horse. "She must eat nothing but candy. Do you think that gives her body a good building foundation? What have you had to eat today, honey?" he asked Ronda. With a look at Bingo she said, "Turkey." This brilliant and wistful lie caused tears to start in Bingo's eyes again. She was afraid the doctor would see, and turned away.

"And look here," he went on. He lifted and parted Ronda's hair, exposing crusts on her scalp. "That's terrible. All those will have to be oiled and dislodged with a fine-toothed comb. Not much fun for Miss Ronda."

Ronda made a face at Bingo, as if it had been Bingo's fault. Bingo didn't even think it was so bad. Nelson and Caroline probably had crusts, too—for all she knew. Crusts, indeed!

"I have to agree that these children are not grossly neglected, at least compared with some we see, but neither are they adequately cared for. The habits they acquire now . . ."

"I'm glad you think they're all right, Doctor," Bingo breathed hypocritically. It dawns on you very quickly, she saw, that a certain amount of craft is required. She was bothered that she did not know the condition of Nelson's and Caroline's scalps.

The doctor told her to go out and wait in the anteroom again while he finished talking with the children. This seemed to take a long time, but time was becoming relative. Her mind, determined to avoid the sloughs of erotic fantasy or despair, desultorily reviewed the subjects it ordinarily employed in dull situations or when falling asleep—Greek transliteration, Russian grammatical paradigms, and the speeding trains from the point of view of the man on the embankment. This new waiting room was furnished entirely in phallic symbols; was this a function of the doctor's mind or of her own? An erect floor lamp capped by a domed plastic prepuce. A picture of phallic lilies in a cheap frame. A ballpoint pen in a stand. Of course, when viewed in a certain way, almost anything could be interpreted as a phallic symbol, a mental configuration subtly encouraged by men themselves: "That'll put lead in my pencil," for instance; one of Barney's coarser expressions. If men could not be serious and reverent about their penises, how could women be? Or perhaps his was the determined levity that really serious subjects, like God, demanded. She wondered if it was true that you could tell the size of a man's genitals from the size of his hands. You didn't really read much in books about the size of a man's penis, probably because men write books and they don't like to suppose that size makes any difference. She had asked Barney once about the relative size of his, and he had looked quite distant and offended. "Big man, big cock; little man, all cock, as the saying goes," he had said, in a dismissive way. It would be nice if Geoffrey Nichols were not a fireman but, say, a famous musical composer, and a lot of amusing, witty, famous people would come to their house, a lot of people around for her to talk to, very brilliantly, and cook great dinners for.

"Do you believe in stealing?" asked Ronda. She had not noticed Ronda and Derek come out. They were sitting again in their chairs. Ronda held a magazine.

"Oh! Ah—under some circumstances, I suppose it's all right," Bingo admitted. "If a person was hungry it would be all right to steal food."

"My mother steals Christmas trees," Ronda said. Bingo

could not tell whether this was said proudly or in defiant shame. Bingo saw that Ronda's magazine, *Today's Health,* was last December's and had a Christmas tree on the cover.

"Ronda," Derek objected. Family secrets. His hands were folded in model-child serenity.

"Do you think it's all right?" Ronda persisted. "My friend thinks it's awful."

"Your friend is just sentimental," Bingo said briefly, though it was a theoretical question that might have interested her in other circumstances.

"I'm awfully hungry," Ronda said. "When are we going to have lunch?"

twenty

Barney checked on Max again. She was dozing, or thinking intently about something, and made no move to speak or remove herself from his bed, either. Barney hung about rather uncertainly, then tiptoed from the room. He retrieved his T-shirt from the bathroom and put it on but found the rest of him surprisingly comfortable towel-wrapped, and so he did not put on his pants. This answered a question that had occasionally occurred to him: what had Mahatma Gandhi worn under that scarf affair? Very comfortable. He had some whiskey from the tray on the edge of the tub and then went to his painting studio to see if he resembled a sheik painting of himself he had done in a caftan. Or sometime he might do himself as a mummy, totally swathed, with desperate eyes peering through a slit: let me out!

Confronted with his paintings, he was immersed again in

the earlier dilemma: which one was the real Barney; and he did not at first hear anybody come in. Then he recognized the dangerous felon, partly from the policeman's photo but more from the drawn and trembling mien as the fellow slid into the laundry room from the carport. Finding himself surrounded by the stretched faces standing at every angle and grimacing down from shelves in robes, in crowns—all, it seemed, with their tormented eyes on him—the felon uttered a faint cry of panic and then, when the towel-wrapped effigy actually spoke, whimpered but seemed too frightened to run.

"Why doesn't anybody ever knock on doors any more? Everybody just barges in," the effigy began petulantly. "Am I square? Am I old-fashioned?" He no longer minded his seminudity, though, and that was a start.

"Say, is Max Gartman here? This is where she told me to come," said the felon, collecting himself, recognizing in Barney a living man.

"In here," Barney said, holding his towel and leading the way uneasily through the kitchen, hating the dangerous felon's being behind him but wanting to get him away from the paintings, and withal discerning in himself a new kind of accepting, blank feeling when it came to this particular day.

Max, sensing an additional presence, lifted her head and said hi. Noel Fish sat down beside her on the edge of the bed, not seeming, even, to notice her bare breasts.

"Hullo, Max, I brought you some speed. Isn't that nice? Only you have to do something for me, one simple little connection."

"This is Noel," Max said, raising herself on her elbows. "It was Noel who turned Hal in, but then he felt bad about it, and he was going to jump off the water tower. He probably would have gone right through Hal's roof, but they busted him first."

"I should of done it, too," Noel said. "It would have been better than prison, and who knows, I might of landed on his beautiful kingly head."

"Noel expects people to love him even when he has put them in jeopardy and almost gets their medical licenses taken away and it costs them a hundred grand in fines."

"They had to come after me, all the way up the little green ladder, all the way around the edge of the tower, like an ant train. I could hear their guns clanging against the side. Twelve cops after me."

This is the dangerous felon, and the cops are looking for him now, Barney thought. Gun battles, he envisioned, or being taken as hostage. He realized that he had begun to sweat.

"See here," he said, "why don't you give Max whatever it is you brought her, and then I think you'd better be going. My wife is due home, and then we'll be having dinner, and . . ."

"Why don't you call the police, then?" Noel said, looking at him.

"Give me the speed, Noel," Max said, sitting up and scratching. Noel extracted some ordinary Methedrine Spansules from his pocket but held them away from her outstretched hand.

"I have to tell you what you have to do."

"Tell me!"

"Not with him here," Noel said. They both looked at Barney and realized, evidently, that they could not make him leave his own bedroom, which was exactly what he was resolving not to do; he encountered their uncertain eyes defiantly, with rising master-of-the-house feelings.

"Now, look," he said.

"Let's shoot it in the bathroom, and you can tell me there," Max said. "Could you get us a candle and a spoon and so on?" To Barney. "We have to cook it. You could watch if you want to see how it's done, but you can't watch us shoot up, because that part is somewhat sacred. But if you are interested in how real junkies cook their stuff . . ."

Barney felt exactly the annoyance of a child excluded from games. "Do you have to do this here?" he said. Max had got up and was leaving the room. Barney followed, expostulating, while she went through the dining room, took a candle from the table, brought a spoon from the kitchen. She was back, quick and catlike, while Barney and Noel were still shuffling uncomfortably around each other in the hallway. Max looked at Barney less sternly.

"Wouldn't you like to try some?" she asked him kindly. "It's just speed. Just try it once. It's the best thing; you'll never want anything else, and it won't hurt you at all. You should experience it just once."

"No, no!" Barney said. "I don't want anything! I don't want *you* to take anything here, either. It's unhealthy and illegal and stupid. What if those police come back or, I don't know . . ."

"There's nothing illegal about Methedrine—you can get it from a doctor. Noel probably has a prescription, even. *You* could prescribe it, right?"

"Hurry up, then," Barney said, realizing from the ardor of her hungry eyes on Noel's hand that it wasn't going to do any good, and it was relieving to realize he could have prescribed it; perfectly true. He followed Noel and Max into the bathroom.

"Go out," Noel said, "while I talk to her." Barney sat on

his bed and could hear their low voices in his bathroom and felt morose and excluded. He had a terrible headache. He would be afraid to inject Methedrine. They were crazy.

He was struck suddenly with the numbing fear that Max was going to kill herself, was too full of drugs to live through this. He had remembered the Propadrine. But he could think of no way to warn her except to cry stagily, "Stop! Stop!" and he didn't. He waited for some sort of death cry from the bathroom. He lay back across the bed and wondered what time it was, too apathetic to open his eyes and look at the bedside clock.

Without opening them he became aware, presently, that Max and Noel had come back and were lying beside him, making happy murmurs. It was Max lying against him, her hand touching his head. Suddenly, without opening his eyes, Barney felt close to tears. It felt as if tears were going to run from underneath his closed lids. These people were going to die, and yet they lay there so complacently. He wanted to tell them something saving, perhaps that it was all right or usual to fail at life, but that one ought not to mind so and take funny things into his body.

"In many ways I am a failure as a man," he said, wanting them to understand. "Or manhood is a failure for me, isolating and bleak. When we were young we took off our clothes and lay on the rocks below Point Lobos and swam. And once, when I was under too long, or it was too cold, they had to pull me out—Horse and Richard, it was—and they, crying, said, 'We almost lost you, Barney,' and tears were in their eyes." Max and Noel made no motion or comment, but Barney's tears overflowed. His stomach felt sick. He must have drunk more whiskey than he had realized.

"The thing you mind the most about modern life is the

way you never see your old friends, and you never get any time to make new ones," he said. He had lost the thread of what he had wanted to tell them. You had to smile at the comradely way these new people sprawled together on the bed with him. It had nothing to do with sex. They had no fear of touching each other, even, like very young people. He had a wistful recollection of the sunny rocks and wrestling, of the brown bodies of his friends, tanned skin covered with faint fair hair; they were, all of them, muscular and brown, unlike this Noel, who was pale and wasted, lying against the inert leg of Max. Still, he liked them. They may be junkies, but they have a kind of trust, he thought.

"Squares are very alone," Max said, but not reproachfully; she did not seem necessarily to mean Barney. "Whereas all men are brothers." But her voice was indolent and flat.

"It *ought* to be so," Barney said anxiously, feeling an emanation from her: love emanating through her passivity.

"Oh, I don't know," she said, with drooping lids. "People just hassle you," and her friend Noel giggled shrilly, also passively, with no motion required of his chest, and he snuggled up to her leg. "I like you, though, Barney," she said, "and your wife."

They had, for all their social deviance, Barney thought, a nice, accepting quality. You felt that you could tell them things. They did not think it odd of you to cry. You also felt, a little, that they did not listen. They would not judge. They liked him and Bingo. It was altogether comfortable. Barney sat up, to talk to them better. His bath towel had come unwound, but he did not adjust it. Deliberately. He sat up, and his head swam. He had been drinking, sipping, he supposed, since lunchtime.

"We used to talk about things a lot when we were younger, very intense long talks, but now I never talk to anyone," he said, sitting naked and cross-legged. "I suppose that's everybody's experience. Except when you get smashed. Then you have these stupid, boozy conversations full of fake profundity and then are ashamed the next day."

"Embarrassing garrulous drunks," Max said agreeably, not opening her eyes. "I like drunks, though. But drinking is not *my* thing."

"Of course I talk to Bingo. Sometimes I think that's half of being married: having someone to talk to."

"Mmmmmmmmmm."

"It's funny how you can't tell your best friend some things, though, if she is of the opposite sex. Some things are untranslatable. I'm thinking of Bingo, whom I'd certainly have to call my best friend, if such terms—if you can still talk that way when you're a middle-aged person, or about the person you're married to."

"Do you think Hal would talk to me if I went over there and asked him again? It wouldn't hurt him; it wouldn't cost him anything," Noel whimpered suddenly.

"No," Max said.

"A doctor is not supposed to refuse the sick. He has to help the sick and needy, which is me," Noel complained.

"It is good, the way you can admit your weakness, this candor that respectable middle-class people seem to lose. All is concealment," Barney said sadly.

"He doesn't care if you love him or not," Noel said, an ugly resentment rising in his voice. "He doesn't care if he cures you or not."

"Your best friend won't cure you," Max said. This seemed to Barney a terrible thing to say, so that his eyes watered again. They all lay quietly a long while, with no one saying anything.

"When I was younger I was a beatnik," Max said. "Literally. That's what they called us. I'm even in *On the Road* and a lot of other books about those times. My best friend was Celestina in *The Sad Angel*. Later she killed herself. A lot of people from those days are dead. Some of us have just gotten older and have children and the ordinary things. Crap. As soon as I can handle my drug problem I guess I'll be very square, but I don't mind."

"You people don't have a drug problem," Noel said. "Compared with me. Speed, hell, it's nothing. In fact, I'm going to have some more."

"Let's have more," Max agreed. "I'll just have some today while Noel is here, because I promised Hal not to have anything, really, and I couldn't have my therapy if he found out. Except he lets me have grass."

"This cat should try some H," Noel said, looking at Barney. His voice sounded to Barney very menacing.

"Did you ever try grass?" Max asked.

"Certainly," Barney said.

"You should try speed, just once. You're a doctor. You know it wouldn't hurt you, especially once. You wouldn't get addicted or anything. We used to talk a lot of mystical shit about it—you don't want that—but you shouldn't be so afraid to try things."

"I am, though," Barney said. "That is my hallmark. I am consistently and continually afraid to try things."

"Shit, man, what can happen to you?" Noel said.

"Well, it depends. Different dangers, different horrors. I can think of a thousand bad things I don't want to happen to me."

"Only one bad thing can happen to you, after all," Max said.

"So you just lay around the house?" Noel asked.

"No! Oh, no, I do the things. I commanded my Coast Guard cutter in the wildest weather. I broke Mach in a small jet fighter, with a pilot who was kind of drunk. That was when I went to Texas for my flight-surgeon training. Bingo doesn't know about it."

"That sounds kind of nutty," Max said. Presently she reminded Noel about the second shot. They roused themselves from the bed and went to the bathroom again. Barney brooded resentfully about his timidity, his fears, and then after a minute went with them, full of unspecified resolution.

They had stuck the candle in a pile of its own wax on the countertop, and Max held a spoon while Noel opened a Spansule. He was clumsy and his hands shook, from the last Methedrine or from excitement. Max took it from him and gave him the spoon to hold. Her hands shook, too. She took the spoon back and held it, with the white powder and a few drops of water, over the candle with a rapt housewifely way of watching it until it boiled. They had taken one of Barney's own syringes and a rubber tourniquet from the medicine cabinet, and Noel rinsed them under the faucet. It was all like preparing any shot. Barney watched, not the loading of the syringe, a perfectly familiar procedure, but Max and Noel. Their excitement showed in the increased movement of their faces, in the agitation of their bodies as they swayed over the collection: needle, syringe, little bits of cotton soaked in alcohol.

Noel wrapped the rubber strip around her arm above the elbow. She made a fist. Barney noticed for the first time the terrible blue-and-yellow swellings on the poor brown Indian arm. It made him sick. They wore glassy, ritual smiles.

Barney could not account for it, but the whole thing made him sick. Max smiled at the needle the way she would smile at a person, only with more passion, as if she saw it more clearly. The thin, cold fingers of the junkie Noel were clumsy with the needle, weak on her arm. She thrust it at him, smiling and panting. They had forgotten all about Barney now. The thin, white fingers, the needle, the candle still burning in his own bathroom, the blighted veins, the clumsy stabbing with the needle for a vein; Barney's ears began to ring. Dark blood on her forearm, her smile unvarying. Noel's apology—"Sorry, Max"—and the stab again. Barney felt cold, felt the ringing in his ears increase. He had been going to tell them he would try it with them, but now he realized he would have to go lie down first. Noel had stuck the thing in Max's arm and was slowly emptying the syringe. She gave an expiration of gladness. Barney left the bathroom with as much composure as he could and then fainted away completely on his bed.

He lay for several moments unconscious, semiconscious, unconscious again, wavering in and out of sick sleep. Little phrases and bed creakings roused him several times. "Homosexual anxiety," he heard Max say. "That's what it means when a man faints at the sight of a needle."

He heard leave-takings, a door somewhere. Max crawled back on the bed with him, a reassuring warmth. He slept, woke, slept, a series of moments. He woke, lying weakly, becoming conscious of the pleasantness of his limp enervation, of the curiously sensitive patterns of warmth and chill on his skin, rough cloth blanket under him. The room spun in a lazy hemisphere when he opened his eyes. In his ears the ringing had subsided to an agreeable low-frequency hum. Next to him Max rustled, so that he became aware of her. She was still high, by the far-off sound of her voice. It was nice having her there.

"Some way for a medical doctor to act: getting sick at the sight of a needle," he said.

"You're not a bad guy," Max said. "Somebody should turn you on."

"I'm too anxious about drugs; I've seen some horrible things they can do. You should see . . . I wish you would realize," Barney murmured, still within himself.

"Yeah, yeah, so climb a mountain, skin-dive," Max said.

"I know what you think," Barney said. "But I'm not one of these thrill-mad guys, not at all. Thrills are not what I need. I can't exactly put my finger on it."

"Oh, we are all so needy," Max said.

"I must be very suggestible," Barney said. "I feel as if I had taken some drug. Kind of a nice feeling but not at all natural."

"Are you sure you wouldn't like to screw?" she asked presently.

Barney lay without answering. "Sort of," he admitted, rather pleased to discover that this was the case. His abdomen warmed. Maybe they could just knock off a little piece; Bingo was away and he wasn't at all afraid. Max's hand, curiously dry and small, reached over to stroke him, intensifying his attraction to the idea. A few pangs of hesitation, trepidation, vanishing before a triumphant sensation of coziness. He rustled, stirred, scratched.

"I'm not really dizzy any more," he said. "Isn't that funny? I actually fainted! I suppose I'm not altogether well yet." But he felt altogether well. He reached over stroked Max, his hand encountering someone naked, soft-fleshed. They stroked each other. Barney was aware that one of them was going to have to move from the supine position and rather hoped it wouldn't be him. His hand engaged large breasts, movable, with big nipples, soft belly, black thatch. He could remember these details without lifting his so comfortable head to confirm what his fingers touched. Her hand engaged his second self, agreeable, growing. It was odd but not unsatisfying to be going to be unfaithful to Bingo; not that he was angry at her, poor girl, but just that he realized he had been meaning to be, and now, with hardly any trouble, he would have been. A very satisfying idea. His obliging body prepared itself. Her hands were pulling at his arms, trying to get him to roll over and get started, but it was rather nice just lying there being stroked. He did, however, roll over on his side to face her. She didn't look very energetic, either, just bare and there, with staring eyes, and that curious heat about her, and an odor, not of sex but faintly of medicine. Or perhaps that was him, his leg ointment. Their odors mingled, their hands stroked, they lay in the low-pitched hum.

This hum in his ears grew louder, and the dizziness came back slightly when he got himself up on his elbow; it was from all the blood rushing to his genitals, he supposed. His heart was pounding. The hot, dry lady beneath him lay languidly and looked up with some interest. They puffed, adjusted; she spread her legs.

Barney paused. He felt embarrassed at not being able to think of anything gallant or reasonably amorous but not phony to say, and he had not kissed her. Nor did he want to; it didn't seem that sort of occasion. He supposed he was a clumsy lover. Her patient immovability was not reproachful. She was smiling. He nuzzled awkwardly under her ear and at the same time thrust between her legs.

And again. It was as if she were sewn up. There seemed to be no opening. He tried to guide himself with his hand and encountered her hand, which he allowed to prevail. She grasped him and guided him to what he could feel as the faintest suggestion of an aperture. Perhaps it was all she had? This panicked him. What would happen? She had wound her legs around him for leverage and was thrusting vigorously against him. She was impenetrable. But she had had children. . . . How could she?

"It'll be all right when you get inside," she said. "I'm just sort of dry right at first." Oh. That was the trouble, of course, all that Propadrine she'd taken, drying to the mucous membranes; it would be impossible for her to exude even a tear. She was crazy and took drugs. Tears came to Barney's eyes.

"Vaseline, maybe," she said. But then they achieved an inch of success. Barney looked at her, and she was smiling, but with a far-off Methedrine smile, making the situation reassuringly impersonal. He closed his eyes, and she became a particular Stanford coed who helped summers in the virus lab and had blue eyes of great sweetness and blankness and a golden quality not unlike Doctor Harris's wife, who, in fact, got tangentially entangled in this fantasy. Then he opened his eyes again and looked into hers, where he could see the faintest yellow cast, a pallor of unhealth, maybe jaundice. This lady was strange and stale and took drugs. He shriveled dryly and could penetrate her no farther.

"I'm sorry," Barney said. "I'm feeling dizzy again." He hung limply above her and felt himself sway on his elbows. She looked up at him with disappointment but without reproach. Her eyebrows did really grow together across her nose.

Barney rolled off her a little way and buried his head.

Her hand came back to offer restorative massage, but it was no use. He was ashamed of the emotion that overtook him: self-pity. He had had in his mind's eye, for so long, someone beautiful, pink, with golden hair and that same expression in her eyes of wondering; but big blue eyes, or even hazel—anyway not yellow.

Max had retired again into her stupor, but Barney became restive and went to look at his pictures again and began to worry about Bingo. It was nearly five o'clock, and she hadn't called in a couple of hours. Nothing to worry about, of course, but you can't help worrying when the person you love has been away for half the day on a peculiar errand.

Presently a feeling of shame and incompleteness prompted him to go back into the bedroom again. Max was pulling her clothes on. Barney watched her, trying to think of the right thing to say.

"Those are nice-looking sandals," he said. Max glanced at him and at her sandals.

"Thanks. I get them from a funny old man, an old, old Indian man. He makes them, and also ankhs and strings of beads, and he gives them away for sex. He never would sell anything he makes. He feels that giving is sacred."

This confounded Barney, so that he said nothing.

"I can get you some if you like them," Max said. "You ought to have sandals, with your cut foot. He's so old he can only have oral sex."

"I, uh, I have a pair of sandals around here someplace," Barney said.

"Do you think my kids are all right? She hasn't called for quite a while. Maybe they all went to the movies or somewhere. They wouldn't still all be at the social-worker place, right?"

"You must be coming down, all this talk about reality," Barney said. "Do you feel all right? You shouldn't take all that stuff. You shouldn't ever take things out of a medicine chest without knowing what they are, and you shouldn't . . ." He stopped, sighed.

"You should eat something," he said. "I'll go heat up some soup." Tenderly.

twenty-one

They were sitting in the antechamber of the principal psychologist's office, a room done up in a deceptively homey way with flowered wallpaper and real, though derelict, sofas and chairs, and a lamp with a drum shade, all ugly, like the inside of a mental hospital furnished to make the patients feel at home with furniture from the nurses' attics. This worked, made Bingo feel more inexorably at home than ever. She felt herself to have faded, like a pattern, into the wall, into the floral design of the wallpaper; to be one more despairing ornament, invisible in her chair and overwhelmed with intensest despondency.

If I live through this, her thoughts would unreasonably begin, and, If I ever get home again, and, Just let me get out of here and I will change my life. At the same time she knew she could go home at any time and change her life. Still she sat. An old woman looked at her with a friendly face, wishing to talk. Bingo tightened her mouth. She thought of her house. She thought of scrubbing it, lovingly. She imagined being suffused with a sentiment of contentment and dutifulness as she scrubbed a floor. She imagined wishing that

Nelson and Caroline would come home from Carmel, or that Barney—she did not know how she would change Barney. She would change herself. She wondered how, if you were in despair and had to sit endlessly in waiting rooms, you could bear living at all? If her home was small, with sour walls and plastic furniture, would she still have this same feeling of intensest longing to return and be safe in it? Yes.

She gathered Ronda, a heavy child, onto her lap. Ronda continued to read but didn't mind, shifted, settled in, a sturdy, consoling weight.

Bingo knew she ought to call Barney again, who must be frantic; always so amusingly, touchingly protective of her, though they both knew she could take care of herself and him, too. His anxiety was real, however, and so was hers when *he* went off to do odd and difficult things, on a ship or hunting, say. She felt she was in a jungle now. The animal panic that had unaccountably overtaken her in the waiting room a few moments ago had still not loosened its hold on her biochemical reactions. When the door opened suddenly and someone came and spoke to her she jumped; something pulled in her eyelid.

"We would like to chat with you some more about the maternal role," someone said. Bingo sighed and got up and trudged down another hall after her, the eyelid flicking, but it probably felt worse than it looked. They went into a big room, where people sat around a table and a map of California stretched across the back wall. The people, four or five of them, were wearing white coats, so Bingo supposed them to be medical rather than clerical; though you could not tell from the faces. A sickening notion—that they had discovered from her urine that she had cancer—irrationally chilled her. Their faces were grave.

"Ah, Mrs. Gartman," they said. "Sit there, dear. Sit down." This was soothing. Bingo found herself smiling socially at them. They smiled back.

"Such a difficult day," said someone sympathetically. Questions, tests. They understood. Bingo expanded. She put her purse on the table and hitched her chair forward a little.

"Oh, I understand," she said. "I know these things are complicated."

"Complicated," they said, in a strange chorus, so that Bingo looked around at them again. They were arranged, when you looked closely, more like a tribunal than like friends. She felt afraid again. The air conditioner in the window started up, intruding its noise, so that they all waited. They all had little piles of papers and folders in front of them. Bingo had a drained and sickish feeling in her stomach.

"What do you mean when you say—you said—you love your children?" began a man, who took his pipe out of his mouth to speak, like a movie psychiatrist. Bingo tried to think very carefully and precisely.

"I mean, I want things to go right for them. I want them to have happy lives, and I want to do what I can to effect this." She folded her hands firmly on her lap. She was to do a good job for Max now.

"But that is a lie or you wouldn't treat them as you do," remarked a woman.

"My intentions are better than my actions," Bingo admitted. These things were as true for herself as for Max. "You asked me what I *meant*."

"If your meanings are always better than your deeds, why don't you change? I mean, since you are aware of it, you could alter your behavior."

"I can't," Bingo said. "But, anyway, my deeds are not so awful. I am sometimes nagged by a feeling of discrepancy, but I am generally adequate. I perform adequately." She was unsure, increasingly unsure of this. She became distracted by the reflections of folded, white-coated arms, upside down, in the high polish of the broad table.

"Now, Maxine," said an immense, full voice, as if someone had instructed it to speak kindly into a megaphone; the unctuous kindness of the loudness, and a ventriloquistic quality, made it hard for her to identify the speaker. "You agree, you have assured us, that your wishes are mainly for the welfare of the children, and that you cannot do as much for them as you would like?"

"Well, that's true. Nobody ever can do as much for his . . ."

"I know it isn't easy, but try to consider for a moment another maternal figure, another home environment, more privileged than yours, a 'regular' place, where the kids could lead a nor—"

"Theoretically there might be another mother, another home," Bingo said. "You can never be so arrogant as to suppose that you are the most ideal for any job, but . . . There would be a lot of worse situations. Love is one thing you have to consider."

"She is so cold," said the kind voice, now unkindly, as if the megaphone had gone dead; a little, clear voice. "The detachment, so abnormal." Bingo was not feeling detached, though. She felt physically cold, iced, frightened. These people were not looking at Maxine Gartman; they were looking, disapproving and powerful, at her.

"Most women would cry," another person said. Bingo glanced around.

"We say, why don't you cry?" someone said.

Bingo struggled for her Radcliffe voice. "I am trying to keep my wits—my temper, I mean—and answer you succinctly. I am not sure why you are being so unkind."

"Most women would cry," declared a stout woman, "if they were about to lose their children." She rose and left, riffling papers. Bingo's panic increased. They hated her. She was trying to be responsible-sounding and calm.

"She's badly scared, I think. Some people react in this calm, collected way."

"Your children barely seem to know you. They are badly disassociated, Maxine. They badly need a stable home situation. Derek is bright but borderline autistic. He needs help. You need help. We're not bad folks here, only wanting to help," a man said. Mr. Peguez.

"Just temporarily, in a good home, until you can get your life straightened around, get back to normal. It will be a lot easier on you knowing they're well taken care of while you get a hold on . . ."

Bingo's heart pounded. "Wait," she cried out. This was crucial. She interrupted, she shouted, not at all calmly, "Why are you saying all this?" Then she realized how agitated, how irrational, she was sounding. She held onto the edge of the table and tried for an apologetic smile.

"We think, your psychological profile suggests," Mr. Peguez said, "that there is every hope of ultimate adjustment. Your disturbances are the sort that, with time . . . But you shouldn't be caring for small children at present. You, why, you have intelligence; you could be a real contribution to society someday. Society doesn't want to lose potentially useful citizens. It acts in its own interest by trying to help, and . . ."

"But why are you saying this to *me*? Is it to *me* you are saying this? Is it my psychological profile or the crusts on my scalp? The messy house? Is it my urine?"

"Well, the psychological tests," they said, "of course. And the mess, too. But mostly the anomie, the feelings of inadequacy, of isolation. You can't tell anything from people's urine."

"Why do you sometimes have thoughts of suicide?"

"Doesn't everybody?" Bingo said. "I was trying very hard to be honest. It's very reasonable to have thoughts of suicide sometimes. It doesn't mean you want to commit suicide. Doesn't everybody think of suicide?"

"No, no," they said. "No."

"Your headaches," someone said.

"Your feelings of hate, your feelings of fear."

"Of isolation."

"But I, that is reasonable. I have feelings of hate and fear and isolation now. That is the reasonable way to feel. You don't seem to understand."

"We do understand, dear," they said.

"No, you don't. I am someone else, a perfectly normal woman, with two children and a nice husband who loves me, and I just agreed to come down here because it would be worse if Max came, poor girl, it sure would have been, and now you are telling me about my psychological profile, and without understanding the situation at all, and . . ."

"Yes, yes," said someone to Bingo.

"Two personalities!" whispered someone else, aside, excitedly. Someone was writing things down.

"And I have answered all the questions as honestly as I could. If you could see my *real* house, if you knew my real thoughts . . ."

"We appreciate your cooperation. You see, we are trying

to help. If you help us we can help you. For the best. For your own good. Promising. You can be helped. That's what we are here for. We are here to." They looked at each other with immense triumph.

"This is terrible," Bingo cried. "How can I explain?"

"Don't worry," they said. "You need more self-respect. 'Unfit mother' is just a technical term."

"Unfit!" Bingo shrieked.

"Only a word, only relative."

"I just came down here to help . . ."

"Your cooperation, very fine . . ."

"Please excuse me," Bingo said, pushing back her chair and standing up. "I think I will go home now." She started to back out, saw her purse left on the table, reached out for it, dropped it, heard a hideous, loud half-yawn, half-groan—a sob—come out of her own mouth.

"Well, it is getting late," Mrs. Kitano said, getting up and putting her arm around Bingo's shoulder. "You go on home tonight, dear, and we'll get together tomorrow about details and things. I think you'll find that everything looks much more possible in the morning. This is all going to work out for the best, you'll see." Bingo allowed herself to be led out.

"Will she split?" someone asked behind her.

"The husband is at home to keep an eye out," said someone else.

Mrs. Kitano led Bingo to the ladies' bathroom, the one she had been in earlier. There she found her own scarf on the basin; evidently she had left it. She wet it and dabbed at her face, and the face in the mirror looked, as usual, like George Eliot's. An unfit woman resembling George Eliot. And George Eliot, at least, had been fit, was accomplished, was famous and wise. Bingo continued, quite shamelessly now, fully aware that the little lady was patiently waiting outside the door, to sob loudly and watched her face's foolish grimaces in the mirror the whole while, until the pressure in her breast was reduced somewhat and she felt, after many deep breaths, up to confronting the outside world.

Mrs. Kitano greeted her with a fixed smile that took no notice of the grotesque streaks on Bingo's face, and led her kindly to the waiting room. She was about to close the door on her, like a hostess to the last guest, when Bingo noticed that Ronda and Derek were gone.

"Where are the children?" Bingo asked. "I'll come back in the morning, but I'm going to take them home now."

"The children will have gone to the Juvenile Hall pending the hearing, I expect, which will, of course, be set at the earliest possible; meanwhile, during which . . ." Bingo, unhearing, staring, repeated her question into the empty waiting room. This was—what? She had no further resources of despair and indignation.

"We explained all that, Maxine. The children will be well looked after, of course."

"You have *taken them?*" Bingo's own voice now high and unfamiliar.

"Getting them some fresh clothes, and then Mr. Brown will take them out for a lovely dinner. It will be such a treat for them."

"You give me those children," Bingo said. These people had taken those children. It was hard to conceive. She thought she could hear, far off down a corridor, the slow, siren wail of a little child.

"Do you hear that? Those taciturn little things, crying. What can they be doing to them? Give them to me at once," Bingo insisted.

"We have taken them away," Mrs. Kitano, in her unvarying patient voice, began. "The State of California . . ."

Bingo, in terror again, felt herself go all canny and full of craft and deceit. She was a mother protecting her children, fierce. Her heart pounded. She was learning, learning. She edged toward the hallway.

"These things are easier, believe me, without a scene," the woman said. "Easier on the children."

Could she take them and run? Would people come running after her, restrain her? She thought of a lot of things at once, the *Diary of Anne Frank,* newspaper photos of people being detained or restrained, frantic writhing people, with contorted faces and twisted clothes, crying.

"Let me see them. Let me call my lawyer. I am calling my lawyer," Bingo said, her voice shrill and uncommanding. She would demand to see them, would take them and run. She could easily pick up this little runt woman and throw her aside.

"Ronda, Derek," she called to them, "come to Mother, come at once," in a loud voice that might be heard anywhere, up and down whichever hall. But she was amazed when Ronda did come, seconds later, crying, running, carrying a Barbie doll someone had given her. Mrs. Kitano had stepped fastidiously back, out of the way of this headlong, gummy child, and Bingo snatched Ronda toward the door, not thinking of Derek. In this violence Bingo saw things in streaks; she thought of hitting.

At the door to the Child Welfare Department, Mr. Tru Brown, coming in, was jostled by Bingo and Ronda, without taking offense. He swooped Ronda up, nodded at the wild-eyed Bingo, and strode with Ronda to a waiting car, hugged her, put her in.

"You cannot do this! You cannot do this!" Bingo screamed. But they already had.

. . .

The policemen sat snugly in their black-and-white car in front of the fire hydrant just around the curve at the top of Lamotte Lane, where they could look down on the Harrises' roof, on the Edwardses' roof, and, far below that, on the city, which, however, was almost obscured in the brown smog or even smoke that had been worsening all day. They were listening to messages on their radio; it was like being in an exciting movie. They could see the pieces in their scheme beginning to fit together. The helicopter came over, dipping slightly. A man walking by the Harrises' driveway looked up at it, shading his eyes. The plain car was parked nearly out of sight at the lower end of Lamotte Lane. The agent's jovial voice explained that the loud crackling they had heard on their radio was him unwrapping his sandwich. He had forgotten to turn off his transmitter. They consoled each other that they were in for a long wait.

Inside the Harrises' house, in the dark kitchen, Doctor Harris, like a half-naked king of the mountain, hairy, leonine, hungry, pawed in the refrigerator for about the ninth time. "Where is my cream?" he complained. "Max said she'd bring it. I haven't had anything to eat all day."

"Pooouh baybee," Irene said. She was in the kitchen making herself a cucumber-and-cream-cheese sandwich. She had pressed a single cucumber slice to the skin under her chin.

"I'm hungry," he said, slapping his belly as if he expected it to sound hollow. "She said she'd bring it."

"Well, you pick such responsible help—what do you expect?"

"Why don't *you* go get it? My stomach hurts. You don't do anything around here." His vague face mirrored a tiny internal discomfort.

"Why don't you eat something else, for Chrissake?"

Irene snapped. She was short-tempered. "What kind of a crazy man only eats cream?"

"And orange juice," Doctor Harris said. "Why not? This way I don't trouble anybody with cooking. Besides, I like cream." He looked surprised and hurt.

"Ah like to cook!" cried Irene. "Ah want you to eat fried chicken and brownies and things. How can ah be a good wife to you when you only eat cream?" She caused tears to stream picturesquely from her baby-blue eyes, to which Hal was of course indifferent.

"If someone could sometime do just a little something for *me,*" he said, in a louder and more bitter voice than he had ever been heard to use. The five-o'clock patient, waiting in the dining room, edged closer to the kitchen door, half-afraid, but forced by some strange compulsion to listen.

"I put out and put out, all day, one way or another, day in and day out, person after person . . ." His white brows were constricting, his underlip beginning to project.

"You might as well not even have a wife, for all you care about a home and . . ."

"Using me! Using me, frankly! The whole goddamn day, person after person, with their drug needs and their love needs and their father-figure needs and their needs for punishment and their needs for approval and their . . ."

"A man of your income, we could have a beautiful home here. Ah've tried very hard. But what kind of a challenge is cream? Ah'm a young woman, Hal, and ah need . . ."

"I need cream. It isn't much. It really isn't much, but is there anyone who will just do me the one little thing? Go to the store—hell, call the milkman. I don't require it to involve personal sacrifice, what the hell. Just arrange it, will you?

Cream, and a little time to spend on my plants, are all I . . ."

"You don't care what this place looks like, you don't care what you eat, you don't care what ah wear, you don't, oh, this house is full of freaks. What do you care about anything?"

"I certainly care about being able to maintain my metabolic functions," Doctor Harris said more quietly, remembering himself. "People are always after me. Every minute of every waking hour someone comes bleeding to me with his needs, and I try to help, but I need to live on something, and now I'm going out for a milkshake, because the Group is coming tonight, and Christ knows I need my strength for that. I'll be back around five."

"You love all these people around. You think you are the only certified Jupiter living on earth," Irene sniffed. "But you surely do take a lot of reminding, every hour on the hour."

"So long," Hal Harris said.

"For someone so *old* you ought to be more secure," Irene hissed after him. Her eye caught that of the five-o'clock patient. Their glances were uneasy. Irene's because she had never before heard her husband express a personal complaint. The five-o'clock patient's because, bearing in mind the crucial transaction of the forthcoming evening, she was terrified that this alteration in Doctor Harris's usually reliable habit—his leaving—might in some way screw things up.

Though it was of no immediate concern, this was the day that a tractor working on the construction of a highway near Studio City, some fifteen miles distant, dragged a chain across a rock, issuing a spark, which touched off what was afterward known as the great Bel Air fire.

twenty-two

Mr. Brown, the social worker, told Bingo to get in his car and he would take her home. He held the car door open for her, very politely, and wore a nice expression of solicitude. "They get a little heavy in there, I'm afraid, don't they? But they mean well. That's what we're here for." Bingo gravely settled herself on the seat and did not look at Mr. Brown or back at the Department of Child Welfare as they drove away. She was composing herself, taking deep breaths, intently relaxing, trying to arrange her features into some more placid attitude. Finally, when she was sure her voice would come out normal, she asked, "Was it all settled before we even came down here?"

"Pardon?"

"I mean, did you put in a report beforehand that settled how they would decide to handle our case? Were all those tests and conversations and things a matter of form, or were they important?"

"Oh, important. The field worker puts in a report, sure, but it's just an opinion, and the people you saw today make the decisions."

"Did you tell them about my messy house? Did you say I took drugs?"

"I gave a description of things as I found them."

"Did you recommend the kids should go to a foster home?"

"Matter of fact, no. I like to avoid that if at all possible."

Bingo, at this, felt oddly, passionately grateful, as if by believing that perhaps Max's children should not be placed in a foster home he became the only person in the world to express confidence in her, Bingo; did not see that she was unfit. She felt almost tearful again but reminded herself that after all her ordeal was, at least temporarily, over, and she must strive to get along in the real world again and understand its ways. She tried to smile.

There was a lot of traffic crowding onto Pico now, and Mr. Brown was paying more attention to that than to her. Trying to be civil and cheery, trying now to think of other things, perhaps trying to intrude herself upon his notice, she remarked that she usually went up Olympic, where the signals were set faster. He agreed politely that it was a good idea and turned up a side street. He was a good driver, confounding the stereotype of the big black man roaring the potent engine of his big car to express a conglomeration of virile and hostile impulses. He drove, in fact, like an adjusted middle-class man, quite a nice-looking one: nice black skin and big neck and head and sloping easy shoulders, very powerful, and one elbow resting on the sill of the open window on the driver's side. Bingo looked at him without his knowing it. On weekends, probably, he would stretch his right arm along the back of the seat, where Bingo could lean against it with her head if it were Bingo with him. Of course, it would not be a middle-aged housewife but a sophisticated blond coed, most likely, on the weekend. This Bingo experienced as yet another in the day's long series of rejections. Mr. Brown fastidiously worked the turn signal.

"The reason I wondered whether they had made their suggestions about placing the children on the basis of your opinion of the apartment instead of their opinion of me is because I'm not really Maxine Gartman at all," she said presently, with a deep breath.

Mr. Brown gave her a sidelong look of surprise and mistrust. "Is that true? Or is this some stunt to drag things on until you can think of something else? Anyhow, the kids called you Mommy and your husband was there and . . ."

Bingo explained why they had done it. There was a certain pleasure in the revelation. He was confused.

"Have you got any identification?" he asked finally.

Bingo got out her billfold and showed him her face through its plastic window. Her head was tilted in the customary way, and her hair needed doing, and her shoulders seemed to grow out of her ears. She must have been nervous when the picture was taken. Do you get your picture before or after you take the driver's test? The written exam? She couldn't remember. She was embarrassed to show him such an ugly picture, but she was always nervous in the Department of Motor Vehicles, because it was a matter of importance with her to get past the eye exam without having them mark "Must wear corrective lenses" on it, because someday she might lose or break her corrective lenses and have to drive, and somehow with those restrictions marked on her license she would be powerless. Before contact lenses it had been harder to deceive; she had had to memorize the eye chart, covertly, while standing in line, and then remove her glasses without being seen. With contact lenses you just stand back from the examiner's window a little and don't turn in profile. In her heart of hearts she knew that she could not drive without corrective lenses and that she saw the world thus modified, as it saw her through the plastic window of her wallet, with her ears growing out of her shoulders, nervously.

Mr. Brown studied it and looked at it and her. "This expires next week, I suppose you noticed." Your license expires every four years on your birthday. Bingo became anxious to know if the face in the plastic looked four years younger.

"It's almost my birthday," she said, bleakly remembering her age.

"When is your birthday?" he said, looking at her with the suspicious scrutiny of a bartender.

"October 28, 1935," she said. "Anyway, it's my face, isn't it?" He handed the billfold back disgustedly.

"And, obviously, I don't really live at Max's house," Bingo remembered. "Could you . . ."

"I know. I noticed. I'll just run you up home to your fancy Bel Air address. Boy. I ought to see that they charge you with something. But I'll just chauffeur you home now. Then I better go get those kids. What a screw-up."

"But you see, don't you, why I wondered about whether you . . . They must have decided that *I* am unfit. Not Max, but me. It was *my* psychological profile, after all. They found me a person unfit to look after small children."

"So if this irresponsible behavior today is any indication . . ."

"They want to re*claim* me," Bingo went on, all her distress renewing. "For society. They said society doesn't want to lose people like me; this they determined from my psychological profile, or else my urine. That must mean that they saw they were in danger of losing me! Sick but redeemable, they think. But where am I sick? I mean, I don't think I am. I'm just so baffled. What did it say? Of course you feel as if you have tight bands around your head when you have a headache. That's what a headache feels like. Sometimes people *are* following you; that's just realistic. I am always faintly pleased if people follow me, if not too far, if they are admiring, just a few steps, smiling . . .

"And then they go and say I am deviant, an unreliable person to entrust with the care of small children. Whereas, in fact, I really do all the things they think are desirable. That's the paradox. I really do go to the P.-T.A. I belong to the Sierra Club and the ACLU. I have a built-in kitchen, just like Mr. Peguez. I am embarrassed about that and about the P.-T.A., but the fact is, I am a conformist. Was. Am a secret conformist, disguised as a deviant."

"Sometimes you get abuse, and sometimes you get nutty sophistry," Mr. Brown said. "You never get cooperation. Nobody really believes that things will get better if they cooperate with us."

"I'm not being sophistical," Bingo said. "I am distressed. I'm upset. Secretly I reverence order and convenience. Now, why couldn't Mr. Peguez tell that? My life is very calm and orderly."

"Order? That motel and that mess?"

"But remember that is not *my* mess. My house is messy, I grant you, but not that messy. And anyway, my mess is only extrinsic. My mind is orderly."

"Apparently not," Mr. Brown sniffed. "Anyway, what are *you* so upset about? It won't make any difference. *Your* kids aren't going to fall into the evil clutches of the Child Welfare Department—they have to take their chances with you, right? Because their parents have bread. White bread. Never mind if the parents are fit or unfit."

"Now you are making very boring, conventional, typical, minority-group allegations about the inadequacy of the middle class, and I won't be intimidated by that," Bingo snapped. "People in Bel Air may be awful, but people in

slums are more awful. Everybody is awful, and I can't bear
it. And I can't bear intimations by pseudo intellectuals that
they aren't. Pseudo intellectuals are awful. Social workers
and . . ."

"I'm just saying that by the criteria of our society you are
as unfit as that poor dame Max, wherever she may be, but
you are rich and she is poor, so you have less excuse, and this
is a beautiful example of the inequities of our society,
which . . ." Mr. Brown had raised his voice.

"All right! But I *wish* to be deviant, so there. I do not
approve of our society. I reject its criteria. But I don't want to
be unfit. There's a difference."

"Deviant and unfit are the same thing," Mr. Brown said
fiercely.

"No, no, no! And, anyway, I'm not deviant. I try and try
to be, but other people all seem to behave and feel as I do.
What is one to do? We had a hedge, but we had to tear it
down. There's nothing a person can do to deviate. Everybody
else is doing it, too."

"How deviate? Drugs? Drink? Adultery?"

"What would be the point? Everybody does them."

"What *is* the point," Mr. Brown asked severely, "of going
to such trouble to distinguish yourself from other people? If
you really want to screw around or turn on, you ought to—
but not just to be different."

"You mean if I did, the Bureau of Social Welfare would
consider me normal—normally deviant, I mean—and . . ."

"I was speaking as a private individual," Mr. Brown said.
"But I also think it would be immature."

Bingo felt hopelessly entangled and incoherent, so she just
leaned her head back on the seat and closed her eyes. She
could imagine Ronda's little crying face as she was driven off

to the institution and felt a wave of maternal compunction for Caroline and Nelson, for weeks away at their grandmother's. Anguish. She should go get Ronda herself.

"I don't suppose you would give Ronda to me. To the real me."

"I suppose *they* would," Mr. Brown said disgustedly. "Deviant profile and secret vices and all. There's no logic whatever, and if you have the money . . ."

"I don't have any secret vices. That's what I can't bear. You don't understand at all." Bingo began to cry again, it seemed to her for the ninetieth time. But, of course, it was all one continuous cry. "I might as well baby-sit. I'm just a useless person, useless, pleasureless. I could help Ronda and Derek at least. Would you consider making love to me?"

His eyes widened. "No, certainly not," he said. "Is this your street? Now I have to go down to the Juvenile Hall, *all* the way downtown, and I had a date at six. I don't know what's going to happen about all this. I suppose it'll be *my* fault for not making sure—oh, shit."

"I suppose it showed up on my psychological profile, my passion for this fireman." Bingo sobbed. "How can I bear this, being so foolish and egocentric? What's the matter with me? I am a sensible woman."

"And I'm surprised a woman of your education believes those racial myths about big black studs and all that," Mr. Brown added.

"What? Oh. I don't. It's just that you're the only man around. I am lost to all shame. And it was a rhetorical question, anyway." Her cheeks burned.

"It's a vulgar, racist cliché," Mr. Brown said.

"I'm *sorry*," Bingo snapped. "I'm sure you're nothing special."

"I didn't say that, either," Mr. Brown sniffed. "You people just have to have the last word."

"*Me* have the last word! You have told me I'm an unstable, racist, nymphomaniac, unfit mother. How would *you* like . . ."

At this Mr. Brown laughed, so that Bingo had to, too, a little. They pulled into her drive. In her sensitive frame of mind she lapsed back into tears again as he drove away, so that she had to stand a few minutes in the garage drying her face on her scarf and taking deep breaths.

twenty-three

Hal Gartman had worked hard all day from the time the social worker had taken the children away but had dozed off a little in the late afternoon, waking up only at the sharp pain when the soldering iron sagged in his relaxed hand and burned his knee. Then the room collected, returned to his consciousness. He had a sensation of the shambles of plates and mismated shoes, mess intruding suddenly upon his reverie, or nap, like an invigorating shock from his own machine, so that he rubbed his burned knee and jumped up quite alertly with a fine, fit sensation in the calves of his legs, and looked all around. His machine sat disconsolately amid its collapsed web of wires and electrodes, resting, discouraged, perhaps, by its failure to give its experimental victims either significant pleasure or a fatal shock. It seemed quite alive to Hal Gartman, and he was not discouraged with it. All he had left to do was fix a few more things and plug it in again. He might need a 220 current, though.

A knock on the door and the children burst in with scrubbed, puckered faces, that black social worker behind them, scowling, looking late and cross, explaining that the Bureau of Social Welfare was returning them to him and would like to know the whereabouts of his wife. Hal Gartman tried to think of Hal Harris's address—she was always around there someplace. The social worker could look it up in the phone book. Hal Gartman saw that their stratagem, sending the children off with the neighbor woman in the morning, had not worked. Mr. Brown, the social worker, left abruptly, with ominous remarks about coming back tomorrow.

Hal Gartman embraced Ronda and Derek with transitory but powerful feelings of guilt. Poor charming things, off at the Bureau of Social Welfare all day, having to sit in chairs, fill out forms. A fatherly indignation seized him. "I will take you up to see Miss Hart!" he promised. His own heart fluttered. Poor little things, sitting virtually alone all day with a strange woman in the labyrinthine Quonset huts of the State of California, watched over by the unknown and plain woman who was not their mother, curse her, or even Miss Hart. They deserved ice cream; they deserved new clothes from Bullock's. They deserved the steadying and inspiring presence of Miss Hart in their infant lives, to correct any impression gleaned from any random sight they might have seen around the halls of social justice that life is irregular and sad.

He did not feel it to be so. He was cheerful. He wondered why he smelled the stench of cat sand when they had no cat. Or perhaps they had a cat. Miss Hart had the pale, gleaming skin and meager chest of a virginal Victorian heroine: stricken, tuberculous, angelic, doomed. Did she know she was doomed? But of course she was not doomed; she was a

nice, strapping girl from Minnesota and could have no conception of herself the way he saw her: as a romantic heroine.
Only as a virgin; of this she had a powerful theoretical grasp.
They had discussed it like theology, like politics, he with a
sage's interest, judicious and sympathetic; she burning with
conviction and old-fashioned principles. Her sweetness,
when you thought of her at all, brought tears to your eyes.

"It is the act of giving yourself, not the mere fact of having
done it. What your husband would mind is that you had
given yourself to someone else," she would say.

"You are not a present but a person. However," he would
say. "However, your scruples are charming." Her scruples
were derived from her mother, who was much spoken of.

"And also our religion feels it is wrong."

"Religion," he would sigh nostalgically. "Virginity. Scruples."

"No, don't take your shoes off, Ronda," he told her.
"Derek, put yours back on. We're going up to see Miss
Hart." Derek sighed, becoming resigned to constraint for
this day only, and put his shoes back on.

"I should think she might have cookies," Gartman continued. "She's a good young woman and loves you, and she'll
want to hear all about your traumatic experiences today."

"They are going to put us in a foster home," Ronda said.
"They looked at our teeth." She bared her teeth. "They took
us to the reform school, but that man came and got us out
again. The lady, Mrs. Edwards, that went with us to the
place was screaming and crying when they took us away."
This had interested them. Hal Gartman thought it interesting, too.

"You kids have got to quit eating so much candy," Gartman said, looking at Ronda's teeth. "We'll keep them from

putting you in a foster home. I'll think of something. Comb your hair. Find me a comb, Ronda, and I'll comb your hair."

Miss Hart had red hair, a color not usually associated with virginity, though come to think of it more suitable and suggestive of purity than either blond hair, with its overtones of suggestibility and folly, or brunette, with the connotations of passion, which was, as he knew, a ridiculous stereotype—witness the frigidity of his swarthy wife—but it might hold in general. You never thought of the Virgin Mary as having hair at all; hair was too erotic, no doubt, and that was probably why she was always represented in veils; nuns, too. Miss Hart, with a sensibility as intact as her membranes, instinctively went about in head scarves, though this was partly also to conceal her curlers after she had washed her fine, long, red hair, as she was constantly doing. Ah.

"I can't find any hairbrush," Ronda wailed, querulous. Long day. He hoped they would behave upstairs, wouldn't turn whiny, though you couldn't blame them after a day of welfare workers peering down their throats.

This thought produced in him a start of self-impatience, renewed his fatigue, reminded him involuntarily that he was an old man. These were his children he ought to be taking better care of, in a real house with a steady income, and you could not conceal the sores of neglect with flute lessons. He had always seen to it that there were flute lessons, but he ought to see to other things. They had—these, his very own children—sad, ghetto eyes. From time to time he saw it.

"Find the goddamn hairbrush," he snarled at Ronda. "Derek, wash, please." A softer voice. Please, Miss Hart or some other reasonable, fastidious, soft-fingered female, preferably Miss Hart, take appropriate maternal pity on this situation. It was true he spent overmuch time tinkering with improbable machines, and he grew bored easily with simple jobs and was, therefore, only an intermittent provider, but he was a victim, too; of his crazy, vicious wife. How was he to have known, how did you know about a tender girl, when you married her, that she would turn out to be a Vedantist and a junkie?

Ronda sat on his knee, trustfully understanding that the hair pulls were not unkindly meant, and neither were his rough injunctions not to wiggle. He tried not to pull her ragged curls.

Miss Hart, her hair in curlers, with no head scarf, seemed embarrassed to see them and turned pink, a feat possible in this day and age, surely, only to the very modest, virginal, and fair-skinned. Gartman did truly adore this girl. His passion was not that revolting prurience stirred in old men by innocence; he was a sophisticated man and had inspected his heart on this point. The contemplation of her chill, thin, big-boned form, inviolate, stimulated not his glands but his philosophy and lent some confidence to his hopes, hopes appropriate in an old man, of serenity, gratitude, repose. Anyway, he got enough on the side, around, if not from his dear frigid wife, to take care of him in other respects. He liked the idea of Miss Hart's untroubled sleep, of her impervious porcelain surface, exuding nothing, absorbing nothing, containing nothing, no one.

Besides, she was a good cook, learned it back on the Minnesota farm—or not a farm, actually, because she came from a small town, but that same sort of extra-calorie part of the world. How her mother had allowed this nineteen-year-old to come to California alone was some mystery.

Miss Hart, Darlene, was stricken to see Mr. Gartman and the children so unexpectedly, bethought herself wildly of what was in the refrigerator to cook for them. The children looked half-starved and surly, as usual, but Mr. Gartman, with his burning, piercing eyes, the most amazing man ever, would not even know if he was hungry or not. Mr. Gartman was the only genius Darlene had ever met.

Flustered, she gathered the children in. She had some sausage, was all, and applesauce; she couldn't remember what else. Mr. Gartman's one chipped tooth, when he smiled, made him boyish, though his maturity showed in his distinguished white hair. She would have to run take out her curlers, but she couldn't think of any way of doing this without making it seem as if she needed to go to the bathroom.

She put the children at the kitchen table, with glasses of milk. Mr. Gartman watched them benignly from the doorway.

"May I offer you something?" she asked, heart still pounding awfully, and dreadfully afraid that he would perceive and understand the significance of the way she was getting soaked with perspiration, so that she didn't dare lift her arms to take anything down from the cupboard.

"Well, I guess I haven't eaten anything today, as usual," he admitted, with his charming, crinkly smile. "Ronda and Derek have been at the Department of Child Welfare all day —that business I told you about—and I got to working. I bought a chicken, however, this morning, and I had a proposal to make to you about it, though I forgot it till now."

"I could fry it—it wouldn't take long," Darlene agreed, grateful that his absence would allow her to run in and take out her hair rollers and renew her deodorant and put a little make-up on. He didn't like much make-up, he had said—his wife didn't wear any at all, though she could sure use it, or at least pluck her eyebrows. Darlene could not think about this poor man's wife without extremest indignation. His wife was his cross. Darlene worshiped him. Literally.

It was hard to say how her odd devotional practices had evolved. She had not been religious in Minnesota, though she had certainly been a regular churchgoer. But she relied upon religion now, and perhaps that was what religion was for: for when you were by yourself two thousand miles from home. All those years of candles and droning voices and crossing herself had had a kind of delayed effect, coming on like an automatic oven to keep her warm and drop her to her knees in Los Angeles, California, in the motel room where she lived, and where she did not talk to God overmuch, even now. But she thought aloud, and if God heard, well and good.

And she had religious pictures, and a silver crucifix and a Bible, and an ivory statue of the Virgin from the Philippines. Stuff she had gotten for Confirmation. It was hard to see how it had come about, but with these things arrayed on her dresser, and the long minutes spent after prayer just leaning back against the bed thinking about things, and her eventual acquisition of a photograph of Mr. Gartman holding his children on the front porch of their unit, which she propped among her devotional objects and to which she began addressing certain of her thoughts, Mr. Gartman had gradually assumed a reliable place in her little ritual. She began to see what people meant by simply worshiping a man.

She had not actually written her mother about all this but knew her mother would approve of her interest in Mr. Gartman and his family. Her mother had given Darlene an important and secret piece of information that most women are not privileged to know. Darlene knew from her mother that whereas the generality of women believes—and, indeed, it often seems true—that in this vale of tears women are victim-ized by men, the actual fact of the matter is that men are victimized by women. And it is this, in the long run, that makes women's lot so difficult, like sinners being visited upon. So Darlene's interest in the Gartmans had, from the beginning, been both personal and, in a way, on behalf of womankind. It angered her that Mrs. Gartman, by dressing so sloppily and never being there, should bring trouble down on all women. And you couldn't help caring about the poor little kids, who were there by themselves so much, and about the tired-looking man. She was a long way from home. She was alone. She didn't at all mind keeping an eye on the kids, poor little things, down there so much alone. She worried at work and hurried home afterward to check on them.

In the bathroom she powdered her rather long, rather red nose, and, because her forehead was high and her own eye-brows were very low and so pale, really invisible, she care-fully penciled two new eyebrows an inch above the unnotice-able ones, in a more aesthetically pleasing relation to her hairline, improving greatly the balance of her face. She un-tucked her blouse from her jeans and powdered her armpits. He was returning with the chicken. Perhaps, after all, this could be the night to give him her virginity.

She had not exactly written to her mother about this, but her mother had alluded to the fact that when you saw the one, you knew. She had not been able to detail the sensation too particularly, but Darlene had a general idea: you felt awe and confidence, and your heart beat rapidly. The man im-pressed you with his attitude of patient suffering and, of course, with his goodness and masculinity. It was better—Darlene had worked it out very carefully—if he was a little older. The tenderest gift you could give was your virginity, and if ever a man was bound to appreciate it Mr. Gartman was, neglected and underfed by his wife, trying to mind those little children by himself, working on his inventions with his genius mind.

"Here it is, Darlene, you dear girl, a frying chicken," he cried, with hearty cheer. Derek made a rude noise and complained that all their food came from Chicken Delight as it was, and Ronda said he was a liar.

"You always take the Chicken Delight money and order pizza," she accused him. Gartman, embarrassed by their tatty manners, told them to shut up, and Darlene, angelic creature, promised them chicken gravy, which you didn't get with chicken-in-a-basket. They put the children in at the television while Darlene cooked.

"I'm glad you're up here," Darlene said. "This guy at work I told you about who's after me wanted to come over. I kind of think he will, and you can get rid of him for me."

"Oh, you ought to have some younger friends, as I've told you many times," Gartman said.

"Well, he isn't a Catholic," Darlene explained, "so why get mixed up with him in the first place?"

"I'm afraid your religious views are going to stand in the way of your worldly success," Gartman said. "Charming. Quaint dilemma. I respect it without understanding it."

"A person has to live by some kind of principles, as you yourself have said," she reminded him. She was not sure what his were. He probably had particular scruples about people's hymens and would not realize that in the long run he would be doing her a kindness. She was not sure of her powers of persuasion on this point. She could try to hug and kiss him into a passionate mood, but she was not sure of those powers, either, his *or* hers. She was not clever or pretty, and he was old.

"It's true, for once and for all, like my wife says, that I'm a square," Gartman said. "It gives me pleasure to contemplate a moral absolute, and even greater pleasure to behold its personification. Virtue. Purity. I'm surprised at myself sometimes. For instance, when you said the words 'saving myself for the man I marry,' I responded to it as to an old bedtime story. Once upon a time . . ."

Terrified, Darlene put down the fork with which she had been turning the chicken and cleared her throat. "I've changed my mind," she said, and looked straight at him. Her ears were ringing with terror as she spoke, and he seemed to her to be toppling heavily off his stool as she cried, "I love you!" Her pale-blue eyes grew tearful. She was a child, really.

Gartman felt rocked, literally swayed on his stool by the directness, the somewhat Joan-of-Arcish heroism, with which she made this announcement, by the other-worldly expression of her eyes, and by the purposeful fanaticism of her expression.

"You are so good," she went on in a rush, "so wise and everything, and I know I'm wicked and sinful, but I just want you to do it to me. I wouldn't let anybody else but you."

"My *dear*," Gartman said, still gaping, shaking his white head, "your virginity . . ."

"I burn," she said. "I mean, I burn candles and pray for my feelings to be conquered or else for us to, you know, but I knew with your honor you'd never think of it."

"I don't want to violate your innocence, really, Darlene," Gartman protested. "There is something particularly beautiful for me about knowing a certified virgin. I vow I haven't known one in forty-five years."

"Know me now," she cried, testifying to the soundness of her Biblical training. She wiped her hands on her jeans and came over to half sit on his knee. The nearness of this part of her—specifically her pure little, or actually big, rather bony but pure and inviolate pelvis to his own—had, with the galvanic intensity of an electric charge, the effect of turning him to marble. Like a boy of sixteen! He nearly dumped her off the stool in his leap to his feet.

"I couldn't, Darlene," he said, frantically burying his face in the delicious, young, surely no more than nineteen-year-old, at least thirty-six-inch bosom. Consternated at his trembling, she supported him. What on earth could he have in his pocket? Oh, Lord. She saw.

She now discovered that she was being urged backward as by a large dog who jumps up on you; in other embarrassing respects, too—pelvic gestures, mainly—this analogy occurred to her. She was attempting to discover some particular local sensation of her own, though she felt bloodless in the head and scared, and Mr. Gartman was saying, "Hold me! Hold me!" which she thought she *was* doing—her arms were holding him up or away or both as they tottered together backward, through the kitchen door into the adjoining bedroom, imperfectly entwined, to become better connected on her crocheted bedspread.

A matter of only about forty-five seconds, for which he apologized and damned himself inwardly (what a way for an old expert to treat a virgin!), but he really had not had any for so long. She was sobbing but, it appeared from cautious inspection, not from bitter disappointment. Up close she appeared to have four eyebrows. He and Darlene revealed to each other how they were in love. Darlene revealed that she was lonesome in far-off Los Angeles, and he that he was often at a loss about his junkie wife and poor kiddies the Child Welfare Department wanted to take away.

It was Ronda who answered the door when the suitor, a Loomis courier, arrived. She told him, in her straightforward six-year-old way, that Darlene was in bed with her father, and the suitor backed away in great confusion. Ronda and Derek, after their tiring day, then fell asleep in the living room even before dinner, which was burned anyway.

Mr. Gartman stayed perhaps a bit later than Darlene, who wanted to be alone with her excited retrospection and her candles, would have liked; but she couldn't deny that she was happy, and there was a certain enchantment—making him an omelette and some biscuits and later some hot chocolate and French toast—and it was so wonderful just sitting there comfortably in the kitchen, him telling her about his machine, and smoking that funny-smelling little cigarette, and not minding that she got a little drowsy and once nearly fell asleep.

twenty-four

Max had left, had wandered through the kitchen and off to get Doctor Harris his cream, trying not to look high. "He gets mad if I'm high." But she looked high: hair wild and shirt on backward. Barney did not tell her she looked high. She looked natural to him; he was used to her, and preoccupied.

Barney sat at the kitchen table with a Scotch-and-water and listened to the kitchen clock behind him without putting himself to the pain of looking at it and forcing himself to realize it was after five and no Bingo. He was worried, but he was more occupied with his own thoughts. Your self played tricks on you and flung you into the arms of ugly ladies whom you did not know, for reasons you did not know. Triste, angst, all those vague words seemed to apply to his vague feeling of distress. He would be glad to get back to work. He wondered if he was right to have become a doctor.

He was thinking that perhaps he should have tried the Methedrine. You cannot know about things until you try them, after all. Assuming there is any virtue in knowing about them at all. You could get a boat and roam the South Seas. You could sit cross-legged by firesides in small Tibetan towns. Why shouldn't you? The pains and exaltations of life mostly go by us, he was thinking. A fine-sounding phrase, "pains and exaltations," though he would have been ashamed to use it in a conversation. It expressed his sense of something that ought to be included in a life. Burning, with a hard, gemlike flame—who had said that? Anyway, that *was* it.

The sound of a car door and Bingo's unmistakable footsteps in the garage relieved and released him. She was back at last! Or maybe not. She didn't come in, causing him to wonder if he had heard right. Then she did come in. He grinned. He was hungry. She would be cross, spending a whole day the way she had. He had told her how it would be.

"Well, our ministering angel back at last."

She looked disarranged, as if she had run home chased by something, and she was smudgy, with uncombed hair. He had in some unaccountable way forgotten how she looked. She was bigger than he had been thinking, and bonier. A thin layer of roundness seemed to have been rubbed off during the day. Otherwise familiar, very familiar; the strangeness disappeared in a second and was replaced by a mixture of irritation and sympathy. Her eyes were all red, and her shape was awkward, as if she was somehow sideways inside her dress.

"It must have been bad," he said. "You look awful. Was it that bad?"

"It was that bad," she said. "It's appalling. The welfare system. Unbelievable. I feel like people who visit prisons. They can never quite tell you what, but they have learned something powerful." She threw her purse on the table. "Where's Max?"

"Gone to get the great doctor cream for supper. That's a very odd bunch over there, I'm telling you. How did everything work out? You aren't accompanied by little kiddies, I'm thankful to see."

"No . . ." she said vaguely.

"Let me get you a drink," Barney offered. "Or, well, if you don't mind—my leg."

"Yes, I'll get it. Sit still. This is one of the few times in my life I have felt as though I need one." She got the half-gallon bottle of wine from the refrigerator and stood it on the table between them, as if she meant to drink a whole lot. Then she went off to the bathroom.

"What is this thing?" she called down the hall. "This thing in the bathtub?"

"It's a Jacuzzi pump. Give it a whirl," Barney called. She came stamping back.

"What's it doing here?" He supposed she was afraid he had bought it, her expression was so cross.

"A crazy friend of Max's brought it, having stolen it, and they made me have a bath with it, for my leg. It was in my horoscope," Barney said, and laughed at her widened eyes. "And the police were here, looking for a dangerous robber, who was also here." He told her about some of it while she was beating eggs for an omelette. The day, when seen retrospectively, cleared of his indecisions and fears, took a form more satisfying to him than it had seemed at the time; it now seemed like an art film, full of symbols and revelations. Bingo's mouth pursed, and she silently worked the egg beater.

"Why didn't you make them take away the pump thing? You have to be careful. I don't like having stolen things around," was her only comment, and Barney didn't reply. The nutlike smell of browning butter mitigated his disappointment that there would be only an omelette; Max had eaten up everything else. There would have been shrimp salad, too. He sighed. Bingo didn't seem hungry; she stayed on her feet, walking around the kitchen while he ate, coming over to the table from time to time to take a sip of her wine, straightening things in the dish cupboard, getting out the broom.

"After I talked to you," she said presently, "there were some more interviews and things, after which they decided I was an unfit mother and took away Max's kids. Just whisked them off. Nothing I could do."

Barney's first reaction—inappropriate, he knew—was to laugh.

"Of *course* you're an unfit mother," he reassured her. "Think what a comment on you if the State of California approved of you! Official views of fitness are practically a definition of mediocrity." He was intensely curious, but afraid to ask, how a definition of Bingo's unfitness had been arrived at.

"Well, it was the ease and assurance with which they decided this. And it was the way I believed them that was the worst of it."

"Poor Boo," Barney said.

Attracted by his sympathetic tone, she put down the broom and came over, clearly intending to sit on his lap. He winced a little in anticipation of the pain to his leg but drew her to him. She seemed to go limp, thereby weighing about forty pounds more, and nestled her head beneath his chin. He understood why she needed comfort.

"Really bad day?" he asked kindly. "Never mind. We'll think of something to do about Max's children, if that bothers you."

She stirred. She seemed to sink into him in a meaningful way. "I need your arms around me," she said awkwardly. The silence stretched out. Her ear was accessible to his lips for a husbandly nibble, but he did not nibble her ear. He knew that he was being ungiving. But he had given a lot that day, somehow. An alien and yet too familiar ear. She half turned to drape her arms around his neck, pressing against him with her soft breasts.

"Dear old Bingo," he said. Limply she lay against him. "Dear?" He jiggled her affectionately up and down with a bouncing motion of his knees, at the cost of great personal pain. She sniffed. He pinched her, to convey his love, affection, understanding—everything, perhaps, but the energy to take her to bed just now, which she was behaving as if she wanted; but it was a strange time. The pinch was perhaps a rather hard one, and she clouted him—smack!—a dazzling smack on the side of the head, catching his ear, dislodging his glasses, bringing tears of pain and astonishment. She had backed off from him. He was standing now, swaying, astonished. Then Bingo put her arms around him the way he always liked, and apologized.

"You just caught me by surprise, and I'm so jumpy," she said. Barney smiled, but he felt the need of silence and reflection for a while. Bingo did the dishes. Presently she dried her hands and took off her apron.

"I suppose I ought to go over and tell Maxine," she said, with distinct resolution, a deep, resolved breath.

"Looks like she's not going to call and ask," Barney said. "If you ask me, she's probably forgotten about them."

"How am I going to tell her, Barney? Her children! I allowed some people to cart her children off, like, oh, Nazi Germany."

"You see how concerned she is," Barney persisted, though the notion, put like that, was appalling.

"She absolutely trusted me to straighten things out. She's probably gone back to her apartment now, expecting to find them there. I can't think of any good way to tell her."

"Well, Bingo, when the police or whoever find out you aren't Max, that she isn't you—you know—then they'll have to give her another chance. So, in a way, it may be for the best. She can pull herself together tomorrow and . . ."

"Maybe *we* should take them. They're nice kids, really, and they—they have a terrible life. She leaves them alone in this filthy motel. We could keep them, and she could come and see them."

"Our own kids might be a little upset to find themselves replaced when they come home. Like some kid nightmare."

"Will you go over to the Harrises' with me? She might still be over there. I'm going to have to tell her."

"Bingo, are you getting really depressed? You sound kind of numb."

"Well, for God's sake, wouldn't you be?"

"Sure." Barney sighed; selfishly, he knew. But it was just that he was feeling increasingly morose himself and wanted to be babied a little, and instead he would have to be brave and cheerful. He took his plate over to the sink and gave her an encouraging, cheerful, loving hug.

twenty-five

They stumbled, holding hands, down the bare earth embankment toward the Harrises' house, stepping in the dark on the young ice plants, which squished beneath their feet. But they knew that ice plants are sturdy and would come back. The city, lovelier at night, twinkled far below them, as though they lived above a milky way in a dark heaven. The eastern horizon was a peculiar rusty orange—must be a big fire somewhere. Barney had trouble climbing down and made grunts of pain. His leg was really a lot worse than it had been that morning. Bingo supported him with her strong arm.

"Barney," she said suddenly, drawing back so that he almost slid. "Barney, there's somebody."

Somebody else, was his immediate and automatic thought. He stared in the dark. Somebody else, naturally, deservedly. He was shot with pain. Why was Bingo giving him this awful news in the night air, with his leg hurting, among the ice plants? This was pitiless. She was not looking at him, but he could imagine the fastidious blankness in which she was holding her features. He made a hoarse sound, meaning to ask who, or perhaps what, in case she hadn't said there was somebody else.

"In those bushes." Her hand took him again—crunch—painfully hard in her fear. "I saw a man move, I'm sure. Then he saw us and went deeper behind the bush. I saw the light on his face and something in his hand, a gun or metal bar."

"Where? Are you sure?"

"Yes. Lurking. Let's go back."

"See here, you, come out of there," Barney said in a loud, experimental voice. Nothing, no one, moved. The bush remained rooted in its black shadow and seemed to grow only more obscure and dense, thicket enough for numerous marauders.

"Let's go on our way," Barney said, again loudly, and whispered, "We can get to the Harrises' more easily than to our house if someone means to leap out at us." He knew she agreed, because she began to lead him again, and they gained the soft light from the Harrises' house, the firm patio, the dark square of normal swimming pool. Bingo looked back up at the bushes by their house.

"Let's go call the *Police*," she said loudly. "Barney, I can't bear it, people lurking," she said, most tremulously for her, who was never tearful or timid. They watched for a time, but nothing moved behind the bush. "Or perhaps I was mistaken," she said. "It's been such a funny day."

They knocked on the Harrises' door, which stood half open. They could hear voices, low numerous voices, but no one answered their knock, so they went in, feeling grateful to be inside. It was the dining room. Rich darkness, food smells from a kitchen to the right of them, below them in the sunken living room, as on a softly lighted stage, a little group of people—actors or conspirators—in a tight ring of sofa and dining-room chairs. People sitting leaning forward on the straight dining-room chairs, their feet and purses tucked under the chairs, and Doctor Harris, bigger than the rest and compelling in a striped T-shirt, like a dockworker, presiding over something they were all watching in the middle. Barney and Bingo started a little when Max came up behind them silently, touching them, taking their arms, and saying "Hush."

"The miracle of life, as they say," she whispered. "Watch." They moved with her to the little railing that marked off the dining room, and moved down the few steps into the living room. The conspirators did not notice them.

"The cat," Max explained. "It's a tribute, really a testimonial."

"What is?" asked Bingo, who could never bear portentousness and yet was whispering like the rest in the reverent hush. Then Bingo and Barney could see on the floor at the feet of the watchers, in the center on the carpet, a cat crouching, purring with a fervid loudness, shivering and looking around at all the people.

"Her time has come," Doctor Harris said, with a brief look at them.

"See," Max said, "she had such a sense of trust and safety that she came into the group—this is group-therapy night— to have her kittens. She's had three already, with us watching." And they could see, beneath the cat, some damp lumps, filmy and bluish, squirming. Bingo and Barney were embarrassed to have come on a neighborly errand in the middle of group-therapy night. They continued to hold hands, as they often did though so long married, and supposed they ought to come back later; but it seemed rude to turn away when someone was giving birth.

"She trusts Doctor Harris, you see. Even an animal can sense," a woman spoke up from the group. The cat gave a howl then, purring fiercely louder, faster, agitated, jungle-like. She positioned her haunches. They watched the bluish fearful bulging, like her intestines, pass from her. No one spoke or moved.

"Oh, she'll step on it," another woman, the housewife Joan Fry, suddenly shrieked, so that everyone started up fearfully and turned on her for her noise. "Look! She's forgotten about the others. Oh, heavens! Oh, God!" The cat delicately curled around the other kittens, not noticing, or not appearing to notice, the thing she had expelled. She licked her own face passionately and did not notice the new kitten, as it trailed out of her. Then finally she turned and began to lick it, too.

"What in the hell," suddenly came a loud, shrill, sarcastic Southern voice—Irene, Mrs. Harris, banging the front door, with her friend the interior decorator in ardent black curls behind her. "What in the hell! Look at mah carpet! Hal, why are you just sitting there letting that animal bleed all over mah carpet?"

"It isn't blood; it's amniotic fluid," Doctor Harris said. No one paid any attention to Irene.

"Here," said a little old lady to Bingo, moving over so that Bingo could sit down by her on the sofa. "It's thrilling. You would think it would be repulsive."

"Hal!" Irene repeated.

"It'll come out," he said.

"You could put it outdoors. You could put some newspapers under it," Irene cried. "Look at the mess! Oh, mah lord, you see what it's like here, Gregson. Mah new carpet!" She led the young man off to the kitchen. They could hear the refrigerator and cupboards banging.

"I think that's the last one," Doctor Harris said.

"Oh, maybe not, maybe not, I hope not!" the housewife, Joan, cried vigorously, and it was impossible not to notice the irrational, beatified expression that had come over her bland moonface. The company felt awkward at this, but Bingo and Barney exchanged one minor glance of astonishment and relish at all of the strangeness. Barney was aware, too, that he felt a core of emotion, some response he did not totally understand. The cat was compelling. The miracle of life indeed, perhaps.

"Oh, let there be another kitten," Joan said, getting off her chair and down on her knees and advancing like someone maimed toward an object of prayer. "Kitty, kitty!" For all her weight she was not clumsy, but people gasped as if they feared that she would, with her fat human hands, crush the new little things. Instead, she took them up with the greatest feeling and delicacy, and then the mother cat, too. Holding her skirt like a sack for them, she sat back against her chair, arranged her legs tailor-fashion, and secreted the kittens in the cozy nest of spread skirt. She looked around at the assembled company in a manner that was satisfied, accomplished. "Maybe she'll have another one, here on my lap. Think of that," she said.

Immediately there was great thundering jealous disagreement. People thought of reasons. "If you touch them too soon the mother will eat them." But objections drained away, because the woman and her kittens looked so happy. The purring of the cat continued like a happy maternal sound from her viscera.

Because no one said anything then and apparently wasn't going to, a thin girl in a plaid dress seized the silence, speaking in the plaintive voice of someone who had been interrupted. Barney, whose fascination with the kittens was something he could not wholly explain, was conscious of wanting to strike or smother her so that he could pursue his mounting emotional response to its explanation without the distraction of listening to her problems. The other watchers shifted immediately to her, as if waking, and began making nods and other signs of their basic sympathies with, after all, human beings. Yes indeed, they seemed to mean, sitting back and folding their hands. Barney realized he had sat down on the one vacant chair, perhaps Max's chair, and a great crease had formed between his eyes as he concentrated on the cat and her kittens. He watched the mother, Joan, rocking them on her lap. The thin girl was talking, and Doctor Harris seemed to be going off to sleep again, or his eyes were drooping in concentration.

"I was trying to make him see that a woman has the same sexual drives a man does, but he just couldn't admit that emotionally. But that's *his* problem, not mine; I mean, why should *I* suffer? So he couldn't accept this, and that's why I had to be unfaithful, and I still don't see anything wrong."

"But you sound so *defensive,* Delores," the little old lady said in a gentle, thin voice. "Of course you shouldn't be sexually frustrated, but you sound so defensive, I'm not sure you're really happy with your solution."

"You should go back to school," said a dark man in a heavy blue suit and horn-rimmed glasses. He was leaning forward in his chair, so that his socks showed at the backs of his shoes. Bright Argyle socks. "My wife went back to school. Before that she was always bitching about something —not getting enough, getting too much, life passing her by, bursitis, the whole bit. But she was a changed woman when she went back to school. Had nothing to do with sex. Intellectual stimulation."

"You lucked out, then," another man interrupted, "because so did my wife go back to school, and it was a real mess. She used to be a good housekeeper, nice with the kids, everything clean, Play-doh. Then she took this class: the oral interpretation of literature."

Laughter from the psychoanalytically sophisticated. Bingo and Barney tittered, too. Doctor Harris opened his eyes briefly to show that laughter was not sanctioned.

"It's true," the man said. "It isn't funny. At San Fernando State. They read plays and reported aloud, and let me tell you, this woman, once she started reporting out loud she never stopped. She used to even recite the plays, and one—it was an odd experience—was about a judge. It was a play by Molière, I think. His wife talked so much that in the end the judge had himself made deaf! The irony of her telling me this play!"

"A deaf judge." Someone laughed. "That *would* be something."

"Justice is not only blind but deaf," Doctor Harris said, opening his eyes.

"Why *should* I go to school? I'm already a college graduate. I'd like a decent sex life," the young woman persisted.

"You should fix your hair different, Delores," another man said.

"At some level you're resisting your femininity, if you ask me," remarked Joan, from the floor.

"How ridiculous," Bingo said loudly, startling Barney. "Why should you say that? Maybe her husband has a hang-up. Why is it nobody ever believes that men have sexual problems? They just say you should get *your* hair done. Maybe her husband has problems, inadequacies. Maybe *he* should be here." Barney felt puzzled and distressed. Was she trying to tell him something? Why was she speaking to these unknown people?

"That's right!" agreed Joan Fry. "My husband complains if I put on a little extra, but he goes around like Orson Welles. He . . ."

"What about the food? Nothing but spaghetti," interrupted a fat man, evidently her husband. "If that isn't an unconscious wish to fatten me to death . . ."

"It's so unfair that all a woman can do sexually is just decorate herself and hope some man, fat or not, will help her out. It's unjust," Bingo said persistently. Nobody responded, perhaps because she was not a member of the group. They looked at her disapprovingly, exclusively. Barney pitied her.

"I bet you're really frigid, Delores," said a man. "You hate men, and you taunt your husband out of hostility, which, of course, turns him off. You want to castrate him."

"I wouldn't need to," she said sadly. "I get no action as it is."

"That's *why* you wear your hair that ugly way. . . ."

Irene bustled her way into the center of the ring of people. "How can you bear," she said to her husband, "to sit around once a week listening to all these boring problems?" She had gone down on her hands and knees and was shaking a substance from a large jar labeled Glamorene. Fumes assaulted them. Barney had seen such corn-meal stuff strewn on carpets where someone—he himself, he remembered, as a child—had thrown up. He felt like throwing up now, the sort of mild impulse of nausea that will go away if you hold perfectly still.

"Pardon me, everybody," Irene said, "but sanctity of life or not, the goddamned cat has ruined the carpet. Pay no attention to me."

Barney's irritation at the thin plaid girl now shifted to Irene, became an almost intolerably strong impulse to hit

Irene suddenly—or kick her, which would have been easier, because her attractive rear was nearest him. He was awestruck at the way the power of this impulse made his foot twitch, even though the rest of him, sickish, was holding perfectly still. He realized he was in the grip of strange powers and racing thoughts; once when he had thrown up and then again, something about kittens, puzzlement about Bingo's strange outbursts in this group, odd things in his head. Fumes from the Glamorene hurt him deep inside, between the eyes. Someone sneezed. Barney still wanted to kick Irene, but she had finished spreading the reeking corn meal and now stood up and walked out. Some combination of emotion and toxicity made sweat break out on Barney's face.

"The kitten! The kittens! I remember!" he cried, leaping to his feet with an expression that caused everyone to turn to him. There was immediate silence, a kind of approving vibration arising in the room as at a revival meeting when someone has suddenly received the Holy Ghost.

"It's just that I've remembered something very important," he said, sitting down again, with apology. "I never thought of it before, a very important thing about my feeling for my wife. My bad feeling for my wife, I mean. I *do* see something to all this—how strange!" He saw Bingo stiffen. He did not look at her.

"You'd better tell us," Doctor Harris said, sensing the enthusiasm of the group, which expressed little interested murmurs for someone who had a new story to tell them. Bingo looked alarmed, which pleased Barney. He was smitten, utterly. He had remembered.

"Yes," he said, "I will tell you. It was like this, entirely available to me in the most vivid detail. This was about four years ago. Maybe three. Our old cat, Tinker Bell. Our old cat was bleeding inside and dropping blood around the house, and though she seemed to feel all right we knew she must be sick, and Bingo said, in her logical way, 'I'm afraid we must put Tinker Bell to sleep.' Or maybe she didn't say 'put to sleep,' a vulgar euphemism Bingo wouldn't use. *I* probably thought 'put her to sleep.' I have a vulgar mind, and that's anyway why I'm an orthopedist: you never have to put anybody to sleep, as it were. I can't stand death. Well, though, I agreed with Bingo that it was necessary, I thought. Poor sick cat. And we were going to spend a month up in Carmel with Bingo's mother. So there was the problem of what to do with Tinker Bell. You can't ask your neighbors to look after somebody who's dropping blood all over, I suppose. Oh, we could have taken her to the vet, but me being a doctor and so on, and we were poor, and Bingo anyway doesn't believe in unnaturally preserving the lives of dumb animals. Well, anyway, we didn't take her to the vet."

"Oh, how terrible," the little old lady said.

"I thought that Bingo had some funny female sense that this was the thing to do, because she knew what was inside Tinker Bell. I mean, she didn't really, and I didn't really suppose she did, but I let myself feel that there was some affinity between Bingo's female organs and Tinker Bell's female organs. Perhaps I thought that Bingo wanted to die or that she wanted to kill Tinker Bell because Tinker Bell kept having babies—kittens—litter after litter. Which Bingo didn't believe in preventing. And I *know* this was because she wouldn't want any knife in her own belly. She admitted that. I had offered, after Tinker Bell's second litter, to fix her myself. It's a simple operation, but Bingo said no. It got so our friends were afraid to come over because we would always press kittens on them."

"Nelson and Caroline were greatly benefited by observing the miracle of life," Bingo said in an acrimonious voice from the sofa, "and they happened to miss seeing the first batch. And Tinker Bell only had three litters, which is not many."

"Is 'miracle of life' a vulgar euphemism?" Barney remarked.

"Not at all," Doctor Harris said, in a reassuring voice, assuming the question had been put to him.

"Seventeen kittens," said Barney. "I knew in some way that Bingo wanted to kill Tinker Bell. That she wanted me to kill Tinker Bell. Tinker Bell to die and me to kill her. Oh, at the time it was agreed; it was the only thing to do."

"Wicked man," whispered Joan, in a baby voice to the cats in her lap. "Wicked man to hurt the kitty-cats."

"Bingo must have known how I would feel, or maybe not—she is so logical. Anyway I got morphine and also some Sodium Pentothal. We couldn't tell the children. Nobody thought the miracle of death very edifying, eh, Bingo? Well, we had agreed that the children might take it rather hard and ought not to think of their father as a cat killer, unnaturally taking the lives of cats.

"We packed the car and made a lot of preparations for the trip when I got home from the hospital that afternoon so we could get a good early start the next morning. And Bingo gave me meaningful glances, or maybe she said, 'Did you bring anything home?' Or maybe nothing was said. But it was in the air. Caroline was only two and wouldn't go to sleep and was excited and fussy, and Nelson made an awful scene about taking his tricycle with us. It was in the air."

"It was not at all like this," Bingo said.

"Then Bingo was putting them to bed, and I couldn't

find Tinker Bell. She was always around but now suddenly not. As if she knew. I waited; I hunted. Then she came home, and my feeling that she knew I was going to kill her was worse than if she had been lying around trustfully somewhere and looked up surprised when I grabbed her. It was as if she had been seized with this irrational fear and then overcome it, telling herself it could not possibly be true that I wanted to kill her, and even if it might be true we could not live together under such conditions—her suspecting me, suspicion between us—and so she had to have it out. Even if it was true.

"So I was sitting there trying to read, and she came in the window and walked up to me and jumped up on my knee, looking directly at me. There was no blood on her, either, and I remember the vigor with which she leaped into the room and up on me.

"I held her and went to get my syringe, very succinctly, no introspection, believe me. A very businesslike murder. Injected her, held her until she looked a little sleepy, put her on the sofa, and went upstairs. Bingo was in the bathroom, with the water running very loudly, very much longer than usual. I guess it must have been ten o'clock already. I sat on our bed for a while, and then I went down to the kitchen for a beer. I had to pass the living-room door, but I didn't look in. I thought, at the time, of when I was little, of getting up for a drink of water on Christmas Eve and passing the living room but on my honor not looking to see if Santa Claus had come, because I should not know that until morning, at the same time as everybody else. What power I felt, when I was little, at not looking. As a grown man I felt my cowardice. I drank the beer in the kitchen and finally figured I might as well go in and carry out the corpse. Water still running upstairs. I remember thinking with satisfaction that the bitch must be showering in ice water by this time, pure ice water.

"I crept sickly up to the couch, and there was Tinker Bell on her side, her paws tucked under her head the way a person sleeps sometimes, purring and snoring, not dead at all, but happy. Obviously happy, smiling, if a cat can smile, having happy dreams."

In the group people stirred. There was in the air the quality of relief. Not dead. Joan looked up from her kittens to smile at him. The kitty still living in her opiate sleep. Barney was oppressed by their fierce attention, more involved with his own visceral memories of Tinker Bell.

"So then I killed her again," he told them firmly. "Without going up to tell Bingo, who had gone to bed, because I heard the bedroom door close. I just watched Tinker Bell for a while and then went out into the kitchen, loaded up my syringe with Sodium Pentothal, and killed her again. I remember I had a terrible pain at the back of my head, is all. I laid her on the sofa again and had another beer, and when I looked at her again she was really dead. So then I didn't know what to do, so I picked her up—she was already colder, heavier—and I rolled her in the newspaper and put her under my arm. I still didn't know what to do, so I took a walk, with the newspaper and our dead and stiffening cat under my arm, her one little hind leg sticking out. I remember I had to stop and wrap her better and almost began to cry, which was stupid. It was chilly out, late, nobody around. I walked around the block a couple of times, past all the houses of people we knew, all inside asleep or having parties, with my murdered cat, and in the end I put her in somebody's garbage can. Just lifted the lid and dumped her in and walked on. I had a terrible fear of being seen. Eyes behind curtains. I walked hastily on. When I got home Bingo was asleep; we had to get an early start in the morning. I had a whiskey-and-soda and a hangover the next day."

"What is his name?" a man asked of someone else.

"Barney," Bingo said, clearly giving Barney meaningful expressions of some kind, which he didn't know how to meet and preferred not to see.

"Barney, that's an affecting tale," the man said. "That's just the kind of thing a man stores up, as I well know, because once when I . . ."

"Oh, come on, Ernest," the thin young woman, Delores, said. "We *don't* want to hear about that, and neither does Barney."

"It was the cat having kittens and then the chemical smell of the rug cleaner that just brought it back to me, sweet smell like morphine," Barney said, and he did feel relieved and loving toward poor old Bingo, whose face, homely and drawn, reflected remorse, perhaps reproach for his not ever having mentioned this before. People said things, various kindly things, to him. They said nothing to Bingo. They had not even wanted to hear her remarks about men. She sat brightly, trying to seem as detached and interested as everyone else in Barney's sensitive nature, but he understood the red patches on her cheeks and a spread of mottled flush on her neck, as if she had clawed herself. Still he could not help it. The thing was, for the moment, quite beyond his control.

"I suppose we should ask ourselves why Bingo had such a determination that I kill Tinker Bell," he heard himself say, in a pompous important voice, hating himself. The group enthusiastically began to discuss it. Bingo got up and went out to the kitchen.

twenty-six

"You wouldn't believe the extraordinary thing I'm watching on television," said the dark and curly lad, Gregson, in his blue striped pants, which the group regarded as if it was the pants, not Gregson himself, who interrupted their meaningful colloquy with Barney.

"I'm watching these houses burning down, right around here, out toward the Valley. They're having a hell of a fire, which is on television, and you can see the houses burning up. It's fantastic."

Abruptly chairs scraped, tipped—some of the group evidently lived in the Valley—and everybody swarmed toward the television, which had, the whole time, been glowing bluely in the corner but with no one paying attention. Now they attended passionately to the speciously urgent, low voice of the commentator, lending drama to the sight of a line of flames burning some grass in a dark landscape.

"Ten thousand acres so far destroyed, and with the winds increasing, hopes for control of the fire diminish! Several houses have been burned; hundreds more are threatened!"

"Wait a minute; they'll show a house going up," Gregson whispered enthusiastically.

"An estimated half a million dollars' damage so far, and the flames are fast approaching the wealthy residential areas of North Bel Air and Beverly Hills." It was now real urgency in his voice. Then on the screen a suddenly illumined rectangle, like an X ray of a house, appeared and vanished in a crumble. People drew in their breath and pressed nearer.

"Where is that? Where is that? That looks like up the street from me!" Machines, trucks, men streaming across the screen carrying things, milling around. Fuzzily, in the background of a smoky street, a woman carrying a television and lamp and what appeared to be a bottle of gin, trying to load them into a Volkswagen. Coils of hose lying around.

"Residents living in the area north of Sunset Boulevard between Laurel Canyon and Sepulveda boulevards are being advised to evacuate their houses. Official estimates . . . the possibilities of control lessen . . . disaster."

"No, that isn't near my house. It looked like it, though. At first I thought . . ."

"It's incredible! It's incredible!"

People had sat down on the floor, crowded around the set, and now they shifted, made themselves comfortable, compelled, eyes never averted, to witness in the comfort of their living room the burning of Bel Air.

"Television coverage nowadays is something," someone said. "Imagine them getting television trucks in there almost as fast as the fire trucks."

Bingo had gone to the kitchen to find Max, and Max was there, a swarthy little figure making orange juice tenderly for her psychiatrist.

"Wow, they really think you're a mean lady in there." She smiled, with genuine sweetness, showing that she thought Bingo an excellent and kindly lady. Her confidence increased Bingo's misery, so that she immediately blurted out the terrible news.

"It didn't work. The people took the children anyway. To the Juvenile Hall. Everything I did seemed to make it worse. I tried to stop them—grotesquely. I even snatched

Ronda up and tried to run away. But they popped them in a car and whisk. No good-byes."

Though Bingo was now bitterly aware of the potentiality for catastrophe in everything, she had not quite expected to see Maxine shrivel and crouch as she did, her thin hands holding onto the kitchen counter as if for support.

"My head is not in the right place," Max said. "Wait a minute. You mean, they aren't home but at the jail?"

"I guess. Is it a jail? Jailers took them, anyway. Ronda was crying, too. They gave her a doll. It was my fault, and I tried to be so articulate and straight. Then at the end they just took them." Bingo felt obliged to include significant detail.

"I haven't even talked to them today. They are locked in somewhere, and they haven't even talked to their mother. Lying in some strange beds in some ugly room, probably not even together. Boys and girls separated, alone somewhere."

"They were going to take them out to dinner. I think they probably go out of their way to be, you know, kind, like the police with lost kids and ice cream. And the kids know what's going on. They're very smart; they probably know that tomorrow we'll come and get them out. I didn't have time to tell them that, but I think they'll know. And your husband saw them before we went and was with them at the park this morning. They're great kids, not at all rattled."

"Oh, ah, hell," Max said, wiping her nose against the back of her hand. Her eyes over her hand were burning, bright eyes. "That's no help. Tomorrow. Tomorrow I'll be just as bad as I am today."

"I'm going to get my lawyer," Bingo said. "It was so grotesque, so unfair. I handled it badly, but it's an impossible system, absurd, dehumanizing . . ."

"We have these pictures of when they were babies. I had

been so straight for a couple of years, so happy just devoting my life to them. I made things for them and ripped off toys and—I was the so-called perfect mother. Me sort of fat, in the pictures, with these dimpled babies, all of us smiling, in the pictures Hal took. He was a professor at UCLA then, in the Engineering Department."

"One night is not really going to hurt them. I'm sure the people are kind, Max, and tomorrow we can . . ."

"Oh, shut up! God!" Max cried, and put her hands to her thin face to think. Bingo was willing to hear angry and reproachful things. She stood waiting for them.

"I know, I know," Max said in a minute. "I can go down there now—you could drive me—and I'll go in and raise hell about how they have taken my kids without even asking me. I'll say you were the baby-sitter, the mentally defective baby-sitter—but responsible—who didn't understand what was going on. Do I look stoned? They'll have to let them out tonight and then tomorrow . . ."

"Max," Doctor Harris said, coming into the kitchen, "I'm sending everybody home. There're some possibilities the roads may be blocked later—fire trucks and things. Just a safety measure, but will you help get everybody together? There's a big fire not too far from here."

"What do you want *me* to do?" She looked worriedly at Bingo. Could not resist any orders from the great man.

"Well, help Miss Cole find her coat, get a box for the kittens so Joan can get up, move the car you parked blocking the driveway, I don't know," he said.

Max grimaced. "We'll go in a minute," she said to Bingo, and hurried off.

"They're advising us all to evacuate our houses," Doctor Harris said. "I suppose we must get things together."

"What are you talking about?" Bingo had the feeling she had just returned from somewhere, had been gone a long time. She did not know why they should evacuate their houses, and she looked around instinctively for Barney, who was not there. She thought of an attack of hydrogen bombs, with the feeling that she had always really expected this.

"The fire, the approaching fire. I'm going to wet things down with the sprinklers. You might do the same up at your house. My plants, I want to get them good and wet. Though I don't expect it will come here."

"My telephone doesn't ring. It doesn't even ring!" a man was screaming in the living room. "My wife, my kids!" Bingo left the kitchen, with heart beating strangely, to find Barney. There was much, she felt, much if not everything, that she did not understand; she had been transformed into an instrument for registering only fear, violation, revulsion, and misery, with no thoughts at all.

"No question about it; our house is gone," the man said, with tears on his fat features. Cars were starting up in the driveway, the door was being opened and closed, footsteps were everywhere, excited voices, a kind of jubilation.

Barney put his arm around Bingo's shoulder and said in a voice only half-assured, "That's right, there's a huge fire, and they're advising people to get their valuables together. It's on the TV, though nobody has come here to tell us. But they say on TV people ought to go somewhere else for the night, because there's no telling where the fire will spread, anywhere in the hills here."

"Let's go home, then," Bingo said.

"It's all stupid," Irene said in a loud voice to everybody. "Ah'm going to bed."

In the living room, amid the departures, the front door

banged and a young man in a fringed leather jacket came running in again and began to shout for Hal before he saw Doctor Harris was not there. "In the bathroom," Max said. She was helping Joan put the kittens carefully, one by one, into a big cardboard box. The young man pounded like Paul Revere on Hal's closed bedroom door and then opened it, revealing to the departing patients like a tableau, like an immobile Dutch prostitute in her window, the beautiful Irene frozen in a position of indignation in bikini panties, drawing an exotic negligee over one ivory arm.

"Sorry, sorry," cried the youth, flinging past the red bed, pounding again on the bathroom door. "Hal, listen, I don't know what's coming off, but the place outside is swarming with pigs. In cars, in the bushes, all over the place. Guys across the street. I can spot these things."

Harris came out of the bathroom, carrying a blooming orchid in a pot.

"Put some of these better plants in the car, just in case. Irene, would you tell Max to put the bishop's blood in my car, too?"

"The cops are outside."

"The fire, probably. They seem to be evacuating the neighborhood."

"Residents are advised . . ." the television told Barney and Bingo, who stood staring at it. Houses burned. "At least fifty-three houses destroyed so far. The fire is moving westward, with seventy-mile-an-hour winds, totally out of control. Relief stations have been established at St. Alban's Episcopal Church in Westwood, the Beverly Hills YMCA, and Emerson Junior High School, the Red Cross announces. So far no lives have been lost. A major disaster of unprecedented . . ."

"They are not here because of the fire, Hal. The guys across the street have guns. You can look out the window."

"I'm clean. I can't worry about that," Doctor Harris said, bringing out a rare Sudanese yucca.

Somebody else came in from the driveway. "The police are outside, searching our cars. We can't get out the driveway. My house! Hal! Do something!"

"Look, oh, look," cried Max, who had pulled aside the curtains on the back picture window and was gazing out over the hills. "Will you look at that fucking fire!"

The garish glow of real flames on the horizon and on the near hills precipitated in the room an agony of shrieks and crashes, as if they were being burned already, a roomful of trapped creatures in a flaming stable, kicking things, crying. The little old lady ran from window to window pulling at things. Men restrained each other, shoved, shouted. Everyone shouted for Doctor Harris, and he, bewildered by the eruption of pandemonium, stood wordlessly, shrinking in the doorway of his bedroom, with the yucca cradled in his arm.

"Save us, Hal, oh, Hal, please."

"What are we going to do? What do we do?"

"We'll be burned alive, Hal. Get us out of here!"

"Police, fire, police!"

Somebody had ripped a curtain down and was wrapping himself in it. "We'll have to run for it. Rescue, rescue, try the phone." Doctor Harris went in the bedroom and locked the door. He set the yucca on the bureau and sat down on the bed, staring confusedly. His patients, crying, pounded on the door. Irene, standing in the window on the street side in her sheer negligee, pulled the curtain closed again and turned to him.

"Hal, now listen to me. They's all kinds of police and

people creeping up on the house. That's right, ah can see them. Now listen, tell me for sure, are there any drugs in this house? Any of those kook patients in trouble? Why are these people creeping up on mah house, and you better tell me now while there's time."

"Oh, Irene, I've . . ." said Hal, his voice trailing off. He got up and went over to the yucca and tamped the soil around it so that it stood straighter in its pot.

"Hal." Her voice rose. "Tell me, what is going on? Is there anything you know of going on? The police are coming!"

"Please, Irene, we need to think how to get all these people out of here. There may be a fire." He sat back down and closed his eyes. She watched him, fiercely ferreting out whether he was thinking or sleeping.

"Sleeping!" She hurled herself on him like a football player. "Sleeping, you bastard! What are we going to do? We have trouble here!" He opened his eyes. "What is the matter with you, you bastard, where is your mind? Where in hell is your mind? It is never in this world, that's for sure! People may be burnt up, police coming, God knows what kind of opium they may have in their pockets—wouldn't you have learned yet? All these crazy lunatics you bring up here. Where is your mind?"

"I don't think the fire will come this way and I don't know anything about any drugs. I suppose somebody might have something but not me. I just can't get excited, Irene."

"Prison is not exciting, either," she screamed. "I can't stand this. You are a mummy; you are a zombie. Isn't there anything that can touch you? Ah used to love you, all these poor people, they love you, and you can't even be bothered to think about them. And now there is something you have to deal with. Will you for Chrissake come down from wherever it is you are at and listen when ah tell you that there's police all around and a fire coming."

"Stop that, Irene," Doctor Harris said, seeming to react more to her noise than to her words. "You cannot understand my mind. It's full of horrors. My thoughts are so full of the horror of things I can't even listen to you. I listen to my patients, and they cannot penetrate my pained and sorrowing thoughts. There is no way that you can understand how I suffer." Irene stared at him, opened her mouth, closed it, stared.

"Oh, suffering. Screwing is all you think about," she snapped.

"Listen, I know things—you are too young to understand, maybe. I could tell you things—there was a little boy, a little orphan boy, and all he ever wanted was to be adopted. Then one day, when he was five, he was going to be adopted —this was in the paper—adopted by a nice family, and it was just before Mother's Day. The day before, and the family was coming for him, only he was killed by a car, because he ran out into the street after something. They found it—it was a card he had bought at the store, and it had blown away. They picked it up—it said Happy Mother's Day To the New Mother. The driver said the little boy just ran out into the street, nothing he could do. The day before he was going to be adopted, the lonely little boy. And on Valentine's Day there was a little girl that didn't come home from school, in Michigan. She was seen getting off the school bus but then she didn't get home. Eight years old, and raped and murdered. They found her little sack of Valentines lying in the rain by the bus stop, and she was dead.

"And another girl—this was in England—was hurt,

beaten and attacked, and she dragged herself out to the road to get help. A woman found her and helped her. They flagged a passing truck, and the driver said he would take her to the hospital. Only she never got there. They found her body farther on, raped and strangled. The driver had done that to the injured girl. Don't you see? And you want me to get excited about the people in the front room, a fire . . . There was a little boy whose stepfather killed him by stepping on his stomach every day, and then they threw his body over a cliff. The mother helped . . ."

"Oh, stop it, stop it, you clown, you idiot," Irene screamed, covering her ears. "That is the newspaper; that is not real. That is horror, melodrama. Is that what it takes to horrify you? You must be pretty numb if it takes all *that* to horrify you. How are we going to get out of here? The fire! Are you sure there aren't any drugs? Where's Max? Oh, I know—Noel Fish." She flung herself against the locked bedroom door, groaned, unlocked it clumsily, and sailed into the midst of the frantic patients in the living room. Great pounding sounds were heard at the front door. More people came in, new men in suits, guns all around, shouts, cries. Irene had fled into the patio, crying for Max. Doctor Harris stood in the bedroom doorway watching the new men in suits writing down the names of all the patients, who were calmer, as if the new men in suits had come to save them, all giving their names and addresses and going outside in an orderly manner, while the light in the room from the far-off fire grew brighter, hotter, and a far-off roaring that sounded like the ocean but was the fire came closer.

"And, Irene, the worst thing of all, that happened to a little boy in . . ." Hal Harris was calling, with great tears in his eyes even to think of these terrible things.

twenty-seven

Bingo and Barney started home without delay, without words. There was no need to speak as they climbed the embankment again because there was so much to see: acres of hills and the fire plainly approaching over them, perhaps a mile away in one spot and threatening the Catholic women's college and convent, curling around its stone skirts like the flames of hell. The scene had a garish, medieval fascination. Bingo had not mentioned Tinker Bell.

"One's lurking hereditary anti-Catholicism, I suppose," Bingo said, "but it would be interesting to see it just go up in flames. All the nuns flapping wildly around."

"It's like the sack of Rome," Barney said. "There's a whole row of houses burning on the downside of that far hill, look!"

"The H-bomb," Bingo said. But it was exciting, strangely exhilarating, now that they were outside and could hear. The whole world was filled with the roar, like a giant gas burner on full blast, and helicopters drove around above in the dark, dropping things in the path of the fire in the farthest hills. Only a few sirens; the trucks were probably already in position, all at work, the firemen all at work. Stretches of low flame, like bright pencil lines across the black distant hills, leaving embers behind, advancing on every hand. Here and there a special larger conflagration, a random bonfire of a house. A hot wind whipped them.

"Bingo," Barney said, "I don't mean to be an alarmist,

but I really do think we ought to load up the car, and then I'm going to try to wet things down outside with the hose." They could see the big shape of Doctor Harris silhouetted against the distant burning as he fumbled in the dark down in his garden for the sprinkler-system switches. Little spurts of water gurgled and died.

"What, the silver and cameras, I guess, and, well, what?"

"I want to put some of my paintings in, but I'll pick them out; don't worry about that. Just go around and you'll notice things we don't want to take any chances about. I suppose it's kind of stupid but . . ." He shrugged and turned to climb the rest of the distance up the embankment. The beam from a flashlight hit him in the eyes. A voice told them to stop. The bright, blinding light approached them; the voice asked them who they were.

"The Edwardses," Barney said, supposing this to be a fire fighter. "We live in this next house here, and we'll get our things together, just in case, but we'd rather stay around, just in case. Of course we'll leave if the fire should come anywhere near in this direction."

"That's not where it is. Walk slowly ahead of me, and we'll see about you up in the light." Barney was, to his surprise, nudged heavily in the ribs with the flashlight. The man, whom they could not see because of his advantage behind the light, walked in back of them and shone the light at their feet so that they could more easily pick their path. They all went in the kitchen door and there saw him to be an ordinary man in a business suit, who continued for some reason to shine the flashlight on them. This had the effect of making them feel he was training a gun on them, so that they stood stock-still, indignant and baffled but subdued.

"You live here? Treasury agent." He showed them something in his billfold.

"Look, our house might burn down. There's a hell of a fire going on," Barney said, but meekly and resigned, so that he was surprised when Bingo quite inexplicably hurled herself against the man and, being a big girl, knocked him across the kitchen and herself as well, as the man grabbed hold of her, so that they landed together in a kind of copulative position on the kitchen floor at Barney's feet. The Treasury man, on top, looked up in amazement at Barney, and Bingo clawed at his face.

"Bingo! Bingo!" Barney cried, afraid the man might be carrying a gun. He leaped forward and pinioned her arms to the linoleum, and the Treasury agent climbed off her.

"I just can't bear it, get him out of here," Bingo said, with a strange expression. Barney released her and she sat up. She did not pull down her dress, which was above her thighs.

"Overwrought," Barney said. "Our house, the danger of fire . . ."

"What does he want? Make him leave us alone," she said.

"U.S. Treasury. We're going to make an arrest. There may be gunfire. I want you to identify yourselves, then I'm going to escort you to a car up the street. We're clearing the area."

"The fire. We have to pack," Bingo said.

"I very much doubt any serious danger of fire, but we are evacuating the immediate neighbors because of gunfire. Identification?" Barney showed him Bingo's billfold and asked if he could go to the bedroom for his own.

"Both of you go, and I will come with you," the man said. Barney felt frightened now as he walked behind them back to the bedroom, farther away from the front door, from neighbors, into the most private and secret part of their house.

"No need to be afraid," the man said, as if he was trained like a bloodhound and could catch the smell of fear off people. They could hear a battery of sirens, maybe turning into their own street, but they could not see because the man was marching them along for Barney's billfold. And Barney was worried about Bingo, who had not said another word and perhaps had been driven mad or something. The sirens were definitely nearer. The air felt hotter. Barney was newly fearful that there might be something—a narcotic smell, perhaps, in the bedroom or some clue the man might see—to do with the dangerous felon. Fingerprints. He had, of course, been sitting right there on their bed.

"Captain Edwards. Okay, that's all right, sir. We've fully investigated you; there's no question of suspicion, sir," the man said. "We will ask you to leave, as I outlined—a normal precaution. We are attempting to make the final arrests in our smashing of an important drug ring; I know you appreciate the importance of that. This crazy fire, it hasn't helped, but we can't let the criminals go now. I know you understand the significance . . ."

"He is not a captain. Don't call him captain. He's only in the Air Force because he's serving his two years, the doctors draft, not the regular military. He . . ."

"Bingo!" Barney cried, not liking the hysteria in her voice.

"Barney, make these people go away," Bingo said, in a loud strange voice, so that the agent gave Barney an understanding look and said, "Or, if you will carefully lock all your doors and windows and remain in some room not accessible by window or easily visible from outside, I could permit you to stay, under the circumstances. I know you want to take precautions against fire."

"Yes, yes, we'll lock up," Barney promised. "We want to stay. We want to stay in our home." This the Treasury agent understood and left them, with a nod of sympathy for Barney.

"Good luck, Captain," he said.

The fire was known to be advancing more by its noise than by heat or light. It seemed to be borne on the wind and accompanied by shouts and the motors of cars, people up and down the street, running feet. Bingo turned the television on, and they stood in the study watching it. The panic in the announcer's voice had increased. Thousands of people were evacuating the hills! Aid stations! Evacuate your house! And then, as they watched, the local man was replaced by a network news broadcast, so that they stood in the heat and noise listening to some calm man in New York telling the world how a fire was laying waste the luxurious suburb of Bel Air in the Los Angeles hills, and thousands of residents, wearing mink, were leading their poodles to safety while embattled firemen, rangers, forestry crews imported for the occasion, helicopters, and sodium bombs combined to bring the thing under control. Fire had destroyed some four million dollars' worth of property to date, no lives.

"Well, we can't stand here. I'm going out to wet down things if I can. You pack."

"You can't go outside. Gunfire," Bingo said numbly.

"The hell. I'm going to get the hose up on the roof—that's the most important part."

"No, we'll get wet blankets," Bingo said. "That's what you do."

They agreed about this, but it was a slow business. No water at all would come out of the tap. They ripped blankets from their beds and from the children's beds and sloshed them in the toilet tanks, a section at a time. Then Barney got a ladder from the garage and carried it around to the front of the house, away from the street and, presumably, from the Treasury men. Fire in the bottom of the gulley, not four hundred yards from their property line but oddly burning along the crevice of the hill, driven that way, perhaps, by the swirling wind. He shouted. Bingo dragged the wet blankets to him, one by one across the living room and through the glass doors, and they hauled them up the ladder. "This is stupid," he kept saying. "There are no sparks. I don't know why we're doing this."

"Barney, it's still burning the other way. It may miss us," Bingo cried. "It's burning away from us, more toward the bend in the road." But a tongue, another front, advanced on their own hill, leaped forward, fell back. The noise was appalling. Bingo was trying to get water out of the garden hose.

"Hey, you dumb son of a bitch," somebody called, "you've got to get out of here."

It was then, from his position on the roof, that Barney noticed that the Harrises' hillside below them was on fire. The fire would reach the Harrises' house, would come to their own house, inevitably, in time, and he climbed frantically down the ladder to get his paintings out of the studio.

twenty-eight

Max did not know if there was still time to get away. The patients were almost gone, the cars were loaded, yet the fire seemed to have appeared suddenly everywhere and might burn them up before they could go. There was no way of knowing if the street was blocked. Maybe they could run away across the smoldering hills, as if they were on trial, innocent, and could walk on coals. Along the curving street below, houses burned on either side, causing heat too extreme, perhaps, for escape in that way. Max went out in the patio to look down the hill, feeling vague curiosity. She saw her friend Barney the neighbor and shouted at him to get down off his roof and save himself, and watched him do it, scurrying down the ladder and limping along without even waving at her. No water at all was coming out of the sprinkler system. Max felt sick to her stomach, not knowing what to do about the fire; but there was something else that worried her more. Inside the house Irene seemed to be screaming. Naturally. Then skinny arms in a white short-sleeved shirt reached out and grabbed her and dragged her into the shed where the pool filter was, and slammed her against the wall.

"What the shit were you doing in there, Max? Max, where is the stuff? The money?"

"Where was your fucking connection, Noel?" Max hissed, breaking free of his fingers and pushing him. He slammed her against the wall again, bumping her head.

"There are flames, there are cops, Max," Noel said. "Give me the money or the stuff. I've got to get out of here. How am I going to get out of here?"

"I sat there and sat there, in Hal's house, with all this stuff on me—I was scared out of my mind, and where was your fucking connection?"

"In there! In there! I saw her go in this afternoon. You mean, she never took the stuff?"

"I've still got it on me, goddamn it," Max said, ripping her blouse open, tearing off the flat packets adhesive-taped to her bare breasts and throwing them down. "Take it and get away out of here." The three packets lay on the ground, but instead of picking them up, Noel suddenly embraced Max in terror.

"There are cops out there," he whimpered. He was bony and smelled like acetone.

"Just because of the fire, you idiot. They aren't looking for junk," Max said. "Take it and go."

"I'll leave it, I'll leave it; it's not worth it," Noel said. "Look at the fire, Max; it's coming right up here!"

"No cop is going to bother you; just go. What if they came and found it here in Hal's yard? Come on, Noel."

"I'm going to leave it, I'm going to leave it," Noel said. They felt the hot wind even in their shelter. The flames, approaching up the hill, were oddly little and pretty, but beyond them was that roar. Helicopters were directly overhead now, dipping, with night lights. "Oh, God, I can't leave it. My life depends on it," he said.

"Heah, now, you," a new voice said, the imperious Southern one, and Irene, like a lace-draped store dummy, pale and unreal in the unreal orange night, was peering in at them, at the flat white packets, in her negligee. "Ah knew it had something to do with you, Max, and ah'm telling you now there isn't going to be any more of this. That's dope, I suppose. Yeah?"

"Go away, baby," Noel said.

"Go away, Irene. Noel is going to take away this stuff like he brought it, and it has nothing to do with you."

"It has nothing to do with Hal, either, but that isn't what those policemen are going to say, as you very well know, and that's if we don't burn to death first. Pick it up."

"*Irene,*" Max said. It was hotter now, the fire was louder now, and a tiny tongue of it attacked the ice plant at the bottom of the garden. That, at least, would be slow to burn, would protect them for a little time.

"Pick it up," she said. Max picked it up. Irene took it. "Why, that's only a little, little bit. We'll just flush it away. There's still time."

"A million dollars' worth, you dumb bitch," squeaked Noel.

"Look." Through the picture window they could look in at the lighted rooms, where policemen in uniform and men in business suits were everywhere and they seemed to have Hal by the arms, Hal looking immense and dignified and dazed. Were they leading him off? Max moaned.

"It's all right. There ain't nothing in there, except if you left something in there," Irene said. "Horrible dope fiends."

"They'll come out here! Either we burn up or they come out and get us!" Noel was crying. Irene withdrew farther into the pool shed with them and partly closed the door. They were layered as if in a coffin in the tiny shed. Irene was strongly perfumed.

"Swaller it," she said between her teeth.

"Don't be out of your skull," Max said. "It would kill you."

"You don't want those police to find it here, swaller it,

what does it matter?" Irene spat. "You call yourself a valuable human being worth preserving?"

"No," Max said.

"If it comes to that, who matters most, you or Hal? You want them to come out here and find it? They're coming, you bet on that."

"I know, I'll throw it in the swimming pool. It'll dissolve," Max said, and she snatched the packets from Irene, gave her a desperate push out of the tiny shed, and plunged herself and the heroin into the swimming pool. She went under, came up, began to splash and laugh. Her dark face and sopping hair and wet black T-shirt made her look, in the darkness and gathering smoke, like a seal in the pool. "And that was fifty thousand dollars, no shit?" Laughter, sputtering.

Noel had chased after her and stood on the edge of the pool sobbing hysterically, "Give it back, Max. Max, that's a million dollars. They were going to give me enough stuff for my whole life, Max!"

"I'm stirring it around." Max laughed, treading water and sloshing the little empty bits of plastic up and down like laundry in the water, and splashing and kicking. "I'm stirring it all up. You'll have to shoot up the whole goddamned swimming pool."

"Max, they'll kill me. They'll kill me if I burn them on this."

"Between the pigs and the syndicate, Noel, what's to choose? The pigs . . ." Max advised.

Irene had climbed onto the diving board, her wrapper streaming out behind her in the hot strong wind, like wings, and she, bare-breasted, like the Winged Victory, was calling, "Every bit, wash it out, swim around," and pointing fiercely.

"The house is catching on fire, lady," a policeman called to her. At this she emitted a scream and dashed inside, negligee still flowing behind. Smoke was coming from somewhere in back of the garage, but no flames could be seen except at the bottom of the garden. Noel Fish, weeping, clapped his hands to his ears and hurtled toward the street. Irene dashed back into the patio with an armload of dishes and flung them into the swimming pool. The smoke was making things darker, the heat was intense, but there were still no flames. Max swam, laughing at Irene, her heart desperate because she could not see what was happening to Hal. In the lighted windows of the house men were visible rifling drawers—dozens of men, like termites, had seemingly emerged from every wall of the doomed house and were having a last feast in the closets, in the undersides of chairs, behind the pictures, with Irene dashing in and out continuously screaming her high wail, like a bat's scream by which she guided herself through the dark and thickening smoke, dumping chairs, radios, paintings, armloads of curtains, rugs, tables, into the swimming pool.

The big walnut coffee table struck Max lightly on the side of the head. She did not lose consciousness entirely but groggily sank in the deep end without Irene noticing. She supposed that she would sink for just a minute and then regain the surface. At the same time, knowing she could not, her mind seized important things. With anguish but resignedly she saw she would not be able to get Ronda and Derek from the Juvenile Hall. She would not know whether Hal was gotten by the police, but if he was gotten he could not come to save her. She washed against the rough poolside, against a sunken lamp. She tried to move her legs but could not find them. She did not mind too much. She thought that Hal would come and save her. She had read that your mind expands to its utmost, but hers faded, constricted. She lost consciousness.

twenty-nine

Several men lingered to save the beautiful Irene, but even the more determined now began to withdraw into the street.

"Come on, Mrs. Harris," a Treasury man shouted. "Get out in front. The whole place is going in minutes."

"Ah'd like to save a few little things now that you all have finished with your looting. Did you find what you was looking for?" She swept by him, nylon wings and hall mirror, splash.

"No," he admitted. Baffled. "We didn't find anything. Come on, lady."

Doctor Harris was already standing in the street clasping the blue bishop's blood in its pot, humming. Irene's Cadillac convertible, top down, was loaded with plants. Doctor Harris was sensible of the enormous inconvenience of all this, the house burning down, but he felt that Irene would know what to do in her own behalf and in his and was therefore not unduly upset. He himself had, the very first thing, attended to flushing the acid, meprobamates, peyote, and cannabis extract regretfully down the toilet, and he had half wanted to tell the policemen this to save them the trouble of tearing up the place—not that it particularly mattered, if it was going to burn up anyway. From the street he could see flames appear in the window. How determined they were, searching away with the house burning up around them.

The four-o'clock patient, whom nobody had noticed

while he was sleeping off his high after a session on scopola-
mine, had waked sometime since and raced jubilantly by
now, clutching to his breast a pair of shoes belonging to the
great doctor. "His shoes, his shoes," he was crying delight-
edly.

"Perhaps I ought to go," said Doctor Harris to the Treasury men. "Delicate plants, the heat, damage." The Treasury
men were climbing into their unmarked Chevrolets and
Fords. "Could you bring my wife?" Then, although feeling it
was not quite the thing to do, he drove away, with difficulty,
down the block until the car could go no farther because of a
battery of parked fire trucks. There he had to walk, joining
the other walkers, sobbing people lugging treasures, passing
the observers, who were walking up the hill, on their subdued journey down it. Doctor Harris and the walkers were
made to jump at the sound of a loud report behind them.
"Wires," someone said, drawing Doctor Harris with him
closer to the fire trucks.

"It sounded like a gunshot," Doctor Harris said, having
guns and police on his mind.

A policeman leaped into their field of vision from behind
a car across the street and walked with an exaggerated
crouch toward a fallen man. "Looters," he told those nearest.
"We've got to watch for this." Doctor Harris saw his own
shoes lying in the street and the four-o'clock patient, too, in a
puddle of water and blood.

"These Nigros. Not careful, we'll have them up here by
the car-load looting," the policeman said. Doctor Harris, not
knowing how or whether to interfere, walked slowly on.

"Mrs. Harris, Mrs. Harris!" Geoffrey Nichols, the fire
chief, called in a cheerful way to Irene, who was standing
picturesquely on the curbing shaking her fist at Hal departing in her car. Geoffrey Nichols, striding up the hill in a

rubber raincoat and stiff black hat, face all grimy, greeted her with steel-blue eyes and great manly shining white teeth.

"Ooh, Jeff, that son of a bitch Hal has gone off and left me," she said. "Ah'm so hurt."

"So much the better. I'll save you myself," he said. "There's not much else to do, God knows. There's nothing anybody can do with these fires. No water, for one thing. Crazy wind. Wouldn't you know, the finest fire of my career and I'm powerless? Anyway, there's nothing I'd rather do than save you."

"Gee, thanks." She smiled at him, modulating her habitual sarcasm to the merest trace.

"Especially in that getup. Like a fire-department recruitment poster," he said, picking her up. "What do you weigh?"

"A hundred and ten," she said.

"Good, I can carry you down as far as the trucks, then, where the television cameras are." He laughed. She laughed too and nestled against him. Geoffrey Nichols was very strong and could carry her cradled in one arm. He put his hand beneath her wrapper and touched her pretty bare breasts. Irene scolded crossly about indignities and snuggled against him; they walked slowly. The last group of Treasury men drove slowly past them without offering a ride. Geoffrey Nichols deposited Irene near the camera truck, rosy and trembling, a beautiful subject for the documentary lens, and went along in some other direction to supervise his men.

In their Volkswagen Barney and Bingo watched this while they waited for the fire truck to be moved so people in cars could escape properly. To their left a house burned, flames coming out the windows and doors, walls melting before their eyes. Firemen stood impotently by with dry hoses. Geoffrey Nichols carried the scantily clad beauty to safety as Bingo watched. A fierce wind blew embers and great ashes, as big as shingles, against the tightly closed windows of the car.

"We could stifle in here," Bingo said. "Do you think that we might? The hot air might just roast us alive."

"No, no, of course not," Barney said, nervously racing the motor. The fire truck was being laboriously positioned, forward, backward, forward, in the driveway of a house that had already been burned down. Then there was enough room for the VW to squeeze by and creep around the curves of the winding street. They were terrified at each turn at what inferno would confront them. Here and there at burst gas lines great ignited jets of flame lighted the way like posted torches. All electricity had failed. Hundreds of people climbed the hill on each side of the street, going up and down by gaslight, firelight, carrying cameras, shovels, armloads of shirts and underwear.

"I've never seen so many—there have probably never *been* so many people on foot before in Los Angeles," Barney said, to rally Bingo, who was shaking. "We're out of the worst of it now, I think," he said.

"There's Doctor Harris. Let's give him a ride," Bingo said. The great shaggy man walking slowly sagged under an armload of heavy clay pots, wild foliage blooming over his shoulders.

"Hardly room, with my paintings and stuff. But we could take his plants for him," Barney said, stopping. Doctor Harris, who seemed unsure who they were at first, was glad to confide these heavy precious things to a car bound for safety. They negotiated the careful installation of the plants in the back seat.

Irene, nose in the air, driving too fast down the street in the abandoned white Cadillac, nearly rear-ended them.

"God damn," she said, and to Hal, "Ah'm not sure ah

should offer *you* a ride. And *surely* not your damn plants."
He did not appear to understand her sarcastic tone but
climbed in beside her, thanking Barney and Bingo cour-
teously for their care of the plants and adding that, should
circumstances keep them separated for any length of time,
the coleus should be watered profusely and the andomentum
sparingly.

At Sunset Boulevard a roadblock, designed mostly to
keep the curious from driving up into the hills and impeding
the fire fighters, delayed their escape. The street below was
bordered with people, perhaps refugees, and cars and taxis.
Now that they were down out of the hills, the ordinary
manner of transacting things seemed still to obtain in Los
Angeles proper. Streetlights worked. There were horrors and
sirens, but unconcerned people could be seen, too. They saw
a man carrying out his trash can to the street for the Tuesday
pickup.

Barney drove the car up the long circular driveway of the
Beverly Hills Hotel. "We owe ourselves a little luxury," he
said firmly, anticipating Bingo's protest about the expense.
But the doorman, as they approached the striped awning,
waved them past.

"Full up here," he said, little evident sympathy in his
tone. "Fire victims," he said, as they slowed anyway.

"We're fire victims," Barney said, stopping, obeying an
impulse to identify himself with the incredible event. Also, if
the Beverly Hills Hotel was opening its humanitarian doors
to the victims, this was where they wanted to be, with their
fellows. Warmth. Community.

"Sorry, sir, we're all filled," the doorman said, leaning in
at them, with his eyes on the back seat full of paintings and
plants. Barney and Bingo drove down to Sunset again.

"I'll head toward Santa Monica. There are lots of motels there," he said. "The Beverly Hills Hotel—it's enormous. Incredible."

"Barney, our house can't be burned. I'll die," Bingo said. "Barney, I forgot the turtles. Oh, Barney."

"Turtle soup," Barney said.

"Oh, Barney, I could have easily taken them. I simply forgot—they're out there in the back yard."

"You don't have a whole lot of sympathy with living things," Barney said, thinking of Tinker Bell. Bingo looked out the window and said nothing.

The Gretna Green Motel at the foot of Tigertail Road was also crowded with refugees, who could watch their homes, burning away above them, from the upstairs balcony.

"A major disaster area," the car radio said. "More than a hundred houses totally destroyed and a hundred million dollars' worth of property damaged, no lives. Estimates include . . . Hopes to bring the blaze under control by morning . . . capricious winds."

"Where are we going to go, for heaven's sake?" Bingo said.

"Let's call somebody. Somebody'll put us up," Barney said.

"No, I couldn't stand it," Bingo said. "I don't want to see anybody."

"Plenty of motels in Santa Monica," Barney said.

Max had washed against a bookcase and lay in the chill water, with her wrecked arms clinging to the wood as to a floating spar. She came to from the feeling of fierce heat against her face. This heat pressed with a force almost great enough to keep her eyes from opening, contrasting with the water in which she shivered as in an alternate version of hell, demanding choice. For a few moments she tried to ignore that a choice was now required. Opening her eyes intensified the sharp pain on the side of her head, and her vision was filled with orange flames.

She lost hold of the bookcase and bobbed in the water weakly, paddling away from the burning wall of the Harrises' house. It seemed likely that it would fall into and fill the shallow end of the pool. Her head was hurting awfully. She lay back in the water to soothe it. She had begun to understand. Around the other three sides of the pool small garden heights of flame flickeringly consumed the grass and shrubs. These gave up their greenness with a collective sigh, a wind of expiration, which beat dryly against Max's wet cheeks. The wind carried chunks of ashes and bits of burning things, which Max had to duck under the water to miss. She was all surrounded by flames and a terrible, terrible noise.

Her legs seemed to have been partly severed from her body by the blow to her head and to depend from threads, like lost teeth, and to have little function. But they washed beneath her with sufficient force to support her head above water. Had she legs? She could not tell. She did not know how she would get out of this place now. Although there is a certain security in being surrounded by four walls of flame there is nowhere to go. She swam toward the deep end so a falling wall would be less likely to hit her, with pained strokes, clutching at treacherous floating picture frames that sank beneath her. Cool water over her face partly helped her head, but she was obliged to come up each time and face the roaring flames and suck a breath of burning air. She considered this: was she really obliged? She might prefer to die. It seemed, with Hal burned up or gone, his very house gone, the children taken by social workers, these were irremediable and troublesome things, and now no legs—or had she legs? She might naturally prefer now rather than some other time to die. Her body was weightless and drifted; she bobbed and sank and rose. She was glad she had seen to it that her children were good swimmers. She could just sink now and lie restfully on the bottom until dead, like a sunken wastebasket.

She remembered dreadfully the sunken and charred wastebasket. At the memory, to her surprise, she heard a great howl or animallike shriek squeeze from her own mouth, expressed by the pressure of the heat against her chest like a great hand on a bellows. The fire seemed all around to grow brighter and hotter in response. A fear now awoke in her, more urgent than the pain in her head. Despite the absence of legs her arms and shoulders were strong, and she knew she could swim long enough to outlast the feebly burning succulents in the side yard. She would not be extinguished by Irene. She swam, coughing and sobbing at the great fire, dog-paddling around and around, conserving her strength. She dog-paddled tirelessly, in a circle, in and out among the drowned furniture, while the flames grew imperceptibly lower all the time, and though she was weak and ached, she knew she was strong enough and had only to keep up this circling over the sunken wrecks of chests and chairs, within the fiery walls, to stay alive after all.

thirty

"Oh, Barney, I'm so tired," Bingo said. "Weary."

"Not just the usual sort of day," he said, giving way to his own weariness, a sort of sensation of evaporation. He sagged in the plastic brocade chair in the worn room. Not the place he had envisioned as a final resting place today. Bingo lay on the bed, fished the pillow out from under the mauve chenille bedspread, adjusted it under her head, and closed her eyes. She opened them in seconds, and Barney discovered her looking at him.

"I'm going to turn on the TV," he said, getting up to position the television, which was suspended on a metal bracket from the ceiling, so that Bingo could see it from the bed. Then he climbed over next to her, and they listened to a developing hum. No picture appeared.

"Maybe you have to put in a quarter," Bingo said. "This is a cheap motel."

"I haven't got a quarter," Barney said. "No change. All home on the dresser, if there is a dresser. If there is a home."

"Worst disaster in the history of the Los Angeles area. Destruction is comparable to . . ." said a ghostly voice from the blank television.

"Just sound, no picture," Barney said. "We'll be spared the sight of our house burning down but we can still hear it."

"Oh, Barney, I forgot the baby pictures. Barney, we can never replace those. Oh, think of it."

"You are looking at the north side of the fourteen hundred block of Lamotte Lane," the announcer said in his lowered, urgent voice. "This is only one of the dozens of infernos in these hills. Ordinary fire-fighting techniques have proved virtually ineffective against the capricious winds and the dry, brush-covered terrain. The sound you hear is of helicopters, dropping bombs of chemical substances."

The screen was still gray. "That's down below us," Barney said. "Does that mean our house is gone?" An implacable expanse of gray glass.

"The fire trucks are being moved to avoid the imminent collapse of the wall you see at the upper right-hand portion of your screen. The cameras must keep at least thirty feet away here, the heat is so intense, and . . ."

"How's your leg, love?" Bingo asked, averting her gaze from the blank screen. Barney was surprised to realize that he had not, through all the excitement, thought of his leg at all. He pulled his trouser leg up a little. The ankle was marked with new ugly red streaks.

"I'll have to go back on penicillin," he said, standing up and taking off his trousers. The thigh was inflamed too. "God damn. I guess I overdid today." An ambiguous snort from Bingo, who was lying on her back with her arm bent over her eyes. She lifted it to raise her head and look at Barney's thigh.

"Do black men have bigger penises than white men?" she asked. It was a funny time for her to think of something like that. Barney frowned.

"I don't think color has anything to do with it. Why?"

"I just wondered." She covered up her eyes again. "I feel very unfit. Unwell, I mean. Weary."

"Move a little. I'm going to get under the covers," Barney

said. "I'm sorry if I embarrassed you, about Tinker Bell. It was as if I couldn't help myself, the memory was so vivid."

"Obviously a meaningful experience for you," Bingo said sharply, uncovering her eyes. She got up and took off her dress and climbed back in under the covers. The elastic on her bra straps and around the top of her panties was brown and rippled from being put in the dryer. Bingo and Barney stared at the gray glass of the television instead of at each other.

"I forgot the Hiroshige print, too," she said presently. "We'll have to start our life all over. I just don't know if I can. I mean, I feel as if I had no base on which to build or, I don't know . . ."

"You feel disoriented, homeless, naturally."

"Residents are urged to use as little water as possible in order to make the maximum available to the fire fighters."

"I was going to have a shower," Bingo said.

"Maybe our house won't burn, Bingo. The fire is capricious—burns, blows out, spares things. There's no reason to suppose it will get *our* house."

"There's no reason to suppose it won't," Bingo said, "and whatever happens, tomorrow we have to see about those kids. Barney, how can so many people, well-meaning people, presumably, get mixed up in such a demented system, the social-welfare system? It doesn't help anybody."

"Well, why do *you* feel determined to go on meddling about Max's kids?" Barney said. "You want to help even when there's nothing you can do. Same with social workers, I guess. Doctors, too."

"I don't even like people. People are awful," Bingo said. "But you just can't abandon them."

"On the lighter side, this is the Red Cross welfare station

at Le Conte School," said the voice. "Red Cross workers find themselves with nine thousand doughnuts, four hundred gallons of coffee—and no takers. Affluent fire victims have meantime repaired to neighboring luxury hotels to solace themselves with fancier fare. Spokesmen say the doughnuts will be distributed free to the residents of Venice and Watts tomorrow. And the coffee? Down the drain."

"You can't just abandon them. Indifference is the wicked thing. I hope I never become indifferent. Like Doctor Harris, for example, or the social workers, callous and uncaring. *You* must care, Barney, even if you *are* a doctor. Actually doctors, when you think about it, seem to care less than other people. These are poor little neglected children—Ronda and Derek—very smart and brave, and I . . ."

"Bingo, honey, what I'm saying is that those poor kids, whatever happens to them, are in for a bad time. What chance do they have for a normal life? Their mother, a dope addict, or going to some foster home—equally bad, surely. It's just brutal fact that they're—how old? Over four, anyhow—all formed, according to the theory. The damage all done. They can never lead a normal life."

"Stop talking about a normal life," Bingo shouted. She stopped. "At least they would be with their mother, who loves them at least, and . . ." In a normal voice.

"Yeah, but so what? Who loves her? She's a sad, lost person, really a sick woman, Bingo. On drugs all the time, unable to function at all except to do a few simple-minded errands for her psychiatrist. I like her, but I can see that she isn't, can't . . ." His voice trailed off. "What about the father?" he asked. Maybe the father.

"I don't know. He looks just like Doctor Harris and has the same name: Hal. That's probably significant, isn't it? He seems eccentric but kindly—maybe he should take them. But why hasn't he before this? I think *we* should have the children, but, of course, I am unfit."

Barney squeezed her hand and wondered at her vulnerable and defeated expression.

"I *am* going to have a shower," she said, beginning to sit up. The homeowner in Barney indignantly pushed her down on the pillow again.

"Water! They need the water for fire fighting." Bingo looked at him a long time, unfastening her hair clip and refastening her hair behind her ears better, silently working some words around in her mouth, which she finally spoke.

"If our house were burning this minute and my not taking a shower would help save it, I would still take one; that's how crawly and dirty I feel. I must wash." She sat up. She looked at him with a sudden dishonest flash behind her eyes, as if she realized some implications of what she had just said and was wondering if he had caught them, too. He had. He felt suddenly cold, with the same sort of clammy chill that he had had before he fainted, but now he was annoyed.

"That's how much you wish our house to burn down," he said. "That's what you're really saying." Better get this out in the open.

"Don't be silly, I just don't think it makes any difference. One shower . . ."

"Well!" Barney said triumphantly. "The fundamental inconsistency of that attitude and what you just said about caring, involvement. What you really are saying is you don't care about other people or their houses, just your own shower. . . ."

"I admit I am so tired I can't feel very intense about our house or other people's houses or anything. But I do care—

how crazy of you! How could I want our house to burn down? I couldn't bear it, starting over, everything. If I could start everything over I would want myself to be different, but not our house."

Barney lost that quick flutter of panic and smiled at her. "Would you? For me it would be the other way around. If something had to change, it would be the place, not myself. Not that I'm so pleased with myself, but I'm used to me, and . . ."

"I understand," Bingo said.

"And I wouldn't want you to be different," Barney said. "I want you and our house to be the same, please." Her smile, though, was very wan, very thin, the eyes looking as if they saw him in patterns. He ran his hand up her back so that she sat up straighter, showing her good breasts. Bingo had a good figure when she sat up straight. Barney unhooked the back of her brassiere and rubbed the red marks on her back. She was marked all over with a chenille design.

"The Harrises' house was definitely burning fully on fire when we got away," Bingo said. "It's peculiar what things people pick to save, isn't it? All those plants. I saw a woman running along with a floor lamp, great tall floor lamp, cord trailing."

"Doctor Harris is a pretty sinister figure, I found out. He treats drug addicts by giving them drugs and screws all his patients. Maybe only the female ones. Maybe not. And only drinks cream, no food. Max's job is to take him his cream. And his patients become his adoring slaves."

"He looks so benign and preoccupied," Bingo said. "Perhaps people think he is treating only them. Really he's tending his plants."

"Cultivate your garden—was it Voltaire who said that?"

"If gardening turns you on. Think of all that damned ice plant I planted, doing no good at all." Barney was still stroking her back. She turned so that he could stroke her breasts as well and expanded her chest voluptuously.

"Doctor Harris must be quite a lover, taking care of all those people. He does look like a very . . . capable man."

Barney laughed and pulled her down onto his chest and kissed her. "I'm sorry, but you're all I can handle. Maybe I should drink cream?" Bingo lay across his chest, and he put his arms around her and kissed her again.

"Love is better than psychotherapy," Bingo said. "He doesn't have to be very smart to have figured that out." Barney could reach her buttocks, smooth in nylon panties. He patted them, pulled the panties down. They kissed and clung. They belonged to each other; they signified this by a close entwining of arms and legs and lips. "It's so good," they told each other.

"It doesn't really matter about the house," Barney whispered. "Don't worry, Bingo."

She kissed him again to show she was not worrying, and stroked his belly. "We have each other," she said.

Barney, intent on the immediate pleasures that lay before them, did not criticize the cliché. The miracle of life. Bingo caressed his stiffened self. He closed his eyes. Bingo raised herself so that her entire weight was not on him and fumbled with him, with herself, fitting them together. Her body swayed outside him.

"Tell us, Captain Nichols, what the basic problem here in Bel Air has been today, why the fire has been out of control, sir," said the announcer's voice from behind the blank glass.

"Well," said the familiar voice of Geoffrey Nichols, "basically the wind, but our efforts have been hampered, too, by inadequate equipment and low water pressure. Basically you can't fight fifty fires at once in Los Angeles with existing equipment and water lines. We just aren't set up for it. But there was no stopping the wind, anyway, and this dry brush. Basically an unquenchable fire."

Bingo's breasts hung against his chest as she worked above him. Barney rather liked this position, occasionally; but tonight he knew—much as he wanted to lie there and enjoy after this long day the somewhat unusual slightly superior friction, the novel sensation produced by Bingo's movements above him—that this was not what Bingo wanted, quite; and with stout thrusts and a simultaneous roll he got on top, hardly missing a stroke; and she, lying beneath him, seemed to him somehow more shining and smiling, stupider but contented, and a great feeling of love and protectiveness welled up in him. Bingo, a passionate woman, his woman, entwined him, making little cries, her hair messy, her eyes closed, their children at their grandmother's. Thoughts fled, were succeeded by forms, pictures, fleeting traces of lurid scenes, so that his mind floated outside him. The blissful condition of his body began to preoccupy him, his woman, a beautiful blond creature with blue eyes moaning beneath him, her eyes, her yellow eyes, jaundiced, her black hair, her thin brown face. Barney's body contracted in a single spasm, rewarding but routine, accompanying Bingo's breathless explanations: "It's like, oh, like those jets of fire, or hot needles. If only you knew," and he sank onto her chest in a sweat of fear. Max's face. Bingo had become Max. Perhaps would always be Max. This was what you got for cowardice and infidelity: a blighted life, a phobia. Why was your mind not ever your own?

"We have each other," he said, embracing her, eyes open,

looking at her dear face. She was crying; great tears trickled down the sides of her face, presumably into her ears. The strain, the day, their house. He closed his eyes, in the back-wash of the pleasant sensation still emanating from his groin. The ugly face of Max grimaced, smiling, surreal, like a face in a film nightmare. He could paint it, it was so clear, so unchangeable. He opened his eyes again to look at the weeping Bingo.

"I'm sorry," she said, sobbing. "I just can't help it."

"Oh, I know, it's terrible," Barney said, tightening his arms about her. He felt his own tears come very readily. "Terrible, terrible, terrible. What will we do?"

"Of course it may not be burned down at all."

"It doesn't matter. We have each other."

"Terrible, terrible. What will we do?"